'I do not tell lies, Your Grace!'

rius quirked a derisive brow over lazily king blue eyes. 'Prove it.'

bella's eyes opened wide at the challenge. g your pardon…?'

y might have been the only two people the room as Darius regarded her from ween narrowed lids. The air between them s charged with expectation as he noted the s of colour to her cheeks, and the shocked certainty that now shone in those previously llious brown eyes. 'I am merely inviting to prove your claim, Arabella,' he repeated s rtly.

'I— But— How am I to do that, Your Grace?'

His mouth twisted humourlessly. 'Surely there is only one way in which a woman might prove her…experience in the matter of physical intimacy?'

AUTHOR NOTE

I feel quite sad to have come to the end of *The Notorious St Claires* quartet.

Hopefully, it will not be the last you hear of the St Claire family. I have no doubt there will be many more family members who'll have their own story to tell, while at the same time you will get brief and tantalising glimpses into the continuing lives of Hawk, Lucian, Sebastian and Arabella. In fact, I couldn't resist setting a story at Christmas, where the family makes a further appearance. Look for my short story CHRISTMAS AT MULBERRY HALL, coming later in 2011.

Thank you for sharing this experience with me, and until next time I wish you happy reading!

LADY ARABELLA'S SCANDALOUS MARRIAGE

Carole Mortimer

First published in Great Britain 2010
Paperback edition 2011
Harlequin Mills & Boon Limited,
Eton House, 18-24 Paradise Road, Richmond, Surrey TW9 1SR

ISBN: 978 0 263 87862 2

Harlequin Mills & Boon policy is to use papers that are natural, renewable and recyclable products and made from wood grown in sustainable forests. The logging and manufacturing process conform to the legal environmental regulations of the country of origin.

Printed and bound in Spain
by Litografia Rosés, S.A., Barcelona

Carole Mortimer was born in England, the youngest of three children. She began writing in 1978, and has now written over one hundred and fifty books for Harlequin Mills & Boon. Carole has six sons: Matthew, Joshua, Timothy, Michael, David and Peter. She says, 'I'm happily married to Peter senior; we're best friends as well as lovers, which is probably the best recipe for a successful relationship. We live in a lovely part of England.'

Previous novels by the same author:

In Mills & Boon® Historical Romance

THE DUKE'S CINDERELLA BRIDE*
THE RAKE'S INDECENT PROPOSAL*
THE ROGUE'S DISGRACED LADY*

*Part of *The Notorious St Claires* mini-series

You've read about
***The Notorious St Claires* in Regency times.**

Now read about the new generation
in Mills & Boon® Modern™ Romance

The Scandalous St Claires

Three arrogant aristocrats—
ready to be tamed!

Don't miss Jordan St Claire in
Jordan St Claire: Dark and Dangerous
January 2011

Lucian St Claire
The Relucant Duke
in February

and Gideon St Claire
Taming the Last St Claire
in March!

For my readers,
for helping to make writing
The Notorious St Claires such a wonderful
and rewarding experience for me.

Chapter One

'How I have come to hate weddings!' Lady Arabella St Claire muttered inelegantly as her partner in the waltz—a dance still considered slightly risqué by the older members of the ton—swept her assuredly amongst the two hundred or so other wedding guests milling about the candlelit ballroom of St Claire House in London.

'Could that be because in the past year you have been three times the sister of the groom rather than being the bride?' drawled Darius Wynter, the Duke of Carlyne.

Arabella looked up sharply, intending to give him a set-down for the mockery she detected in his cynically bored tone. That was her intention, but instead Arabella found her attention caught and held by the hard and perfect male beauty of his face—a face Arabella had once described to one of her sisters-in-law as being that of an angel. Or a devil…

Six or seven inches taller than her own five feet and eight inches in stockinged feet, Darius Wynter had stylishly overlong golden hair, which gleamed in the candle-light, and his eyes were of dark cobalt-blue, edged by long lashes of that same gold. His nose was long and aristocratic, his cheekbones hard, and he possessed perfect sculptured lips above a square and determined jaw.

The stark black of his jacket over snowy-white linen emphasised rather than hid the width of his shoulders, his muscled chest and taut abdomen, and the lean elegance of his hips and thighs was defined by tailored black pantaloons.

Yes, Darius Wynter, Duke of Carlyne, was certainly elegance personified—and he was also the most compellingly handsome man Arabella had met since her coming out the previous year.

Until a few short months ago he had been Lord Darius Wynter, a man well known for his numerous exploits in the bedroom and at the gaming tables. A wild and reckless reputation that had only been added to when he'd married the heiress Sophie Belling a year ago, only to be suddenly widowed one short month later, when his bride was thrown from her horse while out hunting and killed.

As expected, the majority of the ton—marriage-minded mamas especially!—had forgiven Darius Wynter all his previous sins when he'd inherited the title of the Duke of Carlyne on the death of his elder brother seven months ago.

Arabella had been drawn to his decadent good-looks

the first time she'd seen him at a ball some eighteen months ago. An attraction, despite the many social occasions at which they had both been present, that Darius Wynter had unfortunately never given any inclination of returning.

Her top lip curled now with haughty disdain. 'I am sure you did not mean your remark to be so insulting, Your Grace.'

Darius gazed down into the beautiful face of Lady Arabella St Claire. With three brothers older than herself, one of them Hawk, Duke of Stourbridge, Darius knew that this young lady had been petted and spoilt for most if not all of her almost twenty years.

Nevertheless, her beauty was dazzling: a riot of honey-gold curls framed her heart-shaped face, her eyes were the colour of melted chocolate, and she had a tiny up-tilted nose, full and sensuously pouting lips, and a pointedly determined chin. The pale cream gown she wore revealed a spill of creamy breasts above a narrow waist and rounded hips, and her tiny feet were covered in cream satin slippers.

Yes, Lady Arabella St Claire was without doubt a very beautiful and highly desirable young lady. But as the young and so far unattached sister of the Duke of Stourbridge, wealthy in her own right following the death of her father eleven years ago, this haughtily condescending young lady had been hotly pursued by every eligible buck during the past two Seasons. Darius, whilst still only the lowly Lord Wynter, had even made an offer for her himself the previous year. An offer that had been summarily dismissed by this wilful baggage, he recalled grimly.

'Are you so sure?' Darius taunted.

Those deep brown eyes narrowed slightly. 'I am but nineteen years of age, Your Grace, hardly old-maid material yet!'

Darius rather liked the angry flush that had entered her cheeks. It made her eyes appear darker, the fullness of her lips redder. Lips that it would no doubt be a pleasure to kiss and explore, he noted. 'Nevertheless, you have been out for two Seasons now, with no hint of a betrothal being announced.'

Those expressive dark eyes flashed her displeasure. 'Is it your opinion, then, that all young ladies are so giddy and empty-headed that their only aim in life must be to snare themselves a suitable husband?'

He raised enquiring blond brows. 'By *suitable* I presume you mean wealthy, as well as titled?'

Her pointed chin rose challengingly. 'It is the enlightened year of eighteen hundred and seventeen, Your Grace, a time when not all women feel that they need a husband—*any* husband—by which to justify their very existence!'

'Then it is not your intention to marry?' he asked curiously.

'Not for some years, no,' she answered stubbornly.

'A pity.'

Her brows drew together. 'I beg your pardon?'

Darius shrugged broad shoulders. 'At nineteen a woman's body is still firm and ripe—' He broke off as Arabella gave a shocked gasp and attempted to pull away from him, yet Darius easily prevented her withdrawal by tightening his arm about the narrowness of her waist and his fingers about her tiny gloved fingers.

Her eyes glittered up at him angrily when she found herself forced to continue dancing, the softness of her thighs pressed against his much harder ones. 'Release me at once, sir!'

Darius grinned down at her unrepentantly. 'I am merely endeavouring to show you what you are missing by spurning the idea of marriage whilst you are still young enough to enjoy it.'

Arabella had not grown up with three older brothers without learning at least some of the mechanics of a man's body. And at the moment she could feel *exactly* what she would be missing as the hard press of Darius Wynter's thighs became a shocking torment against hers. A shockingly sensual torment…

Her legs felt weakened by the intimacy. Her breasts were swelling against her gown, her palms becoming slightly damp inside her gloves, and her cheeks were burning as she glanced about them self-consciously.

Luckily there was such a crush of people attending the celebration of her brother Sebastian's wedding to his darling Juliet that no one—not one of her brothers or their wives, nor indeed her many aunts and uncles and numerous cousins—seemed to have noticed the Duke's over-familiarity with Arabella.

Arabella's eyes gleamed as she turned back to face him. 'Surely it is not necessary for a woman to marry in order for her to enjoy such…intimacies?' She looked up at him challengingly, hoping to shock him.

The Duke narrowed his eyes. 'Perhaps you have already done so?' he retorted.

Of course Arabella had not. She might not as yet have found any man interesting enough to even think of marrying him, but for her to go to her husband on their wedding night as anything but pure and untouched would cause the most tremendous scandal. Besides which, her three over-protective older brothers would never allow it.

However, she considered this taunting mockery from a contemporary of her eldest brother Hawk intolerable. At one-and-thirty years of age, he should know better! 'Perhaps…' she echoed enigmatically.

Those sculptured lips curved into a hard smile. 'Why is it I find that so very hard to believe, Lady Arabella?'

She drew in a sharp, indignant breath. 'Are you calling me a liar, Your Grace?'

'I believe I am, yes,' Darius murmured.

Arabella St Claire really was a wayward little baggage, he acknowledged with admiration as he continued to twirl her about the magnificent candlelit ballroom. A wilful baggage with a complete disregard for the fact that she was playing with fire by behaving in this flirtatious way with a man she had refused to marry so condescendingly the previous year.

She held herself very erect, her challenging stance pushing up the full swell of those creamy breasts so that Darius now felt their warmth against his chest.

'I do not tell lies, Your Grace.'

He quirked a brow over lazily sensual blue eyes. 'Prove it.'

Her eyes opened wide at the challenge. 'I *beg* your pardon?'

They might have been the only two people in the room as Darius regarded her from between narrowed lids. The air between them was charged with expectation as he noted the loss of colour to her cheeks and the shocked uncertainty that now shone in those previously rebellious brown eyes. 'I am merely inviting you to prove your claim, Arabella,' he repeated softly.

'I— But— How am I to do that, Your Grace?'

His mouth repressed a smile. 'Surely there is only one way in which a woman might prove her...experience in the matter of physical intimacy?'

Arabella stared up at Darius Wynter in disbelief. He could not seriously mean for her to—? He did not expect her to—?

Yes, he *did*!

His intent was blatantly plain for Arabella to read in that single raised brow. In the deep blue of his eyes. In the cynical half-smile on those perfect lips.

Darius Wynter, Duke of Carlyne, was openly challenging her to indulge in physical intimacy with him!

Arabella's heart fluttered wildly in her chest at the mere thought of the muscled strength of this man's hard, naked body pressed against her own; those wide shoulders, the firmness of his chest and stomach, his powerful thighs and the naked glory of his—

'I assure you, sir, that the infamous Darius Wynter is

the very last man I would ever contemplate becoming intimate with,' Arabella bit out with deliberate insult.

He looked down his aristocratic nose at her. 'Is that so?' he responded icily.

She nodded. 'You are undoubtedly the rake everyone believes you to be. A rake and a scoundrel. A man who married for money before being suspiciously widowed only a month later.'

'Suspiciously?' His voice was deceptively, dangerously soft.

'Conveniently, then,' Arabella substituted recklessly. 'As you were then able to keep your heiress's money without the bother of the heiress. In other words, sir, you are a man no decent woman should ever align herself with, as wife or mistress, regardless of your newfound wealth and respectability as the Duke of Carlyne!'

Arabella was instantly aware of her serious error in judgement in insulting this particular man as those dark blue eyes narrowed dangerously in a face gone hard with displeasure. His mouth was a thin, uncompromising line above a clenched and unrelenting jaw. That very stillness was in itself a warning of the coldness and depth of his anger.

Arabella swallowed hard. 'Perhaps I have said too much—'

'Only perhaps?' Darius grated menacingly.

She *had* said too much. Far too much, and most assuredly to the wrong man. That the Duke had challenged her into being so indiscreet Arabella had no doubts. That she should not have taken up that challenge was also beyond doubt. As was the retribution promised in the hard blue of his eyes…

'I believe we should retire somewhere a little less… crowded so that we might continue this conversation in private,' Darius growled, his fingers firmly gripping Arabella's elbow as he left the dance floor to pull her along at his side through the crush of people.

'We cannot be seen leaving the ballroom together,' Arabella hissed self-consciously, hoping that at any moment one or other of her brothers would arrive and demand to know what they were about.

Darius did not so much as falter in his departure as he glanced down at her with cold, remorseless blue eyes. 'I believed you to be unconcerned by such impropriety in this enlightened year of eighteen hundred and seventeen!'

Arabella felt her cheeks warm as he neatly turned her earlier bravado back on her, to good effect. 'I assure you *I* am completely unconcerned, Your Grace, but my brothers may perhaps be less…guarded in voicing their opinions.'

His mouth twisted derisively. 'Sebastian and his bride disappeared some minutes ago, and Hawk and Lucian also seem to be similarly engaged with the charms of their own wives.'

Another hurried glance about the ballroom did indeed show an obvious lack of the presence of Arabella's brothers. How typical! Since her coming out last Season her brothers had made her life almost impossible with their over-protectiveness, and now, when Arabella would actually have welcomed their high-handed interference, they had all disappeared to goodness knew where to dally with their wives. Even Aunt Hammond, her chaperon during these past two Seasons, appeared blind to Arabella's unwilling departure from the ballroom as she stood across the room engrossed in conversation with several of their relatives.

'As I said,' Darius drawled with dry satisfaction, 'I think it better by far that we retire somewhere less crowded in order to continue our present…conversation.'

Arabella had no doubt from the determined tone of his voice that conversation was the last thing the arrogant Duke of Carlyne wished to continue….

Darius strode from the ballroom, pulling Arabella through yet another crush of people where they stood chattering and laughing in the cavernous hallway, although he was not unaware of the expression in her beautiful brown eyes as he looked for a room where he could be alone with this insultingly outspoken young madam. Those eyes of hers, Darius knew, could sparkle with laughter as easily as they now snapped with anger.

So far the former had never happened in his presence….

Whenever he and Arabella St Claire had chanced to meet this past year and a half it had always been at one function of the ton or another. Occasions when this feisty little miss had treated the disreputable Lord Darius Wynter with all the haughty disdain of which a St Claire was capable—if she deigned to acknowledge him at all. Which usually she had not.

The tenuous accuracy of Arabella's recently voiced insults proved that although she had appeared to be completely unaware of him personally, she had obviously not been above listening to the scandalous gossip that so often circulated about him amongst the ton!

It was time—past time—for Darius to demonstrate to her that as the Duke of Carlyne he would no longer tolerate such dismissive behaviour from her or anyone else!

The noise and heat of the wedding party faded, and Darius kept his hand tightly about her elbow as he strode forcefully down a corridor towards the back of the house.

'What is in here?' He indicated a door to the left of the hallway with his free hand.

'It is a linen closet, I believe. Lord Wyn— Your Grace,' she corrected herself hurriedly as she stumbled along beside him, 'this really is most improper—'

'Here?' Darius ignored her protests, his expression grim as he indicated a door to the right.

'Hawk's study. But we cannot go in there!' she protested agitatedly.

Darius thrust the door open before pulling her into the darkened room behind him. 'Now.' He took both her hands in one of his and lifted them over her head as he pushed her back against the closed door and pressed the length of his body against hers. 'Shall we put to the test your claim that I am the very last man you would ever contemplate being intimate with?' His eyes glittered down at her as he slowly lowered his head with the intention of capturing her pouting lips with his own.

Arabella couldn't speak. Couldn't breathe. Her struggles to release her hands from Darius's steely restraint were only causing her body to become pressed more intimately against his. Causing her to feel more closely the hard warmth of his chest and thighs even as those cynical lips claimed hers.

Despite her earlier attempt at sophisticated bravado, Arabella had never even been kissed before. Her own lack of any deep interest, along with the threat of her brothers' wrath raining down on the head of any man who dared take such liberties with their young sister, had been enough, it seemed, to warn off any of the young bucks she had met so far.

Not so in the case of Darius Wynter who, at one and thirty, was most certainly not a young buck. Nor, as the illustrious Duke of Carlyne, was he in awe of any of her brothers.

A mouth that had appeared hard and sculptured was instead softly intimate as Darius kissed Arabella with a thoroughness that made her body tremble and shake even as it burned. Her breasts somehow felt fuller as they pressed against the restraining material of her gown, and there was a heat between her thighs that Arabella had never experienced before. A flowering that caused her to shift her hips in restless need. What she needed exactly, she was unsure. She only knew that she wanted something more than he had so far given her.

Darius raised his head to look down into the flushed and beautiful face reflected in the moonlight that shone so brightly through the window directly across the room. He noted the feverish glitter of Arabella's eyes as she looked up at him. The warmth in her cheeks. The fullness of her lips. The uneven rise and fall of the creamy breasts that spilled so temptingly over the low neckline of her gown.

The burn of Darius's gaze returned to the pout of her mouth. 'Open your lips for me,' he encouraged gruffly.

Arabella frowned. 'Certainly not!'

She was such a little vixen in her condemnation of him. So critical of his reputation. The same reputation that, along with his lack of wealth, had no doubt caused this haughty young lady to refuse his offer for her the previous year.

Darius's grip tightened as he held her hands pressed to the door above her head, his eyes glinting down in promised retribution for all of her earlier slights. 'Open your mouth, Arabella,' he rasped. 'Show me how a real woman kisses,' he added, with challenging scorn for her earlier effort.

He was instantly rewarded by the light of battle that caused Arabella's eyes to shine more brightly in the moonlight as she glared up at him. 'If you will but release my hands, Your Grace?' she snapped angrily.

He gave a hard smile. 'I have no intention of releasing you only to have you use your little claws on me.'

Arabella was furious. More angry than she could ever remember being in her life before. Which, considering how often in the past her brothers had caused her to lose all patience with them, was impressive indeed.

She narrowed her eyes at him. 'Perhaps you might *enjoy* the way I use my little claws on you…'

'Perhaps.' Darius Wynter gave a soft appreciative laugh and slowly released her hands before taking a step back. 'I am waiting, Arabella,' he drawled seconds later, when she made no attempt to make good on her threat.

Arabella's mouth firmed determinedly. She could do this. She could do anything she wished if she set her mind to it.

Even seduce Darius Wynter…

How hard could it really be? The man was, after all, an acknowledged and indiscriminate rake.

Arabella gave a knowing smile as she closed the distance between them, her gaze holding his as her hands moved up to caress lightly across his shoulders before touching the silky softness of that golden hair where it rested on the collar of his jacket. Her fingers became entangled in that silkiness as she pulled his head down to hers so that she might be the one to instigate the kiss. As instructed, she parted her lips this time, immediately aware of the deeper intimacy of their kiss. Of the way her pulse quickened and her body suffused with a new heat as she felt the hot rasp of Darius's tongue against her parted lips, that tongue retreating slightly, only to repeat the heated caress seconds later. Beckoning. Enticing. Encouraging Arabella to do the same to him, perhaps?

How Arabella wished at that moment that she knew more about the intimacies that took place between a man and a woman. How she wanted to bring this arrogant man to his knees in the heat of his desire for her. Longed to have him beg and plead for her capitulation as he became lost to that need.

His need for her, Arabella St Claire, and for no other woman…

She allowed her instincts to take over as she pressed her body against Darius's to run her tongue lightly over his parted lips, at once feeling the leap of the pulse in his throat. A second, deeper penetration of her tongue elicited a low and throaty groan.

Emboldened, empowered by this evidence of Darius's pleasure in the caress, Arabella stroked her tongue into his mouth. Again. Then again. And each time she felt the intriguing pulsing of the firm length of Darius's thighs as they pressed into the welcoming well of her own heat.

What had started out as a game to Darius, a punishment for both that past slight in refusing his offer for her and Arabella's scorn earlier this evening, was a game no longer. His arousal was hard and throbbing inside his pantaloons, and he was consumed by the overwhelming need to carry this interlude to its natural conclusion.

Darius satisfied himself momentarily by using his own tongue to duel for dominance. Finally winning that battle, he returned those delicate strokes of hers with penetrating thrusts.

Yet it was not enough—in light of the many months that Darius had desired this particular young woman perhaps it never would be—and he groaned his frustration with the clothes between them that prevented him from touching every inch of Arabella's firm and ripe body.

Still kissing her, he manoeuvred her away from the door and guided her towards the huge desk that stood in front of the window.

The top of the desk was completely clear of the clutter that littered Darius's own desk in Carlyne House, Belgravia—which of course it would be, this room being the fastidious Hawk St Claire's own private domain!—and Arabella stiffened in surprise as she felt the backs of her thighs came into contact with that sturdy piece of furniture. At least Darius hoped it was sturdy enough for what he had in mind.

This young woman had accused him of being a rake and a scoundrel—amongst other things—and Darius did not intend to disappoint her. His fingers deftly unfastened the buttons on the back of her gown.

Arabella had absolutely no idea how it was that only seconds later she came to be sitting atop her brother's desk, with her dress down about her waist and only the sheer material of her camisole to cover the firm thrust of her breasts.

Although the *how* ceased to matter as Darius gently pushed her gown up and her legs apart to stand between them, his eyes gleaming in the darkness. He slowly lowered his head to run his tongue expertly over the exact spot where the swollen tip of one of Arabella's breasts showed dark against the creamy material.

Arabella gave a breathy gasp as that caress caused pleasure to course through her body, tingling down her arms, the length of her spine, before centring as an ache between her heated thighs.

'You like that?' Darius murmured with satisfaction as he slowly repeated the caress against her other breast.

Of *course* Arabella liked that! What woman would not enjoy such heady pleasure as these caresses aroused in her?

For all her earlier claims, Arabella had certainly never experienced such intimacy. Had never really known what transpired between a man and woman when they were alone together. Her mother had died when she was but eight years of age. And her Aunt Hammond, a widow for some years, had never discussed such matters with her. As for her three older brothers—Hawk, Lucian and Sebastian all considered Arabella to be still too young to even *think* about such things, let alone indulge in them. And Arabella, her outward demeanour deliberately one of a sophisticated young lady about town, was far too embarrassed by her ignorance on the subject to have questioned any of her sisters-in-law.

Which explained why Arabella had reached the age of almost twenty years without knowing of the sheer pleasure, the beauty of physical intimacy…

This time she was prepared for Darius's kiss, but so lost was she in the heat of that kiss that she offered no objection as he slipped the straps of her camisole down her arms and bared her breasts completely for him to cup and caress.

Arabella had never known, never guessed that such

pleasure as this existed. Her back arched as she pressed herself against the caress of Darius's fingers. Light touches that made the rosy tips of her breasts swell to such an aching sensitivity that it sent an echoing surge of pulsing pleasure between her thighs.

Darius broke the kiss to seek out and taste the hollows of her throat, his lips warm, tongue moist, teeth lightly nipping at her sensitised flesh as he moved lower still.

'You are so very beautiful here,' Darius murmured throatily, his breath a warm caress against her bared breasts before he slowly drew one of those pouting tips into his mouth.

Arabella gasped and writhed in pleasure, her fingers becoming entangled in the silky hair at his nape as she held him tightly to her. She felt so hot. So needy. So very needy…

She trembled with that need as Darius pulled back slightly to look at her, and her cheeks were burning as she looked down and saw that her nipple was twice its normal size and much darker in colour than when she sometimes looked at herself in the mirror after bathing.

Her breasts seemed altogether larger, as if they had swollen beneath the caress of Darius's hands and lips. But Darius had said her breasts were beautiful, so perhaps that was supposed to happen?

'May I…?' Arabella now longed to touch Darius as intimately as he had just touched her, and her hands were moving hesitantly to the buttons on the front of his waistcoat as she waited for his reply.

Darius nodded briefly in the darkness and as he straightened, eyes glittering darkly. 'That seems only fair,' he invited huskily.

At that moment, aroused as he was, Darius could have denied Arabella nothing. He drew in his breath on a sharp hiss as she peeled his waistcoat and tailored jacket down his arms to allow them to drop to the carpeted floor, before unbuttoning his shirt down to the middle of his chest, and he felt the first touch of the slender warmth of her exploring hands upon his bared and heated flesh.

Darius gritted his teeth, his jaw clenching as her hands trailed in a soft caress over his chest before she found the hardened nubs nestled amongst the mat of golden hair that lightly covered them.

She looked so beautiful in the moonlight, her bared breasts a proud thrust, her waist so slender, Darius thought he might span it with his two hands. It was all he could do to restrain himself from the urge he had to lay her across the length of the desk before moving between her parted thighs and burying the throbbing ache of his arousal inside her.

'Kiss me, Arabella!' he encouraged hoarsely.

He almost became undone completely when he felt the first moist lap of her little pink tongue against his nipple. As it was Darius had to clench his hands into fists at his sides as he fought to stop from spilling himself like some callow youth.

Instead he reached up and entangled his fingers in Arabella's golden curls to press her mouth harder to his sensitive flesh, drawing in a harsh breath as she copied the caress he had so recently given her.

'I am sure that you must have been mistaken, Lord Redwood,' Hawk St Claire, Duke of Stourbridge remarked pleasantly as he pushed open the study door. 'My sister the Lady Arabella has absolutely no reason to enter the privacy of my study—' The Duke broke off his disclaimer as the candelabra he carried in his hand to light the way clearly revealed that his sister had *every* reason to have entered the privacy of his study….

Chapter Two

'Perhaps you would care to give me your explanation as to *exactly* what Lord Redwood and I interrupted earlier?' Hawk, Duke of Stourbridge, Arabella's beloved eldest brother, was icily calm as he faced her across her bedchamber, but Arabella wasn't fooled.

She did not think she would ever forget the look of horror on her brother's face when, accompanied by Lord Redwood, he had walked into his study to find her and the Duke of Carlyne in a state of undress atop his leather-topped desk!

She gave an embarrassed groan just *thinking* of how her wilful determination to disprove Darius Wynter's mockery of her claim to experience had led to what was now undoubtedly her complete disgrace.

That Hawk, whom Arabella so looked up to and wanted to think well of her, should have found her in such a compromising situation was unbearable. That

Lord Redwood, a member of the government and a man who had campaigned against and spoken in the House on the subject of immorality within Society, should also have been witness to both Arabella and Hawk's shame was beyond enduring….

Regret was an emotion that Darius seemed patently incapable of feeling. He had certainly displayed no indication of it when Hawk had turned to hurriedly usher Lord Redwood from the study. Instead Darius had simply moved away from Arabella to calmly refasten the buttons on his shirt and straighten his cravat, before once again donning his waistcoat and jacket and neatly arranging his snowy white linen at the cuff. A single sweep of one elegant hand through his hair had tousled those golden locks back into their normally rakish style.

And all the time he was doing those things Arabella had been hurriedly straightening her own clothing, her fingers shaking and her face deathly pale as she realised the enormity of her indiscretion. As she considered what the repercussions of her impetuous actions might be…

Immediate banishment to the Stourbridge ducal estate in Gloucestershire would, Arabella felt sure, be the least of those punishments!

Now, she moistened her lips before answering. 'What explanation did Darius—er—the Duke of Carlyne give when the two of you spoke together just now?'

To Arabella's further dismay Hawk had returned alone to his study only minutes after that embarrassing interruption, his disposition stiffly disapproving as he sent her up to her bedchamber so that he and Darius might converse privately together. Until Arabella knew what had been said during that conversation she had no idea what answer to give her brother.

Hawk strode further into the bedchamber, tall and austerely handsome, his eyes a cold, forbidding glitter. 'He offered no explanation at all,' her brother answered testily.

She frowned. 'But he must have said *something*!'

Hawk gave a terse inclination of his head. 'He *offered* marriage.'

Arabella's eyes widened incredulously. Darius had offered for her?

It was the last thing, positively the last thing Arabella had been expecting when she considered Darius's cold and distant behaviour in those minutes after they had been discovered together.

'An offer you will, of course, refuse,' Hawk added autocratically, his top lip curled back with distaste.

Arabella stiffened with resentment at her brother's arrogance. She had already suffered the indignity of being mocked by Darius this evening. Then being made love to by Darius and, once discovered, sent to her bedchamber by Hawk as if she were a naughty child. And now it seemed she was also to suffer being told what to do by her arrogant eldest brother.

In truth, Arabella was not sure that she even *liked* Darius Wynter, let alone wished to marry him. She found his good-looks compelling. His physical attributes exciting. Was intrigued by his reputation. Had been infuriated earlier by his taunting as to her knowledge of physical intimacy. But *like* him? No, Arabella's feelings towards Darius could never be described by an emotion so…so lukewarm as liking!

Even so, her rebellious nature was such that she did not appreciate Hawk telling her what she would or would not do in regard to Darius's offer of marriage…

She held herself proudly. 'Surely that is for me to decide, Hawk, not you?'

Her eldest brother eyed her disapprovingly. 'The man is totally unsuitable.'

'His rank is every bit as prestigious as your own!' Arabella found herself defending the very man she had minutes ago been so angry with.

'His rank, perhaps, but not the man,' Hawk bit out contemptuously. 'Arabella, I cannot tell you how strongly I would disapprove of a match between you and Carlyne.'

She raised her chin in stubborn defiance of that disapproval. 'I am sorry you feel that way.'

Hawk's eyes narrowed. 'It is your intention to accept Carlyne's offer, then?'

'I have not decided,' she answered coolly. 'I will give you my answer once I have given Darius his.'

Her brother straightened, looking every inch the aristocratic Duke of Stourbridge. 'He has asked to speak to you in my study before he leaves.'

Arabella gave a haughty inclination of her head. 'In that case I really must not keep him waiting any longer.' She swept regally from the bedchamber and down the stairs.

Before her courage failed her!

* * *

'Your brother has graciously granted us five minutes alone together in which we might discuss this evening's events,' Darius said dryly when Arabella rejoined him in the now candlelit study.

Hawk St Claire was so damned toplofty. He obviously believed himself to be far superior to Darius in every way. He had seemed not to care a jot for the fact that Darius was himself now a duke, and therefore the other man's social equal, as he'd coldly informed him exactly what he thought of him for daring to dally with his sister.

Until Darius's offer of marriage—his second in regard to Lady Arabella St Claire—had robbed the other man completely of speech!

'So I understand.' Arabella looked at him with the same haughty disdain as her eldest brother had only minutes ago.

Even so, Darius could not help but admire the rebellious glitter in her eyes and the defiant tilt to her chin as she looked down the length of that haughty little nose at him. Not too many women he knew would be half so sure of themselves after being so recently discovered in a compromising situation with a scandalously notorious rake like him.

That Darius had ceased to publicly live up to that reputation since taking on the mantle of the Duke of Carlyne appeared to have gone unnoticed by the majority of the ton; it was a case of once a rake always a rake, it seemed. Not that this reputation was in the least a hindrance to Darius's eligibility. As Arabella's youngest brother Sebastian had once informed him, inheriting a dukedom tended to bring on a bout of amnesia amongst the ton concerning a man's previous indiscretions.

Which brought Darius back full circle to the purpose of this five-minutes conversation with the young lady standing before him…

His mouth compressed. 'I doubt we will need the whole of the allotted five minutes for me to make a formal offer for you and for you to refuse it.' Darius studied her from beneath hooded lids as he clinically admired her undoubted beauty: those deep brown eyes, that pert little nose, the perfect bow of her lips. Lips that had only minutes ago responded to his with a passion that had far exceeded any of Darius's expectations.

He was acquainted well enough with the three St Claire brothers to know that Arabella's earlier claims to physical experience were a complete fabrication. Her brothers would never have tolerated even a hint of licentious behaviour in their young sister. But it had been her defiance that at the time Darius had been unable to resist challenging.

He had never had any serious intention of making love to Arabella, only to exact a little revenge for her dismissal of his offer eighteen months ago. That revenge had neatly rebounded on him when she had responded to his kisses and caresses with a passion that had just been waiting, it seemed, to respond to a lover's touch…

His specific touch?

Somehow Darius doubted that very much. Since

their first meeting Arabella had made her contemptuous opinion of him more than obvious.

'Marriage is not something I either seek or want,' he drawled now. 'Nevertheless, I am aware of the obligation I have to make such an offer. An offer that you, having already assured me that I am a man no decent woman would ever align herself with, need only refuse to bring an end to it.'

Arabella felt a shiver down the length of her spine as she heard the steely edge to Darius's tone as he repeated her earlier insult to him. An insult he had obviously taken exception to….

Enough to have deliberately made love to her a short time ago? No doubt. But it did not alter the fact that she had responded to him in such a wild and abandoned way.

Darius's arrogant certainty that Arabella would refuse his offer rankled in the same way as Hawk's cold assertion that she would refuse it had done earlier. 'Well?' she demanded haughtily.

Those deep blue eyes narrowed. 'Well, what?'

Arabella gave him a pert smile. 'I am waiting for you to make such an offer.'

Blond brows rose mockingly. 'I believe I just did.'

'No, you did not.' Arabella shook her head. 'You have explained that it is an offer you feel socially pressured into making. You have also said that I will refuse such an offer. You have yet to actually *make* me that offer.'

Darius gave an impatient grimace. 'You want your pound of flesh? Is that it?'

Her eyes flashed in temper. 'I merely want my offer!'

'Very well.' He took a deep breath. 'Lady Arabella, would you do me the honour of becoming my wife?' He made no effort to hide the sarcasm behind his proposal, or the cynical twist to his mouth.

It fired Arabella's temper anew. Darius Wynter was one of the most *arrogant* men she had ever met. He was just so absolutely sure of himself. Of Arabella's refusal to even consider his proposal. Of his ability to escape any lasting repercussions concerning their lovemaking—leaving *her* to bear the brunt of them with regard to her immediate family.

All her life, it seemed, Arabella had been surrounded by arrogantly forceful men. Her father, Alexander. Her three older brothers. To tie herself to a husband who possessed that same arrogance would surely be the height of folly.

Or perhaps it would be the height of good sense?

Arabella had enjoyed her two Seasons, but only once during that time had she even come close to finding a man who held her interest beyond their initial meeting. And that man had been Darius Wynter himself…

His Grace was absolutely nothing like the young men who had flattered and flirted with her these past two Seasons, all proclaiming undying love for her until Arabella had become sickened by their attentions.

Darius, making no effort to hide his arrogance or his cynicism, had neither flattered nor flirted with her. Much to her regret…

Arabella's pulse fluttered anew just looking at him:

that golden hair, those dark and unfathomable blue eyes, his arrogant slash of a nose above sculptured lips and jaw. And his perfectly tailored clothes covered what she had discovered such a short time ago was a surprisingly hard and muscled body.

No, Arabella was positive she would never find herself bored in the company of Darius Wynter…

'You are taking a deuced long time to refuse me!' he eventually growled in his impatience with her silence.

Arabella couldn't help giving a taunting, confident smile. 'I am still considering your offer, sir.'

He scowled darkly. 'What is there to consider?'

Arabella could no longer stand looking at the desk which had been the scene of her disgrace, instead strolling over to stand in front of the window to look out across the moonlit garden. 'Well, for one thing, by accepting your offer I would become a duchess.'

'The despised Darius Wynter's duchess, do not forget,' he reminded her harshly.

She gave a haughty inclination of her head as she turned to face him. 'There *is* that to consider, of course.'

His mouth twisted. 'And have you also forgotten that I was so "conveniently" rid of one wife but one short year ago?'

Arabella *had* forgotten!

'You must also be aware that none of the ton has a good word to say about me,' Darius said, pressing his advantage.

Arabella frowned slightly. 'My brother Lucian speaks very highly of you….'

Darius's mouth tightened. 'We are friends. Of a sort.'

She nodded. 'And I know that his wife, Grace, has taken several people to task for daring to criticise you within her hearing.'

His mouth quirked. 'We are related, after all.'

'Only tenuously.' Arabella dismissed the connection of him being Grace's half-uncle by marriage, or some such nonsense. 'My new sister-in-law, Juliet, was also most insistent that you be a guest at her wedding today.'

Darius's expression softened slightly as he thought of the gracious and beautiful Juliet Boyd, now Lady Juliet St Claire. 'Only because it was jealousy of my own friendship with the lady that was instrumental in bringing your brother up to scratch.'

Arabella's eyes widened. 'You had a—a romantic interest in *Juliet*?'

'Not in the least.' Darius gave a firm shake of his head. 'Sebastian *thought* I had a romantic interest in her,' he corrected. 'She and I were both aware at all times that that was not at all the case.'

'Why not?'

He raised surprised blond brows. 'I beg your pardon?'

'*Why* were you not attracted to Juliet?'

'I simply was not.' He snapped his impatience with the subject. 'Contrary to popular belief, I do not set out to seduce every beautiful woman I meet.'

Arabella frowned once more. 'I had not realised you were present at the Bancrofts' house party when Sebastian and Juliet met this past summer.'

Darius gave her an irritated glare. 'I see no reason why you should have been informed.'

Arabella's cheeks burned at the obvious derision in his tone. 'Were you there when the French spy was apprehended?'

It took great effort on Darius's part to keep his outward appearance coolly neutral. 'What French spy?'

Arabella shook her head. 'I have no idea. Sebastian and Juliet deny any knowledge of it. But rumour has it that the man was masquerading as someone's servant before the arrest?'

Rumour, as usual, was wrong. Darius knew with certainty that the French spy in question had been a woman…

'The incident must have happened after I had left,' he said. 'Now, could we get back to our own conversation? Our allotted five minutes was over long ago, and at any moment Hawk is likely to join us and demand to know our decision.' Darius would use any means at his disposal—even reminding her of his marriage offer—to deter Arabella from showing any further interest in that French spy!

'*My* decision,' Arabella corrected haughtily. 'After all, *I* am the one who will decide whether or not we are to be betrothed,' she explained at Darius's questioning glance.

Darius studied her through narrowed lids, easily noting the glitter of challenge in those deep brown eyes, the high colour in her cheeks, the determined set of her mouth and that stubbornly angled chin.

All things that told him Arabella was seriously considering accepting his offer....

An offer she had felt no compunction in refusing the previous year. *Before* he became a rich widower. *Before* he inherited the title of Duke of Carlyne.

Darius's expression hardened. 'And have *you* now decided?'

She drew in a ragged breath. 'I...I believe I need more time in which to consider the matter.'

'How much more time?' Darius rasped harshly.

Arabella shrugged slender shoulders. 'These things cannot be rushed, Your Grace. After all, we are talking of the rest of my life, are we not?'

'And mine,' he grated between clenched teeth.

She eyed him knowingly. 'Perhaps you should have considered that before making love to me earlier?'

'Perhaps I should,' Darius said tersely. He had never met a young lady more deserving of having her backside paddled than Lady Arabella St Claire did at this moment. In hindsight, that was probably what Darius should have administered earlier this evening in response to her challenge, rather than making love to her!

She looked down her tiny nose at him. 'I suggest, Your Grace, that in view of the lateness of the hour I consider your offer overnight and you call on me again tomorrow morning so that I might give you my answer.'

His mouth thinned. 'Whilst you are...*considering*

my offer, might I also suggest you *consider* that any marriage between us would necessarily be of the fullest kind.'

Arabella gave him a frowning glance, colour warming her cheeks as the mockery in his eyes and the twist to his hard mouth told her exactly what he meant by that comment.

Was she seriously considering Darius's marriage proposal? Or was she merely toying with him?

Just as he had toyed with her earlier when he'd made love to her with such deliberation?

For that alone Darius Wynter deserved to suffer at least the overnight torment of uncertainty as to whether or not Arabella would accept him.

She could not deny that becoming a duchess—even the Duchess of the infamous Duke of Carlyne—would be a wonderful matrimonial feather in her bonnet. She was also sure that Darius Wynter was too complex a man ever to bore her. In their marriage bed or out of it.

She gave a gracious inclination of her head. 'That sounds perfectly reasonable in the circumstances.'

His eyes narrowed to icy slits. 'You understand that I would expect my duchess to be amenable to the idea of producing Carlyne heirs?'

'That is the normal consequence of a full marriage, is it not?'

In truth, Arabella could not imagine having a marriage *without* children in it. Having grown up with three older siblings, and with one young nephew already to love and adore, Arabella looked forward to one day having children of her own to pet and spoil and love.

Darius Wynter's children?

If Arabella were honest with herself—and she usually was—then she would have to acknowledge that she had been completely aware of this man from the moment they'd met. It had been impossible not to notice him as he'd done the rounds of the salons and balls. Arabella also knew herself, along with several of the other young ladies out that year, to have become slightly infatuated with the dangerously handsome Lord Wynter.

All of them had certainly heaved a sigh of disappointment when he'd announced his betrothal to the heiress Miss Sophie Belling later that year, before marrying her in a private ceremony in the north of England only weeks later.

To now have him offer for Arabella, for whatever reason, filled her with edgy excitement more than anything else!

Darius had no idea what Arabella was thinking as she stared at him so intently. He could only hope that she was working out how unsuitable this marriage would be for both of them.

Aware that he would have to marry again one day, if only to provide the necessary heir, Darius also knew that now was not the right time for him to even be thinking of matrimony. Not when he had learnt earlier this evening that the French spy Arabella had just alluded to was once again at large…

His mouth tightened. 'Might I also suggest, Arabella,

that you consider the fact that in marrying me you would be tying yourself to a man you do not love, and who does not love you.'

Those brown eyes narrowed. 'Is that not what dalliances outside of marriage are for?'

A red tide of anger passed in front of Darius's eyes at the thought of Arabella taking a lover outside of their marriage.

Damn it, there was *not* going to be a marriage between them! Not if Darius could prevent it.

'Your brothers have all married for love,' he pointed out.

Her expression softened. 'So they have.' Her mouth firmed. 'They have obviously all been more fortunate than I.'

'You are but nineteen, Arabella—'

'Almost twenty,' she reminded him swiftly. 'Although I fail to see what my age has to do with anything.'

'It has to do with the fact that you may yet meet a man for whom you can feel love,' Darius bit out.

Her mouth quirked. 'Take care, Your Grace, you are allowing your own reluctance to take me as your wife more than obvious!'

Was he? If that were the case, then Darius was a better actor than he had ever given himself credit for being! In truth, he had only repeated his offer for Arabella at all because Hawk St Claire's haughty disdain had infuriated him.

But what man in his right mind, given the opportunity, would *not* want to take the beautiful and accomplished, the self-willed and haughty, the emotional and wildly passionate Arabella St Claire as his wife? To spend his days crossing verbal swords with her and his nights revelling in all the wild passion of which Darius now knew she was capable?

No man, in his right mind or otherwise, would even consider passing up the opportunity of marrying such a woman as the magnificent Lady Arabella St Claire!

Unless he was Darius Wynter. A man with whom it had already been proved it was dangerous for any woman to become involved. Especially now…

'Probably because I *am* reluctant,' he drawled scornfully.

'What a pity.' Arabella eyed him mockingly. 'When I am seriously thinking of accepting your offer!'

Darius's jaw tightened. 'Only because you are a contrary little baggage!'

She gave a trill of laughter. 'Do not expect that to change if I *should* decide to marry you.'

He scowled his displeasure. 'Arabella—'

'I believe we have talked on this subject long enough for one evening, Your Grace.' She affected a bored yawn as she crossed to the door. 'As I have said, I will inform you as to my decision in the morning.'

Darius could only stand and stare after Arabella in intense frustration as she left the room.

Would she have the audacity to inform him on the morrow that she had decided to *accept* his marriage proposal?

He realised with a heavy sigh that he was in for a long, sleepless night….

Chapter Three

'I really wish you would reconsider your decision.' Jane, Duchess of Stourbridge, Arabella's sister-in-law, paced agitatedly up and down the nursery as Arabella sat in a chair in the bay window, attempting to soothe the young and teething Alexander, Marquis of Mulberry, as he moved fretfully on her shoulder. 'You may be assured that I have informed Hawk most strongly how wrong he is to allow you to align yourself to a man such as Darius Wynter!'

Arabella had confirmed to Hawk her intention of accepting Darius's offer as they had sat at the breakfast table together earlier this morning. An announcement her eldest brother had listened to in disapproving silence before proceeding to repeat all the reasons he considered the match unsuitable.

She almost never argued with Hawk, and had not enjoyed arguing with him this morning, either. But neither would her pride—that arrogant St Claire pride—allow her to back down in the face of his icy disapproval.

In truth, once she'd learnt of Darius's offer, there had really been very little doubt as to her accepting it….

'I assure you that Hawk has left me in no doubt as to *his* doubts concerning the marriage, dear Jane.' Arabella shot the older woman a rueful smile. 'But the decision ultimately lies with me, does it not?'

'Well… Yes! But—' Jane gave a shake of her red curls. 'Can it be that you are in love with Carlyne, Arabella?'

'Certainly not!' Her expression was one of incredulous indignation.

'Then why think of marrying him?' Jane frowned her consternation.

Arabella gave a dismissive shrug. 'I have to marry someone, Jane, so why not the Duke of Carlyne?'

'Admittedly he is wickedly handsome…'

'My dear Jane!' She arched teasing brows. 'Are you supposed to notice such things when you are so happily married to Hawk?'

'This is not a teasing matter, Arabella.' Jane's expression was reproving. 'And being happily married, to Hawk or otherwise, does not render a woman blind to the fact that Darius Wynter *is* devilishly handsome.'

'He is rather,' Arabella acknowledged thoughtfully, a smile of satisfaction playing about her lips as she considered his golden hair, deep blue eyes, his wickedly sensual mouth and his hard and muscled body.

Jane eyed her uncertainly. 'Even if the two of you

have…have anticipated the wedding vows, it does not mean you have to marry the man.'

Arabella smiled wickedly. 'My dear Jane, I believe the Duke and I had barely begun to "anticipate the wedding vows" when Hawk and Lord Redwood interrupted us yesterday evening!'

'In that case why consider tying yourself to him for a lifetime?'

Indeed. It was a question Arabella had already asked herself many times. Yesterday evening. During the long, sleepless night she had endured. And again this morning, before she'd informed Hawk of her decision.

She had finally come to the conclusion that there was no single answer to that question. Although it could perhaps best be summed up by the fact that, after two Seasons spent being flattered and fawned over by all manner of eligible men, Arabella knew that Darius was the only man that she had found to be in the least exciting or intriguing. And dangerous…

'Not all women can expect to find a marriage of love, as you, Grace and Juliet have done with my brothers,' she answered Jane evasively.

Arabella knew she could not explain to anyone the strange satisfaction she felt in her decision to marry Darius—or the feeling of fluttering excitement she felt at the thought of becoming his wife. Of sharing his home and his bed.

Most especially his bed!

Far from repulsing her, as Darius had so obviously hoped that it might, the promise of sharing his bed on a regular basis filled Arabella with a delicious anticipation that made her tremble just to think of it.

Although it would not do to allow Darius himself to know of the eagerness of her feelings in that regard…

'There are several matters that need to be settled before I feel able to give you an answer to your offer of marriage.'

Darius looked between narrowed lids at the young and haughty miss before him as she stood up to receive him in the drawing room of St Claire House at precisely eleven o'clock. Arabella had offered him no word of greeting, instead simply proceeded to continue their conversation from the evening before as if there had been no break in their discussion.

Wearing a gown of the deepest gold, a colour that seemed reflected in her eyes, and with her golden curls arranged artfully at her crown with several tantalising wisps at her nape and temples, Lady Arabella St Claire was this morning in possession of an air of self-sufficiency and confidence that Darius found less than reassuring.

'Good morning to you, too, Arabella,' Darius said pointedly as he gave her a sweeping elegant bow.

Irritation creased her creamy brow, and she gave no curtsy in response to that formality. 'I had believed our present situation to have put us beyond the need for such inanities, Darius.'

'Had you?' He strolled further into the room, its cream-and-gold décor a perfect foil for Arabella's appearance, of which this self-possessed young lady was no doubt fully aware. 'Exactly what situation would that be?' His voice had hardened perceptively.

Irritation coloured her cheeks. 'Do not attempt to play games with me, Darius.'

His gaze was icy. 'I have no intention of attempting to play games with you, Arabella, considering what happened the last time I rose—quite literally—to your challenge.'

The colour deepened in her cheeks. 'There is no need for—for such indelicacy!'

'No?' He looked at her coldly. 'What would you rather I be?' He deliberately broke social etiquette by sitting down in one of the gold brocade armchairs whilst she still stood, leaning his elbows on the arms of that chair to steeple his fingers together in front of him as he looked up at her. 'The besotted lover, perhaps? We both know I am far from being that,' he said scathingly. 'The man resigned to his fate? But I am *not* resigned, Arabella,' he assured her, with a tightening of his jaw. 'Far from it!'

Faced once again with the flesh-and-blood man—a rakishly sophisticated man, far beyond her experience—Arabella could only wonder at her own temerity in daring to challenge him.

Once again he was dressed all in black, with snowy white linen and black Hessians, the sombre and perfectly tailored clothing giving him the appearance of that blond-haired devil Arabella had once considered him to be—still did.

'Might I remind you, Darius, that you were not forced into offering for me?'

He gave a hard, mocking smile. 'I thought it worth it just to see the look of outrage on Stourbridge's face.'

Her eyes widened. 'You *expected* me to refuse?'

He gave a dismissive shrug. 'Of course.'

'You would rather bring disgrace down upon both our heads than marry me?' Arabella said slowly, her anger rising.

Darius shrugged. 'I am no stranger to disgrace, Arabella. On the contrary, in the past I have considered it my duty to provide such scandalous diversions as I can, for the ton's entertainment.' He looked bored. 'On the basis that if they are gossiping and speculating about *my* behaviour then they are at least leaving some poor innocent alone.'

'*I* am an innocent, Your Grace—and if our actions yesterday evening are made public then I very much doubt the gossiping tongues of the ton will leave *me* alone!'

Darius shook his head. 'You are far from innocent, Arabella.'

Her eyes flashed. 'You still doubt my virtue?'

'Not in the least,' he said. 'I was referring to the fact that you are hardly the epitome of a young and innocent miss,' he pointed out. 'Neither did I say I would not marry you, if your decision is to accept. I merely stated that I am not resigned to such a fate.'

Arabella felt a shiver of apprehension down the length of her spine at the cold anger she read so easily in the harshness of Darius's expression.

Yet her own anger increased each time Darius voiced his reluctance to marry her!

What choice did she have?

Marriage to Darius, or eventual marriage to one of those young bucks of the ton with whom Arabella already knew she could never find any real happiness? A life of mediocrity, of boredom, when all the time she was aware that she could instead have had the exciting Darius Wynter, Duke of Carlyne, as her husband?

A man whose very presence in a room both thrilled and excited her.

A man who made love to her with a finesse and skill that left her hot and aching.

A man she had gazed at longingly from afar for far too long already…

Besides, his very reluctance to marry her was an insult. A challenge no St Claire would refuse….

She straightened determinedly. 'Then it is a pity I have decided to accept your offer, is it not?'

Darius's eyes narrowed speculatively on the young woman who faced him so defiantly across the drawing-room. The beautiful and feisty Arabella St Claire, a young woman that at any other time Darius would have enjoyed taking for his wife. No, would have revelled in taking as his wife. Most especially the 'taking' part!

But now was not the time for Darius to publicly tie himself down with emotional entanglement. To announce to the world at large that he had aligned himself to a young, and consequently vulnerable, wife.

Although he had no doubts that Arabella would dispute that she was in the least vulnerable!

'Why?' he bit out harshly.

She raised those haughty brows. 'I am sorry, I do not understand?'

His gaze narrowed. 'Did I inadvertently deliver some unintended insult to you in the past that you now feel I should be made to suffer? Some slight upon your person for which you feel I need to make suitable reparation?'

Her mouth twisted. 'Your obvious joy in my acceptance of your offer is overwhelming, Darius.'

He gave a hard grin at her sarcasm. 'It is difficult to feel joy when one feels one has a loaded gun placed against one's temple.'

Her cheeks flushed angrily. 'How flattering!'

He gave a mocking inclination of his head. 'Strange, when I intended to insult.'

Arabella was completely aware of what this man had intended. 'No one is forcing you to do anything, Darius. No matter what my own decision is, you have only to inform Hawk that you have changed your mind and now refuse to marry me.'

Darius gave a humourless laugh. 'And so allow him the pleasure of pulling the trigger?'

Arabella gave an inelegant snort. 'I assure you that Hawk has no more desire to see you become a member of his family than you have to become one.'

Darius did not doubt it. He had known for a long time—eighteen months, at least—that Hawk St Claire held him in complete contempt.

'Lucian is not so disapproving, however,' Arabella added slowly.

'Lucian?' Darius echoed slowly. 'Lucian has spoken on my behalf?'

'I believe he talked with Hawk after breakfast.' She nodded.

Darius didn't much like the sound of that. He didn't like the sound of it at all! So much so that he made a note to himself to talk to Lucian at the earliest opportunity. Damn it, if Lucian had dared to break the promise he had made to Darius seven months ago…

He had no doubt that Arabella would make an admirable duchess. That as both the daughter and the sister of a duke she was more than capable of fulfilling that role with grace and confidence.

Any duchess but Darius's!

He had made certain decisions concerning his life eight years ago. Decisions totally private to himself and a few chosen others. Immune, or simply uncaring of the danger those decisions represented to himself, he was nevertheless aware that they could become a threat to anyone with whom he became intimately involved. Most especially, it seemed, to any woman he became betrothed to or married!

Darius stood up impatiently, his eyes narrowing shrewdly at the way Arabella immediately took a deliberate and nervous step back from him. His mouth tightened as he mercilessly went for the attack. 'Am I right in thinking that a wealthy duke is a more attractive marriage prospect than a penniless lord?'

Arabella eyed him warily. 'Any woman who did not think so would be very foolish indeed,' she replied honestly.

'How unfortunate, then, that you are not a foolish woman,' Darius rasped bitterly.

Arabella gave a puzzled shake of her head. 'I fail to understand what—'

'Do not play the innocent with me, Arabella,' he growled.

'I am not—'

'I advise you to be absolutely certain that you are completely happy with your decision.'

'I have said that I am...'

'You have taken into account, I hope, that—as you have said—my previous wife "conveniently" died within a month of the marriage and left me all the richer for it?' he reminded her grimly.

Arabella felt all the colour drain from her cheeks.

Of course she had not forgotten that this man's first wife had died in a hunting accident a year ago, only weeks after becoming Darius Wynter's wife. Nor was she unaware of the suspicions that had been voiced amongst the ton about the suddenness of the other woman's death.

Suspicions that she had voiced to Darius herself, only the previous evening!

But she was sure he had only brought that up to try and make her change her mind about accepting his offer! She eyed him closely. 'I have no idea as to your first wife's family circumstances, but I have no doubt that my own brothers, Lucian included, would deal with you most severely were anything...untoward ever to happen to me,' Arabella told him firmly.

Once again Darius could not help but admire her.

Whether Arabella believed those rumours concerning his wife's untimely death or not, she obviously had no intention of being deterred from marrying him herself. 'In other words you are hoping that the threat of your brothers' retribution will ensure that it does not?'

'Exactly.' She nodded coolly.

Darius gave a rueful shake of his head. 'I fail to see of what possible comfort that retribution could be to you if you were already dead.'

She gave a blithe smile. 'I assure you, knowing that Hawk, Lucian and Sebastian would instantly consign you to the devil is of tremendous comfort to me!'

Darius's mouth thinned. 'And if I were to admit to you right now that I *was* indeed responsible for my first wife's early demise?'

Arabella drew in a sharp breath and looked at him searchingly. 'Why would you do such a thing?' she finally murmured.

Darius shifted impatiently. 'Possibly because it is the truth?'

She frowned. 'I believe you are trying to frighten me into refusing you!'

'Am I succeeding?' He scowled darkly.

'No,' she answered pertly. 'Now, if you have quite finished voicing your reservations concerning our marriage—'

'I do not recall voicing *any* of my reservations as yet,' Darius rasped harshly. 'The main one being, of course, that I have no use for a wife. Not now. Or in the foreseeable future.'

She blinked. 'Yesterday evening you mentioned the necessity for heirs.'

His mouth compressed. 'Which I would be just as capable of fathering in ten—twenty years as I am now. Arabella, have you seriously considered what it will mean to become my wife?' he continued impatiently. 'I am a man most of the ton still believe beyond the pale. A man who has only attained a tenuous respectability because of a title which should never have become mine.' His expression darkened. 'That would not have become mine if my brother had not died so suddenly and his legitimate heir, my nephew Simon, had not already been slain at Waterloo.'

Yes, of course Arabella had considered all of those things during the long hours of a sleepless night. But ultimately they had all been rendered insignificant against her own inexplicable desire to become this man's wife.

Inexplicable because Arabella refused to search her heart too deeply in order to find the answers to that particular puzzle…

'In that case, marriage to a St Claire can only but add to your newfound but shaky respectability!'

Darius could see from the firm tilt of those highly kissable lips and the stubborn light in those deep brown eyes that Arabella would not be swayed from her decision, that she was wilfully determined to become his wife whether he desired it or not.

And he most certainly did not.

But not for any of the reasons he had so far stated…

He admired Arabella St Claire. Desired her. He would not have offered for her eighteen months ago if he had not—an offer she had not hesitated to refuse when he was penniless and lacked a dukedom, he reminded himself testily.

He crossed the room in two long strides to reach out and grasp the tops of her arms, totally impervious to her sudden look of alarm. 'I advise you to be sure of exactly what you would be doing by marrying me, Arabella,' he growled.

Her throat moved convulsively as she swallowed nervously. 'What do you mean?'

'I am a man used to doing as I please. Going where I please, when I please, as I please. A circumstance I would see no reason to change simply because I have a wife.'

Arabella's eyes widened. 'You are telling me before we are even wed that you intend to continue your relationships outside of our marriage? That you perhaps already have a mistress you intend to continue to visit?'

Darius almost laughed at the ludicrousness of those questions.

Ludicrous because there had been no women in his life, mistresses or otherwise, for some time now. His brief foray into marriage had shown Darius how unwise it was for him to have an intimate relationship with any woman. How detrimental that very intimacy could be to her health…

He looked down at Arabella. She was so very young. So beautiful. So utterly and completely desirable…

Darius suddenly realised how he could dissuade the stubbornly determined Arabella from going ahead with their betrothal and marriage. He had only to ruthlessly demonstrate how unsuitable a candidate he was as a prospective husband to send her running back to the safe and welcoming arms of her three over-protective brothers.

Yes, Darius knew exactly how to go about achieving that end. But he also knew that having done so he would be giving up any chance of renewing his addresses to her in the future, however far ahead he was looking. That, believing herself rejected by Darius, Arabella was contrary enough to accept the next suitor who made an offer for her and in doing so making it impossible for Darius to ever claim her.

No, as inconvenient and risky as it was for Darius to marry Arabella now, for him not to do so would certainly mean losing her for ever. A possibility that he found was even more unacceptable to him than this forced betrothal, than knowing that she only wanted to marry him now because he was the wealthy Duke of Carlyne…

'I do not expect to need a mistress once we are married, Arabella.' He finally answered her previous question. 'I would expect you to cater to my physical needs. Whatever those might be.'

Arabella felt a shiver of apprehension down the length of her spine as she looked up into the hard implacability of his face. His mouth was a thin, uncompromising line. His eyes as hard and glittering as the sapphires in the necklace left to her by her mother.

It was the face of a man who would brook no challenge to his indomitable will. Least of all from a wife he felt had been foisted on him by the dictates of Society rather than one he had chosen for himself.

Any woman not born a St Claire would have been daunted by the risk that he represented at that moment. Yet it only made Arabella all the more determined to penetrate his arrogant façade. To poke and prod at that mockery and cynicism until she reached the man beneath that apparently impenetrable shield.

Perhaps if she had not had the cynically remote Hawk and Lucian as her brothers, or the softer but just as arrogant Sebastian, then Arabella may have believed that outer shell to be all there was to Darius Wynter. But, as their petted and spoilt younger sister, Arabella had come to know her brothers' natures well, and she knew all of them to be capable of deep and tumultuous emotions. To be men who were all deeply and irrevocably in love with their wives....

Was she hoping, once they married, that Darius would similarly fall in love with her?

Arabella stifled a disbelieving gasp at even the suggestion of such a hope. Did that mean she had feelings for Darius she hadn't even dared to suspect existed?

Darius raised a brow as he saw Arabella's reaction to his suggestion that she alone would satisfy his physical needs. 'My physical needs are really not as debauched as the ton would have you believe.' He eyed her teasingly. 'I can at least assure you that there will be no whips or chains involved!'

'Whips or chains?' she gasped breathlessly, her face paling.

It was a response that reminded Darius more than any other, despite her claims to the contrary yesterday evening, just how innocent she really was when it came to physical intimacy. 'I am sure you will very quickly learn to satisfy all my *very normal* sexual appetites, Arabella.'

Once again her throat moved convulsively as she swallowed before raising her chin proudly. 'As, no doubt, *you* will learn to satisfy mine?'

She was a vixen. A little hellcat. Verbally spitting and clawing despite her obvious unease at discussing such an intimate subject with him. 'That part of marriage I am already looking forward to with the greatest of pleasure,' Darius assured her throatily.

A challenge entered the deep brown depths of her eyes. 'I would prefer us to have a lengthy betrothal in order that we might become better acquainted with each other on a social level before—'

'No.'

She eyed him uncertainly. 'No?'

Darius looked down at her between hooded lids. 'No,' he repeated firmly. 'If we are to marry at all, then it must be immediately.'

'I— But— Why?' Arabella didn't even attempt to hide her bewilderment.

She had been envisaging spending the winter months as Darius's betrothed. With perhaps the wedding planned for next spring or summer. Six, possibly nine months when the two of them could spend time together, tormenting and challenging each other if they must, before contemplating the complete intimacy of marriage.

The implacability of Darius's expression told her that such an arrangement was totally unacceptable to him. 'Take it or leave it, Arabella,' he stated uncompromisingly. 'You will either marry me by special licence next week or we will not marry at all.'

Next week? Was he *insane*?

Arabella pulled out of Darius's grasp to move away from him. 'I cannot possibly organise a wedding by next week!'

'I fail to see why not.' Darius appeared unmoved by her obvious shock. 'Obtaining a special licence should pose no problem. All of your family and the majority of the ton have already gathered in town in order to attend your brother's nuptials yesterday. Hawk's duchess has proved she is capable of being hostess to a wedding supper at short notice. As I see it, a week is more than time enough for you to obtain a suitable wedding gown.'

As *he* saw it, perhaps. As *Arabella* saw it the idea of marrying this man as early as next week was unacceptable. Terrifyingly soon, in fact.

'Why the rush, Darius?' She made her tone deliberately light. 'I realise that this situation has been thrust upon us by—by certain actions that took place between us yesterday evening, but we both know that there is no real reason for such a hasty wedding to take place.' Her cheeks burned at the memory of the intimacies the two of them had shared the previous evening.

Darius felt a sharp stab of sympathy for Arabella's obvious bewilderment as to his insistence on a short betrothal and a hasty wedding. Reminding him that for all Arabella was a St Claire, and as such in possession of the same arrogant self-confidence as her three older brothers, she was nevertheless still only nineteen years of age. A very young and innocent nineteen years, despite her previous claim otherwise.

He wished that he could grant Arabella the lengthy betrothal she so obviously desired—months during which the little minx had no doubt intended to tempt and bedevil him!—but the truth was, once their betrothal was publicly announced, Darius simply dared not leave her for any length of time without his full protection.

He dared not.

'Next week, Arabella. Or there will be no wedding.'

Arabella looked up at him searchingly, knowing by the grimness of Darius's expression—the stern set of his mouth and the coldness of his blue eyes—that he was unshakeable in his decision that she would marry him next week and be damned, or the two of them would not marry at all.

She drew in a deep breath. 'Very well, Darius.' She gave a tiny inclination of her head. 'I will inform Hawk that we have decided to marry as early as possible next week.'

'*I* will be the one to inform your brother as to our intentions, Arabella,' Darius cut in decisively, a cynical curl to his top lip. 'As is my right as your future husband.' He quirked one arrogant brow.

Arabella bit back the argument that had been hovering upon her lips, wisely deciding that prudence was probably the better course at this point in time. There would be plenty of opportunity after they were married for her to show Darius that she had no intention of being a conventional meek or obedient wife….

Chapter Four

'It is still not too late to change your mind, Arabella, if you have a single doubt as to the wisdom of marrying Carlyne.'

Arabella turned to look across her bedchamber as Hawk, her tall and imposing brother, stood in the doorway dressed in his own wedding finery of snowy white linen beneath a tailored claret-coloured jacket of the very finest velvet, black pantaloons and shiny black Hessians.

The rest of the family had already departed for St George's Church in Hanover Square, but as the eldest of her brothers Hawk was to ride with Arabella in the bridal carriage, and then accompany her down the aisle before handing her into the care of her husband-to-be.

Into Darius Wynter's care.

Arabella swallowed down her feelings of nervousness as she presented her brother with a widely confident smile. 'I have no doubts at all, Hawk.'

This past week had been a busy one of hectic arrangements. Arabella had never been left alone for a moment as the dressmaker was visited, the ivory silk chosen for her gown and fittings arranged, flowers obtained, and the menu for the wedding breakfast decided upon in consultation with Jane.

There had been little or no time for second or third thoughts, and with everything there had been to arrange or decide upon, Arabella had seen very little of Darius himself. Despite that, Arabella was more convinced than ever that her choice of husband was the correct one. For her.

Arabella knew herself well enough to realise that she could never be happy with a weak man, a man she could bend to her will by artifice or design. And Darius would never be such a man.

Despite their lack of opportunity to spend time together, Arabella had nevertheless had the chance to witness for herself what she viewed as the strengths of Darius's character. His arrogance was more than a match for any of her brothers whenever they chanced to meet. He had been charm itself on meeting Jane and being faced with her obvious uncertainties as to his suitability as a husband for Arabella.

Most surprising had been Darius's consideration and gentleness with his brother's widow, the Dowager Duchess of Carlyne, when she had arrived in London three days ago for the wedding and the betrothed couple had been invited to dine with her that evening.

Arabella had reassured herself that any man capable of showing such kindness as Darius had to Margaret Wynter, even a man who preferred the ton to think of him as a rake and a cynic, could not possibly be all bad.

Hawk's austere expression softened slightly as he stepped further into the bedchamber. 'You look so much like Mama today.' He gazed down at her admiringly in the ivory silk gown, her golden curls enhanced by a matching bonnet, her bouquet a simple arrangement of deep yellow roses from the St Claire hot-house.

'Really?' Arabella glowed; she had been aged only eight when her mother and father were killed in a carriage accident, and over the years her memories of her warm and beautiful mother had become hazy at best.

'Very much so,' Hawk assured her gruffly as he reached out to take both her hands in his own. 'How I wish our parents could be here to see how beautiful you look on your wedding day.'

Arabella squeezed his hands. 'Perhaps they can.'

'Perhaps,' Hawk allowed gently.

She gave her brother a searching glance. 'I *am* going to be happy, Hawk.'

'So Lucian never fails to assure me.' His eyes narrowed. 'Even so, I am sure I have made no secret of the fact that Carlyne is not the man I ever envisaged as a husband for you.'

'No.' Arabella smiled slightly as she thought of the battle of wills that had ensued between Darius and Hawk on the few occasions the two men had met during this past week. Battles which Darius had—surprisingly—invariably won…

Her brother gave a rueful shake of his head. 'Perhaps if I had known of your preference for him then I would not have been so hasty in refusing him when he last offered for you.'

Arabella's eyed widened incredulously. 'Darius has offered for me *before*?'

'During your first Season,' Hawk acknowledged heavily, releasing her hands to cross the bedchamber and stand with his back towards her as he stared out of the window into the busy street below.

'I— But— Why did you not tell me?' Arabella frowned in disbelief as she stared at the implacability of Hawk's stiffly erect back and shoulders.

Darius had offered for her the previous year?

Before he had made a similar offer for Sophie Belling and been accepted, obviously.

Hawk turned, the sternness of his features twisted into a grimace. 'I did not tell you because I was not—am still not—convinced as Lucien appears to be as to Carlyne's suitability as a husband for you.'

'So you refused his first offer for me without even consulting me?' Arabella accused.

'I did.' Hawk looked haughtily unrepentant. 'And I would have done so again this time if the—the circumstances had not been as they were. If you had not informed me it was your sincere wish to marry him.' His expression was grim. 'The fact that Carlyne offered for Sophie Belling too last summer, and then married her after approaching me in regard to you such a short time before, only confirmed to me that his reasons for offering for you then were of a mercenary nature rather than because his emotions were truly engaged.'

Arabella knew she couldn't refute that claim. She doubted that Darius could, either. But for Hawk to have refused Darius's offer without even asking her opinion was beyond belief.

Although it went some way to explaining Darius's remark a week ago that a wealthy duke was obviously a more attractive marriage prospect than a penniless lord. He obviously believed Arabella's only reason for accepting him now was because he *was* now a wealthy duke!

Would she have accepted if she had known of Darius's offer a year ago?

At the time he had been known as a rake and a gambler. A man who, with little personal wealth left at his disposal, was deeply in debt. A man whose only means of alleviating that debt had appeared to be in the taking of a wealthy woman to wife.

Hawk was Arabella's guardian, charged with her welfare, and she knew that he had been perfectly justified in refusing him on her behalf when Darius had offered for her last summer.

But as the young woman who had compared every man she had met these past two Seasons with the devilish good-looks and magnetic charisma of Lord Darius Wynter—and found them all wanting!—Arabella could not help but feel resentful at Hawk's highhandedness. She might not be in love with Darius, or he with her, but Arabella had absolutely no doubt that she would have accepted him the previous summer.

Much as she hated Darius to think badly of her, Arabella knew she would be wise to make sure Darius didn't discover that she had not known until today of his previous offer for her, and to keep to herself her reasons for marrying him. The battle of wills that existed between them would be lost before it had even begun in earnest if Darius were ever to guess that Arabella was entering into their marriage with an eagerness for her husband's kisses and caresses that would be shocking if the anticipation did not feel so deliciously exciting…

'You are looking very lovely today,' Darius remarked dryly to his wife of two hours.

Hours during which he had smiled and been polite to both Arabella's family—all those St Claire aunts and uncles and cousins—and numerous members of the ton, who ordinarily would have returned to their country estates this late in the year, but had instead stayed on in town to attend two fashionable St Claire weddings.

No doubt gossip and speculation about the second of the two weddings would sustain many a conversation on a cold winter's evening before the ton returned to London *en masse* in the spring—with the added and erroneous assumption that the heir to the Carlyne dukedom would be born an indecently short time after the wedding!

'Thank you.' Arabella had no intention of returning the compliment by telling Darius how breathtakingly handsome *he* looked, in his snowy-white linen and austere black jacket and thigh-hugging black pantaloons, with his hair gleaming deeply gold in the reflection of the hundreds of candles illuminating the ballroom at St Claire House.

Seeing Darius in church earlier, as he'd stood at the altar waiting for her to join him, had literally robbed Arabella of her breath. So much so that for a few brief moments she had been unable to move as the organ began to play. Only the recently acquired knowledge of Darius's previous offer for her, one that had been made *willingly*, had prompted her into moving forward on silk-slippered feet.

Apart from her three brothers, Darius now stood head and shoulders above their wedding guests. Even if he had not, the deep gold of his hair and the handsomeness of his features would have distinguished him from every other man in the room.

Or perhaps that was only Arabella's biased opinion?

'When can we decently take our leave, do you think?' Darius looked bored by the whole proceeding.

Arabella arched blond brows. 'Decently?' she prodded.

Darius shrugged broad shoulders. 'Or indecently?'

'I would have thought, having been through this once before, that you would have more knowledge of the correct etiquette than I? Or perhaps your previous marriage was of such short duration that you have simply forgotten?' she taunted.

His eyes narrowed. 'Have a care, Arabella,' he warned her softly.

'Or what, Your Grace?'

'Or I might give myself the pleasure, once we are alone, of placing you over my knee and administering suitable punishment,' Darius murmured huskily, and was instantly rewarded by the flush that appeared in Arabella's cheeks.

Of anger? Or *anticipation*?

This past week had shown Darius that his new bride possessed all the courage he had imagined and more, as she had steadfastly refused to be daunted by any of the underlying displeasure of the ton in her choice of husband. Just as she had withstood all the gossip and speculation that had circulated around town after their wedding was announced. She had also, without fuss or ado, aided her sister-in-law Jane with the arrangements of that wedding. Best of all, she had been gracious and compassionate to Margaret, his brother's widow, a lady that Darius himself held in high regard, when they had dined with her.

In fact, Darius could not fault Arabella's behaviour towards everything and everyone this past week. Everyone but himself, that was…

Whenever the two of them had chanced to be alone—which, admittedly, had not been often—Arabella had tended to be either sharply critical or coolly dismissive, giving him little idea as to how she really felt about him. But Darius had every intention of rectifying the coolness of her manner towards him later this evening, once they were finally alone together at Carlyne House.

In fact, the anticipation of at last being alone with her was only adding to Darius's frustration with the social expectations it was so necessary to fulfil at one's own wedding. He physically ached to finish what the two of them had started in Hawk St Claire's study a week ago. Especially when he considered it had been that intimacy which had forced him into having to offer Arabella marriage!

His promised conversation with Lucian St Claire, once he'd finally managed to get the other man alone, had assured him of the other man's silence. Lucian had confirmed that he had not in any way broken the promise he had given to Darius six months ago. Nor would he.

Arabella looked down her provocative little nose at him. 'Am I to assume from that remark that I should expect to be beaten on a regular basis in our marriage, Your Grace?'

'You can expect to receive *something* on a regular basis in our marriage, Arabella,' he warned harshly. 'Especially if you intend to continue addressing me as "Your Grace" in that patronising manner.'

Her cheeks coloured prettily. 'I am not sure that I altogether approve of a man who would threaten to beat his wife.'

Darius raised blond brows. 'I do not believe I have ever asked for your approval, Arabella.'

No, he never had, Arabella acknowledged with a frown. In fact, she could never remember Darius, either as the disreputable Lord Wynter or the more respectable Duke of Carlyne, ever asking for, or indeed needing, anyone's approval. Least of all her own.

Arabella grudgingly admitted that it was this very arrogance, the feeling of dangerous uncertainty whenever she was in Darius's company, that made him so fascinatingly attractive to her....

'Nor,' Darius continued softly as he moved to stand in front of her, and so effectively shut the two of them off from their guests' curiosity, 'did I, in fact, threaten to beat you in the manner you describe. I assure you, Arabella, that I would endeavour to ensure that you thoroughly enjoy any...punishment that I choose to administer to you.'

Arabella felt colour blaze in her cheeks at the bluntness of his conversation. 'Perhaps the women you are used to associating with enjoy such—such rough treatment, Darius, but I assure you that I do not.'

'I hope you will come to appreciate at least a little sport in our marriage bed, Arabella.' His eyes gleamed down at her mockingly. 'I assure you, there is nothing quite like it for rousing the blood.'

Arabella felt herself becoming flustered. Had she, after all, taken on more of a challenge in becoming Darius's wife than she was capable of dealing with?

Darius had been married before, and had indulged in a prodigious number of affairs with ladies both in the ton and out of it. In comparison to those women Arabella knew herself to be very young and inexperienced. Perhaps too much so to sustain the interest of a man as experienced as Darius undoubtedly was?

It was a little late for her to be having second thoughts now, when the wedding had already taken place and she would shortly be retiring for the night with her husband to Carlyne House!

She looked searchingly into his face. 'I believe, sir, that you are deliberately trying to alarm me…'

His mouth quirked. 'Am I?'

'Yes.' Arabella felt more and more confident of the fact as she saw the humour deepen in his vivid blue eyes. 'It is very cruel of you to tease me in this way, Darius.'

He raised a wicked brow. 'Perhaps in the same way it was cruel of *you* to tease *me* this past week?'

Her eyes widened. 'I was not aware of indulging in any such teasing.'

She was so very young, Darius realised ruefully. And so completely unaware, it seemed, of the physical provocation of the creamy swell of her breasts and the way her hips swayed so seductively beneath the soft material of her gown when she walked. Of the perfume that he had begun to associate only with her—a soft and enticing floral, womanly scent that he knew belonged uniquely to Arabella.

Of how the soft gold of her curls enticed him to release those tresses from their pins and allow them to tumble down the length of her slender spine.

Of how the soft fullness of her mouth just begged to be kissed.

In fact, it was all he could do now not to totally scandalise their wedding guests by taking his wife in his arms and kissing her in a thorough manner that was guaranteed to shock the avidly watching ton and no doubt confirm all their suspicions!

'I assure you, I have been well and truly teased by you,' he confirmed abruptly. 'Although I have high hopes of that situation changing very shortly—'

'I am sorry to interrupt, Carlyne.' William Bancroft, Earl of Banford and an active member of the House, had approached them unobserved. 'I wonder if I might steal your husband away for just a few moments, Your Grace?' He smiled warmly at Arabella.

Arabella instantly found herself blushing at being addressed by her new title for the first time, but at the same time recognised that she would appreciate a few minutes' respite from Darius's overwhelming presence. 'Of course, Lord Bancroft.' She smiled graciously at the other man in an effort to make up for the fact that Darius looked intensely annoyed at the interruption.

Which was less than gracious of him, considering that the Earl and Countess of Banford had been on Darius's guest list rather than Arabella's own.

It was a fact that Arabella had found curious to say the least, and she had wondered if it was not *Lady* Bancroft, a woman reputed to have been mistress to several high-ranking male members of the ton before her marriage to the Earl three years ago, with whom Darius was better acquainted...

'Can this really not wait, Bancroft?' Darius felt no qualms about voicing his displeasure. 'It is, after all, my wedding day.'

'I require only two minutes of your time, I assure you,' the older man placated him lightly.

'I really should circulate amongst our other guests anyway, Darius.' Arabella looked up at him reproachfully.

'We will shortly be leaving, Arabella.' Darius said. 'Before anyone else feels themselves urgently in need of my company.' He scowled darkly at the other man.

Arabella shot the Earl a reassuring smile before taking her leave, but that smile was replaced by a frown as she could not help but overhear Darius's muttered words to the other man.

'What the hell can be so urgent, Bancroft,' he rasped impatiently, 'that you feel the need to bring it to my attention during my wedding celebrations?'

'I thought, before you left town, that you should be apprised of how events are developing concerning a certain matter,' the older man answered softly.

Arabella had moved too far across the ballroom by this time to be able to hear what Darius said in reply. But that did not stop her from wondering to what 'events' Lord Bancroft was referring. Or in what way they had 'developed'.

Although the conversation *did* imply that it was the deeply respected Earl of Banford, after all, with whom Darius was acquainted, and not the other man's beautiful wife…

It was an indication to Arabella that there was still much she did not know about the man to whom she was now well and truly married….

'Did you and Lord Bancroft manage to settle your differences earlier?' Arabella asked Darius lightly.

They were travelling together in the Carlyne ducal carriage some half an hour later, having just departed St Claire House to the cheers and well wishes of both their families and friends after Arabella threw her bouquet into a group of young unmarried ladies.

The curtains were drawn across the windows, but a lighted lamp prevented the inside of the carriage from being in complete darkness. The reflection given off by the flickering light threw Darius's face into darkly satanic relief as he scowled across at her. 'I do not remember either of us stating that any such differences existed.'

'No, of course you did not,' Arabella accepted with a frown. 'But you did not seem very pleased at his interruption.'

'I believe my irritation with his intrusion to have been completely merited, considering this is our wedding day.'

Darius rose suddenly to cross the carriage and sit beside Arabella on the cushioned seat, the hard length of his muscled thigh pressed intimately against her much softer one.

Very intimately. Far too intimately for comfort. For Arabella's comfort, anyway. Enough to once again make her feel flustered and a little unsure of herself. A little? Arabella was a *lot* unsure of herself!

She moistened dry lips. 'I admit it will be a relief to reach Carlyne House and remove all this wedding finery…' Arabella's words trailed off into embarrassed awkwardness as she realised that she had unwittingly broached the very subject she had been trying to avoid. 'I meant, of course—'

'I know exactly what you meant, Arabella,' Darius drawled, deliberately moving closer to her as he turned in the seat to look at her before raising a hand and touching the flushed heat of her cheek. 'As your husband, I assure you I consider it my duty to aid you in removing your wedding finery at the earliest opportunity.'

'I had not thought you to be a man to whom duty meant very much.' Her eyes gleamed challengingly.

For all her youth and inexperience his little wife had the tongue of a viper!

A tongue Darius was sure could be put to much better use than deliberately insulting him…

'Usually only in regard to entertaining the ton,' he reminded her. 'But I am willing to make an exception when it comes to the comfort of my wife.'

Darius held that snapping brown gaze as his hand moved to deliberately pull on the ribbon that untied the bow of Arabella's bonnet, before removing it completely to reveal those enticing golden curls, long fingers moving confidently as he systematically removed the pins that held those curls in place.

'I— What are you doing…?' Arabella raised a hand in half-hearted protest as her hair began to fall wildly about her shoulders.

Darius smiled. 'I believe it is called making love to one's wife.'

The creaminess of Arabella's throat moved convulsively as she swallowed nervously. 'Can you not wait until we reach Carlyne House and the privacy of our bedchamber?'

'Why should I?' Darius retorted. 'You are mine now, Arabella. To do with as I wish, when I wish—remember?'

Arabella felt a shiver of—of what…? Was it apprehension? Or excitement?

This past week, despite all the rush and bustle of the wedding arrangements, Arabella had still found herself thinking of her wedding night whenever there was the slightest lull in those arrangements. Thinking of it. Anticipating it. Longing for it. For the touch of Darius's lips and hands upon her once again. In the certain knowledge that this time he would not stop at touching but would take their lovemaking to its fullest conclusion.

Yet now that the time had come Arabella found herself both shy and not a little apprehensive!

To their obvious embarrassment—and Arabella's own, if the truth be told—she had spoken with all of her sisters-in-law this past week concerning what her role should be in the bedchamber.

Jane had advised that lovemaking was a mutual giving and receiving of physical pleasure.

Grace had said that it was perhaps best if Arabella allowed her husband to take all the initiative until they knew each other's likes and dislikes.

Juliet's slightly flustered opinion, when Arabella had questioned her shortly after her arrival this morning, was that husbands were sometimes appreciative of the woman taking the initiative.

Advice which had left Arabella more confused than ever as to what Darius might expect of her in the marriage bed.

So far there had certainly been no mention at all of what Darius might expect of her as they travelled in the coach to Carlyne House!

'Better,' he murmured appreciatively now, as he ran his fingers through the heavy thickness of her hair so that it cascaded loosely over her shoulders and down the length of her spine. 'Whenever we are alone, Arabella, I would prefer that you wear your hair just so.'

She touched her loosened curls self-consciously. 'I—What would the servants think?'

He raised blond brows. 'I do not pay them to think, Arabella.'

'Yes, but—' Her words ceased as Darius's hands cupped either side of her face, the soft pads of his thumbs a light and evocative caress against the softness of her lips. 'Darius…?'

Darius was fully aware of Arabella's uncertainty, knew she had no idea how sexually provocative she looked at this moment, with her golden curls wild about her shoulders, eyes dark and uncertain beneath lowered lashes, and her parted moist lips in a full and inviting pout.

He had begun this flirtation with his wife as a means of diverting her from questioning him any further as to his earlier conversation with Bancroft, but now Darius found that his gaze was fixed upon the invitation of Arabella's parted lips, and ruefully he recognised that his only desire now was to taste them.

Arabella felt small and slightly fragile as he curved his arms about her waist and crushed her breasts against his chest, pulling her hard against him before lowering his head to capture those pouting lips with his own.

She tasted of wine and peaches, which Darius now recalled were the only two things Arabella had consumed at their wedding feast. The wine perhaps to allay some of her nervousness? The peaches because they were light and exotic? Whatever the reason for Arabella's choice, they were a heady combination to Darius's senses. Intoxicating, as well as inviting.

As Arabella herself was intoxicating and inviting.

It seemed to Arabella at that moment as if no time had elapsed at all since Darius had made love to her in Hawk's study a week ago. The desire she had known then was once again bursting into flames as he kissed her with a thoroughness that took her breath away and made her body burn.

All of her sisters-in-laws' contradictory advice fled as Arabella returned the heat of those devouring kisses, pressing against Darius to make even closer contact as her arms entwined about his neck and her fingers became entangled in the thick silkiness of the hair at his nape.

His lips were firm and commanding against her own, teeth gently biting, tongue tasting as it explored the shape of her lips before slipping into the heated cavern of her mouth.

Arabella gasped slightly when she felt Darius's hand curve around one of her breasts as he continued to kiss her. His thumb caressed unerringly over its sensitive tip as it pressed against the soft material of her gown, sending rivulets of desire coursing down between her thighs, readying her, she felt sure, for even deeper intimacies.

It was—

There was a sudden shifting, a lurching of the ducal coach, and it tilted precariously to one side, tossing Darius back against the door, his arm still about Arabella's waist. Her eyes went wide with shock and fear as Darius pulled her down on top of him to land on the floor of the coach in a tangle of arms and legs. The lamp swayed precariously for several long seconds before it too fell to the floor beside them, extinguishing the candle inside and plunging them into complete darkness.

Arabella began to scream.

Chapter Five

'Calm down, Arabella! Arabella, I order you to stop that noise instantly and allow me to think!' Darius said firmly.

His words had no effect on her obvious hysteria. Not that he could exactly blame her for her distress, when they were blanketed in darkness inside the tilting carriage with a cacophony of noise outside made up of men shouting, dogs barking, and horses whinnying in a horrible manner that seemed to imply at least one of them had been injured in the crash.

For a crash it had most certainly been. Whether they had collided with another vehicle or not, the precarious tilt of the Carlyne carriage proclaimed that the vehicle had somehow either been damaged or had lost a wheel and was now lurched dangerously to one side.

The door above them on the other side of the carriage was suddenly wrenched open and one of the grooms, his grey wig askew, peered down at them in the darkness. 'Your Grace?' he gasped as he gazed in upon the tangle of legs, arms and bodies. 'Are you injured?'

'I myself am not,' Darius answered grimly as he attempted to sit up and found Arabella's arms so tightly clutched about his neck he could barely move. 'Are *you* hurt, Arabella?' he asked with concern, and he released her clinging fingers and held her slightly away from him so that he might inspect her for obvious injury.

'I do not—do not know.' Her voice was faint and slightly shaky. 'Please get me out of here, Darius.' Her eyes glittered wildly in the darkness as she reached up and clung to him once again. 'Please!'

Darius had become accustomed to her stoicism this past week, her bewitching and tempting air of self-sufficiency that challenged him into wanting to tame her. In his bed, if not out of it. To see her reduced to such trembling distress by a simple carriage accident seemed totally out of character.

Until, that was, he suddenly recalled that the ninth Duke of Stourbridge and his duchess, Arabella's parents, had both been killed in a carriage accident eleven years ago….

Darius's face was like stone as he turned to look up at the groom. 'I am going to lift my wife so that you can remove her to safety.' He wasted no time in suiting his actions to his words as he placed his hands about Arabella's waist and lifted her up, allowing the other man to pull her outside into the darkened night. Darius quickly followed by placing his hands either side of the open doorway and levering himself up and out of the badly listing carriage.

Another of the grooms had managed to quieten the horses by the time Darius lowered himself down onto the cobbled road beside a now quietly sobbing Arabella. He moved to place his arms protectively about her as he turned to take in the scene of the accident.

There was no other carriage in sight, but one of their nearside back wheels had come completely adrift and lay some distance away. The terrible screeching noise Darius had heard earlier had obviously been that of the axle of the carriage as it was dragged along the cobbles for several feet before the groom had managed to bring the horses to a halt.

Luckily they had not been travelling at any speed when the wheel had parted company with the carriage, which accounted for the lack of any serious injury. Even so, Darius's face was stern as he turned his attention back to his distraught young wife. 'You really must calm yourself, Arabella.' He frowned as he realised how harsh his voice sounded. 'It is all over now and there is no harm done,' he added in a much gentler tone.

Arabella was shaking so badly, her teeth chattering together so loudly, that for a moment she didn't hear Darius, let alone comprehend what he had just said to her. Even once she did understand his reassurances she could not stop the trembling of her body or the shaking of her hands as she still clung to—and no doubt ruined—the lapels of his jacket. 'I thought—I believed we were about to—to—' She broke off with a telling shudder.

'I understand, Arabella.'

Looking up into Darius's face, Arabella saw that he did indeed understand the reason for the depth of her distress. Understood it, perhaps, but the harshness of his expression implied that he also found her hysteria less than becoming in his wife. In his duchess. His rigidly controlled demeanour was so like Hawk's would have been in the same circumstances that Arabella instantly calmed, straightening her back and shoulders and releasing Darius's jacket before turning to look at the carriage.

'The grooms and horses also escaped injury?'

'Yes. But at a guess more by luck than judgement.' Darius nodded, his eyes narrowed as he looked again at the precariously tilted carriage.

'What do you mean?' Arabella frowned her confusion as she turned back to him.

Darius forced his anger over the accident to the back of his emotions, to be dealt with at a later date rather than expressing it here and now in front of Arabella. 'I was merely questioning the care that was taken in preparing the carriage for our use today,' he explained.

Her breath drew in sharply. 'I am sure that none of your grooms would have been negligent, Darius. After all, they were travelling on the coach too.'

'Of course.' Darius forced a tight smile. 'It was just an accident, as you say. One that unfortunately seems to have left us a little distance from arriving outside Carlyne House,' he added ruefully, realising they still had a quarter of a mile or so to travel before they reached his—their—London home.

'I doubt that a walk will do either of us any lasting harm.' Arabella tucked her hand into the crook of his arm with the obvious intention of beginning that walk immediately.

The dignity of her expression prevented Darius from pointing out how much in disarray was her appearance, with her hair loose and falling wildly down the length of her spine, and her gown less than pristine. It had several dirty smudges down its front and a slight tear in the material along one side. In that moment, dishevelled and still slightly unnerved by the accident, Arabella still managed to look every inch a duchess.

His duchess.

'At least you now have a valid reason for the dishevelled state of your hair,' he teased lightly as they began to walk along the street with every appearance of simply being out for an afternoon stroll.

Arabella had visited Carlyne House several times this past week, to be introduced to all of the household staff, as well as become acquainted with one of the houses that would become her home once she and Darius were married.

Having decided that the spring, when hopefully the weather would be more clement, was a much nicer time to honeymoon on the Continent, Arabella and Darius had instead made arrangements to travel to Winton Hall on the day following the wedding. They would spend several weeks there before travelling into Gloucestershire in December, to spend the Christmas season with Arabella's family.

Arabella's cheeks warmed slightly as she recalled the reason her hair was tumbled loosely about her shoulders and down her spine. That soft thrumming resumed in her body as she recalled the ardour of Darius's kisses. Her heart started pounding as she wondered how much further he would have gone in his lovemaking if the accident had not brought such an abrupt end to their intimacy.

Then the warmth in her cheeks became due to embarrassment as Arabella recalled, and deeply regretted, her behaviour following the accident. That she had the excuse of her parents' death in a carriage accident to explain her hysteria did not make it any less undignified.

She drew in a sharp breath. 'I can only apologise for behaving like a—a ninny just now, Darius. It was inexcusable of me to take on so. I should not have screamed or clung to you in the way I did.'

'I assure you I found your behaviour highly diverting,' he said.

'Diverting?' she echoed sharply.

'Why, yes.' The humour that curved Darius's mouth was also reflected in his eyes. 'It is not every day that one sees the Lady Arabella St Claire appearing less than composed.'

'You forget, Darius, that I am now Arabella Wynter, Duchess of Carlyne!' she reminded him tartly, stung by his amusement at her expense.

He snorted. 'That is even more reason to marvel at your recent loss of control.'

'I am pleased to have provided you with some amusement!' she huffed.

'Are you?'

'No!' Arabella glared up at him in the moonlight.

'Perhaps that is as well—as I am actually far from amused.' His expression turned suddenly grim once more, his eyes taking on the cold sheen of ice.

A frown creased the creaminess of her brow as she looked up at him searchingly. 'You are angry with me, Darius?'

With her usual intelligence Arabella had managed to pierce straight to the heart of Darius's mood! It *was* anger he felt. Cold. Steely. Implacable. Remorseless anger. But he was not angry with *her*.

What had just happened only proved to Darius that he should never have persuaded himself into believing the best course of action to keep Arabella safe was for him to marry her. In his defence, it had been done in the mistaken belief that once their intimate interlude in Hawk's study had become public knowledge—as it invariably would have done, thanks to Lord Redwood—it would be far safer for her if they married and then shortly thereafter removed themselves from London and became ensconced in the privacy and safety of Winton Hall.

Darius had certainly not expected the first attempt at an 'accident' to occur before they had even had a chance to leave London.

It was too much of a coincidence, too soon after his

earlier conversation with William Bancroft, for Darius to believe that the wheel coming loose from his carriage was truly the accident it gave every appearance of being.

He knew he had made enemies this past eight years. Dozens of people, traitors to their country, who had every reason to want to cause him harm. Now that Arabella had become his wife, those same people might wish to cause her harm too.

One person in particular, perhaps…

But Arabella must be kept in ignorance of that, at least for now—she was still not recovered from her shock after the accident, and Darius had no intention of alarming her further with tales of possible mortal danger. He would have to tell her something else instead, to explain his mood to her.

'There are so many reasons for the present state of my emotions, Arabella, that I hardly know where to begin,' Darius commented as he came to a halt beneath the lamp in front of Carlyne House. 'I have been treated with icy disdain this past week by at least one of your brothers, and with an equal amount of suspicion by your sisters-in-law. I have also just been forced into a marriage not of my choosing to a woman also not of my choosing.'

'You did not seem to feel that same reluctance a year ago, when you offered for me!' Arabella was stung into defending herself heatedly.

Ah.

Darius's mouth compressed. 'An offer I seem to recall that you did not hesitate to refuse.'

Arabella opened her mouth to protest. And then closed it again. Not only would it be disloyal of her to admit that Hawk had not even consulted her over that offer, but it would also allow Darius to pose the question as to whether or not she would have accepted the offer if she *had* known of it—and she wasn't ready to answer that yet…

She looked up at him haughtily. 'No woman of good sense would have accepted such an offer.' Which meant, perhaps, that Arabella was not a woman of good sense—because she most certainly *would* have accepted a marriage offer from him!

Darius's eyes gleamed coldly in the moonlight as he looked down at her. 'No doubt because my…circumstances were far different a year ago from what they are today?

'In that you mean you had not yet *conveniently* inherited the fortune of the woman who *was* stupid enough to accept your offer?" Arabella snapped back—only to draw back in dismay as she saw the way Darius's face had darkened ominously.

'This is the second occasion upon which you have voiced such slanderous accusations, Arabella.' His tone had become as icy as his demeanour. 'I would advise, for your own sake, that there not be a third.'

Arabella felt a shiver of apprehension down the length of her spine as she realised she really did not know the man who was now her husband. 'You are right, Darius. This is not the best time for such a discussion. Nerves are obviously frayed, and tempers even more so.'

'On the contrary,' he drawled in a deceptively soft tone. 'It has been my experience that it is exactly when nerves are frayed and tempers roused that the truth tends to be spoken.'

Perhaps, Arabella allowed heavily. But she would far rather her words had remained unspoken tonight of all nights!

She gave a heavy sigh. 'I spoke in the heat of the moment only, Darius.'

'If that is in the nature of an apology, Arabella, then let me assure you that it falls far short of the mark.' Darius didn't know which of them he was more angry with. Arabella—or himself, for actually allowing her words to pierce the guard he invariably kept about his emotions.

In truth, her accusations were not so different from the many others levelled at him over the years. He was a rake. A womaniser. A gambler. A fortune-hunter. A possible murderer.

Hearing them spoken by one's own wife, however, was extremely unpleasant.

He looked down the length of his nose at her. 'Perhaps you even believe that *I* arranged the carriage accident just now, in the hope of ridding myself of my second unwanted wife?'

Her shocked frown showed him that the idea had not even occurred to her until he had voiced it. She recovered quickly. 'Not when you were a passenger in the carriage, too!'

Darius sighed heavily. 'I believe it is past time we went inside.' He curled his fingers about her upper arm and ascended the steps to Carlyne House; if someone was watching them, possibly the perpetrator of the coach 'accident', then they had already lingered far too long outside than was wise.

Arabella had no idea what to do or say in order to dispel the tension that now existed between herself and Darius. A tension that was so at odds with the intensity of passion they had shared in the carriage such a short time ago.

The cold and remote man who swept so arrogantly into the marbled hallway of Carlyne House the moment the door was opened by a footman brandishing a candelabra was not the man who had made love to Arabella either a week ago or earlier this evening. *This* man was a stranger to her. A cold, aloof stranger to whom she was now married and who questioned her belief over whether the carriage accident had even been an accident at all…

'Ah, Reynolds,' Darius spoke to the butler as he appeared in the hallway. 'There has been a accident. No one was injured,' he assured the butler quickly as the man looked alarmed. 'But I am afraid we were forced to abandon the carriage and walk home. It is my intention to return to the scene and check on progress with the carriage. I am sure Her Grace would appreciate being shown to her bedchamber, and then provided with a tray of tea and dainties.' Darius's expression was forbidding as he released Arabella to turn back towards the front door, which the footman instantly swept open once again, allowing a blast of cold night air to swirl about the hallway.

Arabella shivered as that coldness pierced the thin material of her gown in accompaniment to the ice creeping through her veins at Darius's announcement that he intended leaving the house. Leaving her on their wedding night!

'Darius?'

Narrowed lids hid the expression in the deep blue of his eyes as he paused in the open doorway to turn and look at her. 'What is it, Arabella?'

Pride—the St Claire pride so embedded in her own nature, as well as that of her brothers—dictated that she could not demand an explanation in front of the listening butler and footman as to why Darius felt it necessary to return to the broken carriage tonight of all nights.

Yet incredulity at his obvious intent of leaving the house on such a fool's errand, rather than remaining with his bride of but a few hours, dictated that she could not just let him leave the house without some show of disapproval at his actions, either!

On top of which, Darius had absolutely no right to instruct that she be 'shown to her bedchamber' in what was effectively now her own home!

She forced a cool smile to her lips, although the blaze in her eyes as she looked across at him gave the lie to that air of serenity she was projecting. 'Perhaps you would care to join me in a reviving cup of tea before venturing back out into the cold?'

At any other time Darius would have enjoyed taking the time to indulge his wife's request for his company—

as he would no doubt have enjoyed even more the consequences of quelling her obvious sparks of temper!

At this moment, however, he had far more pressing matters to attend to—he had to think about her safety above all else, even if she wasn't aware of it.

'I think not, thank you, Arabella,' he drawled. 'It's probably best if you do not wait up for me,' he added dryly. 'I have no idea when I will return, and you are no doubt tired after the excitement of the day.'

Darius could only regret the way her cheeks paled at his obvious dismissal, and he made a mental promise to himself—and her—to make up for the disaster of this, their wedding night, as soon as could be. As soon as they were both safely away from London…

Her dismay did not last long, however, as two bright spots of colour appeared in the pallor of her cheeks. 'What a considerate husband you are, to be sure, Darius.' The sweetness of her tone did not match the anger glinting in her golden-brown eyes.

He could only eye her appreciatively, even as he once again privately regretted his need to leave her. 'I have no doubt that you intend being as considerate a wife as I am a husband.'

'Oh, undoubtedly!' she retorted.

Darius bit back a smile at the promise of retribution glittering in those bright golden eyes. 'Pleasant dreams, Arabella.'

She gave him a sweetly saccharine smile. 'I have no doubt they will all be of you, my dear Darius!'

In that case he very much doubted they would be pleasant dreams, but rather ones of a violent nature, no doubt culminating in some painful punishment dealt him by her for his desertion.

All humour left Darius's expression as he strode back towards the disabled carriage, pondering what he was sure was an attempt on his life. And not just on his life, but Arabella's too. Darius considered himself more than capable of taking care of himself. Indeed he had been doing so for some years now. But endangering Arabella in this way was unacceptable.

Someone would pay for this evening's mischief.

Someone would pay dearly, he vowed grimly.

Arabella ignored the tray of tea things that had been brought up to her as she paced restlessly, agitatedly, angrily, up and down the spacious bedchamber that, as the Duchess of Carlyne, was now her own. It was a graciously appointed bedchamber that had been hurriedly decorated to her tastes in gold and cream this past week, in preparation for her arrival this evening, and it possessed an adjoining door to the room of her husband.

A husband whom, at this particular moment, Arabella dearly wished to throttle within an inch of his life!

Admittedly the broken carriage had to be removed from the street. The grooms must be returned to the house. The horses stabled and calmed after their ordeal.

Yet it was simply beyond Arabella's understanding that Darius considered those grooms and horses more deserving at present of his solicitude than his own wife.

Surely a senior member of his household could have sorted out the mess?

How could he treat her in this callous way?

How could he just turn her welfare over to the care of servants after the scare she had suffered such a short time ago?

How *dared* he just abandon her on their wedding night?

Arabella sat down abruptly on the gold brocade coverlet draped over the blankets of the huge four-poster bed that dominated the bedchamber. A four-poster bed in which she was expected to sleep alone.

On her wedding night…

After days, a week, of nervousness as she imagined herself and Darius going to bed together on the night of their wedding, Arabella instead found herself abandoned and alone. It was an unforgivable insult. A humiliation beyond endurance!

Arabella was well aware of the gossip of servants. They would all know that the Duke had not cared to share the Duchess's bed on their wedding night. From which piece of delectable gossip certain conclusions would no doubt be made…

Either that the rumours were all true, and the Duke had already shared his bride's bed before their marriage and so felt no particular compunction to share it again on their wedding night. Or—more humiliating still—having dallied with her and then been forced into a marriage not of his choosing, the Duke felt no inclination to claim what was now his by right.

Darius would pay for insulting her in this way, Arabella vowed fiercely.

He would most definitely be made to pay!

Chapter Six

'You are very quiet today, Arabella.' Darius eyed his young wife across the width of the carriage—the second-best carriage, as the main ducal vehicle was once again safely in the stables at Carlyne House and awaiting repair—as they travelled from London to Worcestershire in the early-morning gloom.

Arabella turned from looking out of the window and returned his gaze coolly. 'I prefer to think of it as being introspective, Your Grace.'

Oh, dear, they were back to the formality of Your Grace! 'No doubt you have much to think on?' he pressed.

'No doubt.' The smile that accompanied her reply did not reach the coldness of her eyes.

Everything about Arabella was cool today. The pale green gown and matching bonnet she wore for travelling. The pristine white lace gloves that covered her tiny hands. The pale, smooth alabaster of her face and throat. The deep, unfathomable brown of her eyes.

Not that Darius did not fully deserve Arabella's coldness after the way he had left her so abruptly the night before—a desertion that had ultimately proved fruitless.

There had been nothing to gain from examining the wheel and axle of the carriage once it had been returned to the stables. Except to tell Darius what he had already guessed: the rivets that held the wheel in place had come loose. Whether by accident or design it had been utterly impossible to tell.

A visit to the home of William Bancroft, recently returned home from Darius and Arabella's wedding celebrations, to continue their earlier discussion in view of this latest 'accident' had been of little help, either. Bancroft had no new information as to the whereabouts of Helena Jourdan, the French spy whose existence Darius had denied to Arabella, following her escape from custody the previous week. If, indeed, it *was* she who was trying to kill Darius. There was a second possibility, much closer to home, that Darius found even more unpalatable.

His younger brother Francis…

Disgraced and banished, could Francis have returned to England somehow and even now be plotting Darius's and Arabella's deaths?

His mouth thinned at the thought of the danger he might have placed Arabella in simply by marrying her. The same danger that Sophie had found herself in the moment Darius had taken her as his wife a year ago…

Was Darius *never* to be allowed any personal happiness?

Last night's 'accident' gave every indication that was the case!

He sighed heavily. 'You are still angry with me because of last night.' It had been very late when Darius had returned to Carlyne House after seeing Bancroft, almost two o'clock in the morning, and as promised, rather than disturb Arabella, he had instead retired directly to his own bedchamber.

Only to remain restless and virtually sleepless for the remainder of the night as he regretted telling her he would not be joining her in her bedchamber. It had been impossible to sleep when he could so easily imagine how beautiful, how desirable, his wife would look as she lay back against downy pillows, with that gloriously golden hair spread out beneath her….

Darius still ached at the vividness of that image!

Arabella raised haughty blond brows. 'What happened last night, Darius? Admittedly, the carriage accident was a little—bothersome, but I assure you I slept surprisingly well, considering.' The dark shadows visible beneath those dark brown eyes gave the lie to her claim.

A fact that Darius was well aware of. Just as he was aware that it was the St Claire pride that sustained Arabella in the face of what she no doubt saw as Darius's abandonment of her after she had been so shaken by the carriage accident, and also his rejection of her on their wedding night.

It was not Arabella that Darius had rejected, it was the taking of a wife at all when his own life was being dogged by someone who wished him harm and did not care if his young and beautiful wife shared that same fate, that caused Darius to guard his thoughts and deeds. But he dared not share that information with her.

'In that case you will have no need of sleep once we have arrived at the coaching inn,' he murmured.

'I do not understand, sir.' But the delicate colour that crept up Arabella's throat and into her cheeks said she understood his huskily spoken words only too well!

Darius sat forward on the padded bench-seat so that his face was only inches away from hers. 'I am sure we will both benefit from retiring to our bedchambers for the rest of the afternoon. In order that we might bathe and…rest after travelling.'

Arabella stared at Darius. Was he seriously suggesting that they amuse themselves in bed all afternoon? Did he really dare to think that she would be willing to participate in the pleasures of the bedchamber after the way he'd treated her?

Her disappointment at Darius's desertion the evening before, followed by outrage as his absence continued long after she might have expected his return, had sustained Arabella through the long night that had just passed. She certainly had no intention of allowing Darius to make love to her for the first time in a coaching inn, of that she was sure. As was the case in most inns, it would offer little comfort and absolutely no privacy!

Arabella's intention to treat Darius with dismissive coldness for the dreary and lengthy duration of their journey into Worcestershire, in an effort to show him how contemptible was his behaviour of the night before, was completely forgotten as she bristled indignantly. 'You may choose to pander to your mistress rather than your wife, Darius, but I assure you that I am not someone who can be discarded and then picked up again when it suits your own needs!'

Amusement darkened the blue of his eyes to cobalt. 'And what do you know of the treatment of mistresses, Arabella?'

Her eyes snapped with temper. 'You seem to forget, Darius, that I have three older brothers.'

'And?'

'Do not treat me like a backward child, Darius,' she warned tartly, her mouth thin. 'It is well known that the men of the ton change their mistresses as often as they change their linen.'

'Oftener, in some cases,' Darius allowed, and he sat back against the upholstered seat, arms folded across the muscled width of his chest as he gazed at her speculatively. 'And you count me in their number, do you, Arabella?'

She gave an inelegant snort. 'Your own actions have placed you in their number.'

'Indeed?'

Arabella was completely aware of the underlying steel in Darius's tone. But she felt perfectly justified in ignoring the warning in view of his desertion of her the previous night. Long hours which Arabella had spent alone in her bedchamber. Hours when her imagination had provided her with thoughts of whether or not it was actually another woman rather than the broken carriage that had drawn Darius's attention away from his new wife so soon....

It had also occurred to Arabella some time during her sleepless night that when she'd questioned Darius the previous week he had not denied having a mistress at present, only the need to continue to keep one after they were married. Perhaps last night had been the end of their affair? Perhaps the woman had even been a guest at their wedding!

Once the idea had presented itself to her, Arabella had found her imagination taking flight to the extent that she had clearly been able to visualise Darius in bed with the other woman. To imagine the two of them lying naked and entwined, satiated from their lovemaking, as they perhaps laughed together at the thought of Darius's abandoned lonely bride.

The mere thought of that being the case made Arabella's blood boil anew!

She looked across at Darius coldly. 'I take it you feel no desire for me to produce your heirs immediately?'

He frowned. 'Not particularly, no.' He didn't want to give his enemies yet another innocent, vulnerable target!

Arabella nodded abruptly. 'In that case I see no reason to share your bed at the present time.' She turned to once again stare out of the window at the now softly falling rain. The gloomy weather was reflective of her own mood.

Darius continued to study Arabella through narrowed lids and he realised from her remarks, as well as from the things she had left unsaid, that she had drawn her own conclusions concerning his lengthy absence from Carlyne House the night before. He was experienced enough to know that her anger at the thought that he'd visited his mistress was merely a shield for the much deeper hurt she felt at his apparent shunning of her on their wedding night.

The obvious thing to do to put things right between them would be for Darius to offer Arabella reassurances as to his whereabouts the night before. Unfortunately, in doing that he would also have to explain his reasons for having gone to see Bancroft. An explanation that even now Darius would not—could not—share with anyone. Even his young wife.

Eight years ago, in the midst of those bloody years of England's battles against Napoleon, Darius had known that as the second son he was expected to take up a commission in the army. Tired of Society, jaded from his years of drinking and gambling, disenchanted with the women who frequently shared his bed, it had been an action Darius had been only too willing to take.

However, before he had been able to do so he had been approached by a member of the English government—a man who had explained that he recruited a widespread group of men and women, both in England and France, who, despite the danger to their own lives, had become spies for their country rather than overtly displaying their patriotism on the battlefield.

The work was dangerous, the man had explained, the rewards few, and the thanks non-existent as the role those people played in the fight against Napoleon could never be made public.

All that was required of Darius was for him to continue to live the debauched and profligate life he was already leading. To lull the public in general, and the ton in particular, into believing he was nothing more than a wastrel and a rake. He would be surprised, the man had assured him, how indiscreet a traitor could be when in the company of a man they considered too drunk or uninterested to pay any attention to their conversation.

They had been prophetic words, Darius now acknowledged wryly.

For six years the ton had continued to believe him too lazy or cowardly to fight for his country. During those same six years Darius had become adept at discovering a man's—or a woman's—secret alliances. More so than he could ever have imagined. His success had been such that he had moved quickly up the rank and file of this secret organisation, until he had eventually found himself as the head of one of the networks of England's spies.

Two years after Napoleon's final defeat Darius still headed that network. William Bancroft, Earl of Banford, was only one of their number.

None of which Darius was at liberty to share with anyone—not even his own wife. Not even when the work he had done, and continued to do, might have placed Arabella in that same danger as Darius himself….

There was one thing he *could* make clear to her, however. 'I do *not* have a mistress, Arabella.'

Her expression was scornful as she turned to look at him with hard brown eyes. 'Perhaps not now, no. But only because you probably ended it just last night!'

'Not for some time,' he stated firmly, his expression intent as he leaned forward again. 'Arabella, there has been no woman in my life, or my bed, since Sophie's death.'

Arabella's eyes widened. Did Darius seriously expect her to believe he had been celibate for a whole year? A man who, despite having gained respectability since inheriting a dukedom, was still known for his womanising. For his carousing. For his gambling.

Had he been womanising, carousing or gambling during the week of their betrothal?

Not to Arabella's knowledge. Or that of her brothers, she felt sure. For Arabella had no doubt that one or all of them would have brought it to her attention if he had.

But just because he had behaved himself in the week before their wedding it did not necessarily mean that Darius had remained celibate for this past year.

Then why would he say that he had?

Darius was still very much a puzzle to her, and did many things she could not approve of, but she had no reason to believe he had ever lied to her. More truthfully, Darius was arrogant enough never to feel the need to lie about any of his actions.

Her chin rose challengingly. 'Did you love your first wife so much, then?'

He gave a rueful shake of his head. 'I can always rely on you to ask the unexpected, can't I?'

Her brows rose. 'In that case you will not find me tedious.'

'Far from it!'

'Did you love your first wife?' she repeated determinedly.

'For my sins—no.' Darius grimaced.

Arabella gave a graceful inclination of her head—as if the answer were just as she had expected. 'You have been widowed a year. Even before you became a duke you were considered highly eligible. So why have you not taken advantage of that rank and fortune this past year to secure yourself a mistress?'

Darius mouth twisted with distaste. 'Perhaps because I preferred it when I knew a woman's partiality was only to me rather than due to a title or a fortune.'

Arabella bristled. 'Your implication being that *I* only married you for your title?'

'There can be no other reason,' he pointed out calmly. 'Not when I have been reliably informed by Hawk that you have no need of my fortune when considerable personal wealth became yours upon our marriage yesterday.'

It was true, of course. Arabella's parents had been more enlightened than most, and had considered their daughter to have as much right to financial independence as any of their three sons. Consequently her father had left her a vast fortune in his will, which

Hawk had managed for her these past eleven years, and a small estate in Norfolk, which Hawk had also taken care of by putting in a manager. The estate had become part of Arabella's husband's lands upon her marriage, of course, but the fortune would remain in trust for her children, with the interest set aside for her personal use.

Her wedding yesterday had made Arabella an even wealthier and more independent woman than ever she had been before that marriage.

She smiled tightly. She could not—would not—allow this arrogant and sarcastic man to know that she would probably have married him a year ago, whatever his wealth or title, if she had known of his offer.

'How clever of you to guess!'

He looked at her coldly. 'Cleverness has nothing to do with it.'

'If you say so.' She nodded coolly. 'Did you have a particular reason for confiding your celibacy to me now?'

Amusement now danced in those cobalt-blue eyes. 'I was merely trying to reassure you that you may expect my complete fidelity, Arabella.'

Arabella wasn't yet ready to forgive him for leaving her so abruptly on their wedding night. 'Surely that is something any new bride might expect?'

'Expect, perhaps,' he said ruefully. 'But never be truthfully assured of.'

She raised a sarcastic brow. 'In that case I should no doubt consider myself fortunate that you feel able to offer me such assurances.'

Once again Darius was tempted to lift her skirts and paddle her bottom until she screamed for mercy. After which he would enjoy nothing more than making love to her until they were both thoroughly satisfied!

She was a little madam. A minx. And he found her completely enchanting. She was a temptress who had occupied far too many of his waking thoughts—and his dreams—this past week.

Perhaps if she had not Darius might have been more on his guard yesterday. More expectant regarding the sabotage of their coach…

He would not relax his guard again until they were safely ensconced at Winton Hall. Once there, he had the necessary security in place to ensure Arabella's safety at least.

Darius's expression hardened as he once again regretted that he had allowed himself to be beguiled into marrying her. By doing so he had brought her into the web of deceit and danger that had necessarily become his own life these past eight years.

He would not have been so tempted beyond resistance if Arabella were not so beautiful. So delectable. So spirited. And if he had not wanted her so badly in his bed for years…

'I am pleased to hear you are wise to the honour,' he bit out in response to her sarcasm. 'If you will excuse me, Arabella? I believe I might nap for the rest of the journey.' He lowered his lids, deliberately shutting out the vision of loveliness that was his brand-new bride.

Except Darius could still see her and feel her behind

those closed lids, as she glared rebelliously across the width of the carriage at him.

The silky gold of her hair was tempting him into releasing it. The pout of her lips was begging to be kissed. The full swell of her breasts was spilling over the low neckline of her gown. A fullness that Darius ached to cup in his hands. To kiss and caress once more as he had that evening a week ago in Hawk St Claire's study.

Dear God, he had no need to fear meeting death at the hands of his enemies when this desire for Arabella was sure to drive him into an early grave!

'I am very tired, Darius. I believe I will retire for the night.' Arabella placed her napkin on the dinner table before standing up.

She had found herself becoming more and more tense, and their conversation had reflected that tension as the two of them dined privately in the warm comfort of the secluded parlour the landlord of the inn had provided for their use. As bedtime had approached, that tension had reached breaking point…

Having suggested that once they reached the inn they might retire for the afternoon together to their bedchambers, Darius had once again busied himself—unnecessarily so, Arabella had felt—in seeing to the stabling of the horses and the securing of the coach. Leaving Arabella to be shown upstairs to the privacy of her bedchamber and the attentions of her maid, who had been sent on ahead to the inn with Darius's valet and their luggage. Having bathed and changed into her robe, Arabella had lain down upon her bed and managed to fall asleep, waking only when her maid came back into the room to help her dress for dinner.

Darius had obviously found time to shave and bathe, and his hair was freshly washed and gleaming deeply gold as it curled in meticulous disarray about his stunning face. He had also changed from his dark travelling clothes into a tailored superfine the same colour blue as his eyes, his impeccable linen was snowy-white, and his buff-coloured pantaloons moulded to the muscled length of his thighs above shiny black Hessians.

On first seeing him thus, Arabella had had to allow that Darius was the handsomest man in England!

The knowledge that this man was also her husband, and that the second night of their marriage was fast approaching, had made Arabella all the more aware of him as each second of the meal progressed, resulting in her doing little more than pick at the food placed before her. That Darius's hooded blue eyes had settled on her often, and no doubt noted her lack of appetite, had only added to her increasing nervousness.

Darius also now rose from the table. 'I will join you shortly.' He nodded coolly, the expression in those deep blue eyes unreadable.

Arabella swallowed hard even as she eyed him shyly from beneath lowered lashes. 'I...' Her voice sounded reedy, and too high even to her own ears. Completely unlike her usual forthright tone. She drew in a controlling breath. 'I really am exceedingly tired, Darius.'

'I do not see how you can possibly be tired when you

slept most of the afternoon and early evening away,' he pointed out as he moved away from the table.

Irritation creased her brow as she raised her chin to look at him fully. 'And how would you know how I spent my afternoon when you were engaged elsewhere?'

Darius did not need the warning glitter in Arabella's eyes to tell him that he had displeased her yet again. This time by the lack of the attention he had promised to her this afternoon. 'I sincerely hope that you are not going to be one of those wives who expects to be told of her husband's every move?'

Angry colour entered the previous pallor of her cheeks. 'Unless I am mistaken, Darius, I am not, as yet, a wife of any kind!'

Now, with Arabella's temper on the rise, was not the time to smile, Darius knew. But it was hard not to do so when she looked so put out, so disgruntled by the fact that he had not yet made her his wife in the fullest sense.

He gave a mocking inclination of his head. 'I assure you, Arabella, that I have every intention of remedying that omission as soon as we are alone together upstairs.'

Her throat moved convulsively at she realised it was Darius's intention to make love to her once they were in her bedchamber. More evidence, if Darius had needed it, of her youth and inexperience.

He did not need it when he knew Arabella had been under the fierce protection of Hawk St Claire these past eleven years. Added to which, while Arabella's ardour had not been in doubt when Darius had kissed her the previous week, her inexperience had been evident to him.

And in equal part arousing…

Arabella's eyes widened slightly as she watched Darius approach her with all the smooth and predatory elegance of a cat stalking its prey, and it took every effort of will on her part not to make herself look completely ridiculous by taking a step backwards. Especially when to have done so would have brought her up against the wall of the shabby parlour!

Darius stood in front of her now, the lean and muscled length of his body only inches away from her own. The heat of his body and the tantalising smell of his cologne caused Arabella's pulse to beat erratically, her heart to pound loudly, and her head to spin. She moistened stiff lips. 'I would rather you waited until we are upstairs before any—any intimacies take place.'

He raised blond brows. 'Surely a kiss from one's own wife cannot be classed as an *intimacy*?'

If it in any way resembled the way he had kissed her—and she had kissed him back—a week ago, then, yes, it most certainly could!

Arabella shook her head. 'I would rather wait, Darius.'

His eyes glittered down at her with amusement. 'And if I would rather not?'

Her eyes narrowed. 'I do not appreciate being played with in this odious way.'

'No?' He reached up to trail a finger down the creamy length of her throat, that finger lingering in the deep and sensitive well at its base. 'That is a pity—when I so much enjoy playing with you!'

Arabella found it difficult to breathe, and her skin burned where he touched it. 'Stop it, Darius!' She was becoming agitated by his easy arousal of her senses.

'Your skin is like velvet, Arabella,' he murmured appreciatively, his gaze now following the line of his finger as it moved lower still, to skim lightly across the top of her rapidly rising and falling breasts as they swelled over the peach material of her gown.

Breasts that became fuller, heavier, the tips tightening, becoming as hard as berries against the silk of her shift as he stroked her.

'You have to stop, Darius!' Arabella's agitation increased in tandem with her arousal.

Darius looked at her from beneath lowered lids, recognising the rapid beating at her temple, the fever-brightness of her eyes, the flush to her cheeks and the full arousal of her breasts for exactly what they were. Signs of desire. The same desire that thrummed through his own body, hardening his thighs so that his arousal throbbed and ached beneath his breeches.

He stepped back abruptly. 'As you wish, Arabella.' His jaw was tight, the expression in his eyes hidden beneath narrowed lids. 'You may have ten minutes before I join you in your bedchamber.' Darius only hoped that he could control his desire to possess her for longer than that allotted time….

Chapter Seven

Arabella was standing in front of the window, looking out into the darkness below, when she heard the door of her bedchamber softly open and close behind her—evidence that Darius, after the briefest of knocks, had entered the candlelit room.

She had toyed with the idea of already being in bed when Darius joined her, but once beneath the bedcovers had decided she appeared far too much the willing sacrifice. Or at best far too eager!

Having decided earlier that a roadside inn was the last place in which she wished Darius to make love to her for the first time, Arabella now found she wanted him to touch and kiss her with such an aching intensity that she no longer cared where he made love to her, only that he should do so as soon as possible.

'Arabella.'

She turned slowly, her breath catching in her throat

as she looked across the warmly lit bedchamber and took in Darius's appearance. He wore a dark and paler blue fitted robe of rich brocade which fastened at the waist with three buttons. The deep vee of the dark blue lapels revealed that his chest was bare beneath, hard and muscled, and covered in fine dark blond hair. As Darius moved to put a tray containing a decanter of brandy and two glasses down onto the table beside the door, before stepping further into the bedchamber, Arabella saw that the long and muscled length of his legs were also bare.

Leaving her with no doubt that Darius was completely naked beneath that brocade robe! 'Did you walk down the hallway dressed like that?'

He regarded her teasingly. 'I believe I am well past the age of climbing up the ivy outside the window in order to reach my wife's bedchamber!'

Arabella felt no amusement at Darius's self-deprecation, only a fierce shaft of jealousy that pierced through her as she imagined one of the other female guests at the inn seeing Darius walking down the hallway wearing so little clothing and looking so rakishly handsome!

He quirked a brow. 'Arabella…?'

'I— But anyone might have seen you!'

He gave a dismissive shrug. 'Anyone did not.'

'That really is not the point, Darius—'

'Then what *is* your point?'

Her point was that if another woman had seen him walking down the hallway wearing only this magnificent brocade robe, then that woman could not have helped but want him. Desire him.

As Arabella desired him.

Her jealousy faded as her earlier nervousness returned with a vengeance. She made an evasive movement with her hand. 'If it does not bother you, then I see no reason why it should bother me.'

Darius looked unconvinced. 'No?'

She glared at him frustratedly. 'Where would you like me?'

Darius raised mocking brows at her bluntness. 'Where would I *like* you?' he echoed with considerable amusement.

Her cheeks burned hotly. 'Well…yes. Lovemaking does not necessarily need to be confined to the bed, does it?'

Darius instantly had visions of Arabella seated on the window as he knelt between her parted thighs and pleasured her with his lips and tongue. Or, once pleasured, draping her over the back of the armchair in the corner of the room as he entered her from behind. Or perhaps against the wall, her fingers clinging to his shoulders and her legs clasped about his waist, as he thrust into her again and again…

But no, pleasurable as any or all of those things might be for him, Darius intended indulging in none of them tonight. Far better that Arabella be introduced to pleasure slowly. With tenderness and care. After all, he had a lifetime in which to introduce his young wife to all the pleasures of her body, as well as his own.

He did not need to frighten her before they had even begun!

Although it was a little difficult to turn his thoughts from those vivid and erotic images when Arabella's hair was once again cascading loosely down the slender length of her spine, and she wore only a sheer white silk and lace robe over an equally diaphanous nightgown. The low and rounded neckline of both garments clearly revealed the firm swell of her unconfined breasts.

He swallowed hard. 'I had thought we might share a glass of brandy together first.' He moved to the tray he had brought in with him and poured some of the rich amber liquid from the decanter into the two glasses.

Arabella could have wept with relief at this short respite. Her nerves were so jittery now that her hand shook slightly as she took the glass of brandy from Darius's long and annoyingly steady fingers.

Not one of her sisters-in-law had thought to tell Arabella of the painful nervousness edged with anticipation she would feel when Darius came to her bedchamber for the first time. No doubt that was because Jane, Grace and Juliet had known they were loved by the men to whom they were married. They had felt reassured by that love, and secure in the knowledge that their husbands would never do anything that would either hurt or frighten them.

Arabella knew that Darius would be an accomplished lover—his rakish reputation amongst the women of the ton was testament to that—but would he be a gentle and a patient one?

Darius did not in the least care for the way in which

Arabella was looking at him over the rim of her glass as she took a sip of the brandy. Almost as if she expected that at any moment he might throw her to the floor and pounce upon her!

Darius was fully cognisant of his scandalous reputation amongst the ton—after all, was it not a reputation he had deliberately nurtured these past eight years? But he was sure he had never heard himself described as a cruel or violent man. Why, then, did Arabella now look at him with such a look of apprehension in her beautiful eyes?

'You—'

'You—'

Both broke off as suddenly as they'd started speaking. 'You first,' Darius invited.

Arabella drew in an audibly ragged breath. 'I was about to say that you must be tired after your disturbed night and this day's travel.'

He hid a smile. 'Not too tired to make love to my wife, I assure you.'

'Oh.' Those golden-brown eyes dropped demurely to the carpeted floor.

This awkwardness between them was intolerable, Darius decided impatiently. Unaccountable, even, when Arabella certainly had enough to say to him out of the bedchamber!

He swallowed down a liberal amount of brandy before trying again. 'Do you want me to make love to you, Arabella?'

Those dark lashes rose sharply as she looked at him once again, heated colour in her cheeks. 'I— What sort of question is that to ask the woman you have been married to for only one day?' she exclaimed, falling back on defensive anger in her obvious embarrassment.

His mouth twisted ruefully. 'A valid one, I would have thought, given the circumstances.'

Arabella looked more irritated than upset now. 'And what circumstances are those?'

'I am sure there is no need for us to discuss the reason for our marriage any further tonight, Arabella. Or indeed any other night,' Darius said as he placed his empty brandy glass back onto the silver tray. 'Either you wish me to make love to you, or you do not. I am not an unfeeling monster. Neither do I intend to force the issue. If you do not want me here, then it is for you to say that you do not.'

'But we are married!'

He sighed. 'Even so, I have never yet made love to a woman who did not wish it, and I do not intend to start with my own wife. No matter what the provocation…' he added huskily.

Arabella swallowed hard. 'Provocation…?'

Darius's eyes darkened. 'Do you have any idea how desirable you look in the candle-light, dressed just so and with your hair loose about your shoulders in that wild and wanton way?'

Until Darius had said so, no—Arabella had *not* known that he found her appearance to be in the least desirable….

She moistened dry lips with the tip of her tongue. 'Do you have any idea how desirable *you* look in the candle-light, dressed just so and with your hair rakishly ruffled in that wildly attractive way?' she returned softly.

Darius's expression softened even as his eyes flashed with admiration. 'You are a woman like no other I have ever met, Arabella,' he said gruffly.

For now that was enough…

It had to be enough. Darius was her husband, and if Arabella did not wish him to turn to the arms of another woman as soon as the honeymoon period could decently be called over—and she most certainly did not—then she must become his wife in the fullest sense of the word.

She took hesitant steps towards him, her courage instantly fuelled by the flare of desire Darius allowed her to see burning in the cobalt-blue of his eyes. Her head went back proudly as she came to a halt only inches in front of him. 'Make love to me, Darius.' Her voice was low and inviting. 'Show me—teach me how to make love to you too.'

Darius had long admired Arabella. Her beauty was all too apparent. Her strength of character was much more subtle.

Looking down at her now, seeing the unwavering courage in the depths of those deep brown eyes as she met his own gaze unflinchingly, Darius knew her to be a woman who was more than a match for him. In every way, he hoped.

His thighs were hard just at the thought of making love to her. 'I need to make love to you first, Arabella.' His voice was a husky, unrecognisable groan. 'I have to!' he muttered achingly as he drew her fiercely into his arms.

It seemed to Arabella, as Darius's mouth claimed hers, that it had been far longer than a week that she had hungered for him to make love to her again. Hungered. Ached. Yearned...

She heatedly returned his kisses, her hands sliding up the muscled hardness of his chest before her fingers dug into his shoulders as he tasted her, gently biting the swell of her bottom lip before sucking it deep into the heat of his mouth.

Arabella was aroused, her breasts full and aching, the rosy tips hard and tingling for Darius's touch. So much so that she offered no resistance as one of his hands moved from about her waist and she felt his fingers untying the ribbon at the front of her robe to slide the silk material down the length of her arms before allowing it to drop to the floor at her feet.

Darius drew back slightly, his eyes intent as he looked down at her standing so proudly before him, so unflinchingly, in the sheer white nightgown that showed more than it hid; her breasts were firm and pouting, tipped by dark, rose-coloured nipples that stood hard and inviting against the soft material of that gown. Her waist was slender, her hips a gentle swell, with a triangle of dark blond curls between her thighs that begged for more intimate exploration.

Just looking at her, aware of his increasing desire, made Darius question the wisdom of his past year of celibacy. Would he be able to hold his own needs in check long enough to give Arabella the attention she deserved?

He absolutely would, Darius instructed himself firmly. He must maintain control. He had to. For Arabella's sake. He had to prepare her. Make her ready. To ensure that she was as aroused as he was, so that when he did enter her, breaching her virginity, he caused her as little pain as possible.

He slid one of the ribbon straps of her gown from her shoulder and allowed the material to slip slightly, baring one of her breasts. His gaze feasted hungrily on that exposed flesh. Arabella's skin was so creamy-white, her breast round and perfect, the rosy nipple unbearably tempting. 'May I?' he prompted huskily.

Arabella stared straight ahead, but Darius could feel the way she trembled slightly beneath the touch of his hands. 'Please,' she whispered.

Darius slowly lowered his head, his tongue flicking lightly, across that rosy nipple in a moist caress, and he was able to feel and see Arabella's response as her trembling increased and her back arched slightly so that her breast thrust against his mouth in a silent plea.

Darius went slowly at first, until his hunger far outweighed his need for caution and his hand moved to cup Arabella's other breast. He captured that second nipple between thumb and finger and began caressing it gently.

Arabella's earlier nervousness disappeared completely as she looked down at that golden head lying so close against her breast, Darius's lashes were resting on the hardness of his cheekbones, his face unusually flushed as he concentrated on pleasuring her.

Emboldened by his complete absorption, Arabella let her fingers became entangled in the thick golden hair at his nape, and she watched in fascination as his mouth moved against her nipple like a thirsty man in a desert as his other hand squeezed and caressed its twin.

There was heat between her thighs, a pulsing, throbbing heat, and Arabella could feel herself blossoming there in a way she never had before. Shockingly, she began wanting to take Darius's hand and place it against her, have him caress away the ache that was growing there.

As if aware of that desire, Darius moved back to swing her up in his arms and carry her over to the bed, before sitting her gently down upon the covers.

Her eyes widened as Darius removed one of the pillows before lying her head back again. They widened even further still as Darius raised her slightly, to place that pillow beneath her bottom and elevate her thighs to a shocking degree before gently folding back the soft material of her nightgown to bare the lower half of her body his heated gaze.

'What are you—?' Her exclamation choked in her throat as Darius gently pushed her legs apart before moving to kneel between them. She voiced her uncertainty. 'Darius…?'

His eyes glittered darkly as looked up at her. 'I will not hurt you, Arabella,' he assured huskily. 'Believe me when I say I will never hurt you.'

Arabella wanted to believe him. To trust in him. It was only that these intimacies were so much more than— 'Ah…!' Her breath left her in a strangled gasp as both Darius's hands moved to touch gently between her legs, just as Arabella had instinctively longed for him to do only seconds ago.

Long and sensitive fingers parted her silky curls, and instead of feeling exposed Arabella instead felt an ache that burned. 'Please…!' Her own fingers dug into the sheet beside her and her head turned restlessly on the pillow. Seeking. Wanting. So desperately needing something she didn't really understand. Arabella gave an incomprehensible groan, her hips rising in sweet surrender as Darius lowered his head and the soft rasp of his tongue touched that part of her that was so swollen and sensitive.

Instantly sending Arabella to both heaven and hell!

Heaven because she had never known such pleasure as this existed. Hell because she thought she might die if Darius should stop!

Darius had not meant to move so fast. He had meant to go slowly. To gently introduce Arabella to this intimacy. But, having once lain her upon the bed, he had not been able to resist baring the softness of her thighs and allowing himself to gaze hungrily upon the silkiness of her naked curls. She was so pretty there. So beautiful. Plump and delicious, and just begging to be touched. To be kissed.

The first rasp of his tongue against her caused her to groan and move restlessly, rhythmically, into that caress. Darius continued until he was plundering her with his tongue—until Arabella hung poised on the edge of release.

Darius moved his mouth and slid one finger inside her moist heat. Slowly. Oh-so-slowly. Stilling once that finger was fully inside her so that she might accustom herself to how it felt to have her sensitive flesh invaded.

'Please, Darius…!' Arabella had lost all sense of where or who she was. Darius was her only reality as she felt something pooling deep inside her, building, growing and growing, until it seemed she might explode into a million pieces. 'Darius, please, I want—I need—' She groaned in protest as Darius slid that finger out of her, only to moan low in her throat as that first finger was joined by a second. He slowly began to thrust them inside her in a rhythm Arabella's hips moved up to meet even as Darius's tongue returned to the swollen nubbin above.

She bit her bottom lip painfully as she felt a need to cry out, to scream and shout at the top of her lungs as the pleasure built to an impossible degree, taking her higher, ever higher, to a place she had never been before.

She sat up, her hair wild, eyes even more so, and the eroticism of having Darius look up at her from between her naked thighs was enough to send her over the edge of that pleasure. She cried out in ecstasy.

Darius ensured that he drew every last vestige of what he was certain was Arabella's first ever orgasm, long after she had collapsed against the pillow to roll her head from side to side in mindless and uncontrollable pleasure.

Finally his caresses gentled, became soothing, as Arabella sobbed ever so softly.

Arabella lay back when Darius finally ceased and moved up beside her, looking for all the world like a wanton, with her hair tangled about her shoulders, one breast bared, and her nightgown thrown up about her waist.

He frowned as he saw that several tears had escaped from beneath her lashes and now lay wet upon her cheeks. 'Arabella?' Darius smoothed those tears away with the tips of his fingers. 'Did I hurt you after all?'

She raised long lashes, her eyes a deep unfocused brown. 'If you did then I believe I wish for you to hurt me in that way every night for the rest of my life!'

Darius laughed at her complete lack of guile. 'We have nowhere near finished this night yet.'

'No?' Her eyes widened with unconcealed interest.

'No,' he promised huskily. 'There is still so much more for us to share, Arabella. To explore together.'

She looked almost shy. 'I am to be allowed to touch you in the way you just touched me?'

'Oh, yes,' he assured her with feeling.

Darius had put his own fierce arousal to the back of his mind as he'd concentrated on giving Arabella pleasure. But it came back with a vengeance now. So much so that Darius doubted he would be able to hold long enough for Arabella to place even one delicate little finger upon his throbbing flesh!

'I—am I still a virgin?' Uncertainty creased Arabella's brow.

Darius sobered as Arabella once again revealed that her bravado of their first evening together had been a fabrication. 'I am afraid so.'

'Oh. Then—touching me—in that intimate way—?' Her cheeks were flushed. 'It did not—it did not—?'

'No,' he confirmed regretfully. 'But I promise when the time comes I will endeavour not to hurt you unduly. Do you believe me—?' Darius broke off, frowning darkly as the sound of shouting could be heard outside in the hallway. 'What the hell…?' He sprang lithely from the bed to scowl in the direction of the closed door.

'Fire! Fire!' The shouts became more audible as someone was heard running past in the hallway outside. 'The inn is on fire!'

Arabella sat up abruptly in the bed, her face pale, her eyes wide with fear as she hastily tidied her nightgown before standing up.

The inn was on fire?

Chapter Eight

'Do you suppose that everyone managed to get out?' Arabella asked worriedly some time later, as Darius joined her where stood huddled in the cloak she had managed to gather up before leaving the inn.

The two of them stood outside the front of the inn, staring up at the blaze that had once been the thatched roof above their bedchambers. The flames were so intense that they lit up the night sky and reflected on the faces of the dozen or so other people who stood gathered together in various states of undress—Arabella's maid and Darius's valet amongst them, thank goodness.

'The innkeeper seems to think so,' Darius replied. 'There were only ten guests, including our own party, and they are all accounted for. Fortunately we were able to prevent the stables from catching alight too,' he added grimly.

Arabella turned to look at Darius, still dressed only in his brocade robe. As were most of the other guests. There simply hadn't been time for anyone to dress, the fire having already spread to the hallway outside Arabella's bedchamber by the time Darius threw open the door to see what all the fuss was about. Now, in the light from the fire, it was possible to see that Darius's face was blackened in several places from where he had assisted the other men in getting the horses out of the stables, before helping to keep the blaze from spreading to the outer buildings.

'That is good news.' A shiver moved down her spine at the memory of the neighing and snorting of the trapped horses before Darius and several of the other men had managed to go into the stables and lead them out to safety.

The inn itself was beyond saving, several parts of the roof having already fallen in and so adding to the force of the fire as it blazed unrelentingly. The numbed innkeeper had accepted it was a losing battle too, and he now stood speechlessly beside his wife as the two of them looked up at the flames destroying not only their home but also their livelihood.

'Those poor people have lost everything,' Arabella murmured emotionally as she saw that loss upon the elderly couple's faces. 'And all because someone no doubt allowed a candle to fall onto the floor, or left it burning too close to the curtains.' She gave a sorrowful shake of her head.

Yes, Darius reflected grimly, no doubt someone *had* allowed the fire to start. Deliberately…

First the carriage accident the night before, and now a fire at the inn where they stayed tonight. Darius was far too aware of the unlikelihood of two such coincidences to accept that they were completely separate or random events.

If the two were connected, then it would appear that someone had known of his every move these past two days. And that someone had either followed Darius and Arabella to the inn earlier today, or they had already known where the two of them would be staying the night and had acted accordingly.

Neither explanation was acceptable. The former implied that Darius, too preoccupied by his young wife's beauty, had been lax in his usual caution of repeatedly checking to see whether or not they were being followed. The latter implied that one of his own servants had been loose-tongued concerning the movements of their employer. Or possibly been persuaded to be so by monetary reward. The fact that Darius had placed two of his grooms on guard outside the inn after their arrival yesterday only made the starting of this fire all the more suspect.

His past eight years as an agent for the crown had evoked a cynicism inside Darius that had taught him to trust no one. Not even those closest to him. Especially those closest to him!

Darius's gaze was icy-hard as he looked down at Arabella. 'Admittedly it will take time, but rest assured I will ensure that the landlord has enough funds to rebuild. A gift in honour of our marriage,' he added, as he saw the way Arabella had turned to him in surprise at his apparent largesse.

It was only fair to make reparation to the innkeeper, as Darius suspected that the inn had been burnt down with the intention of trapping him inside. Which might so easily have become the case, seeing as he had allowed himself to become so engrossed in Arabella's magnificent charms…

'That is—very generous of you, Darius.' Arabella laid a hand warmly upon his arm.

He gave a hard smile. 'No doubt I have inhaled too much smoke, and will come to my senses come the dawn.'

She gave him a chiding look. 'I do not believe you.'

'But talking of the dawn… Bearing in mind that we now have no inn in which to spend the night, and no clothes in which to dress ourselves come morning, I have ordered that both carriages be made ready so that we might all continue with our journey to Winton Hall tonight,' Darius informed her.

Arabella's eyes widened. 'Tonight? But—'

'You would rather sleep in the straw in the stables, perhaps?' Darius asked. 'With the other survivors of the fire? Along with any number of vermin—and I do not allude to the human kind!—nibbling at your feet in the darkness?'

Arabella repressed a shiver at the thought of the rats and mice, let alone the fleas and lice, that probably inhabited the stables. 'No, of course I would not prefer to do that. It is only—what will the servants at Winton

Hall think when, come morning, the Duke and Duchess of Carlyne arrive clothed only in their night robes?'

Darius gave a humourless laugh. 'Personally, I do not give a damn what they think!'

No, Arabella was sure Darius would not care a jot for the censure or otherwise of his servants. He had made it more than obvious during their short acquaintance that he cared little for anyone's opinion concerning his behaviour. Including her own! But Arabella, having had such wonderful imaginings of arriving at Winton Hall as its new duchess, could not help but feel dismayed at the thought of this unorthodox introduction as the new mistress to the servants.

'Or perhaps you had imagined that we might *enjoy* spending a night in the stables, where we might finish what we started earlier?' Darius's eyes glittered down at her mockingly.

Arabella recoiled at his harsh words, the colour first burning in her cheeks and then as rapidly fading, to leave her face pale and her eyes a dark and haunted brown. 'Darius…?'

'Yes?' he snapped.

Arabella stared up at him. Was this really the man who had made love to her so gently such a short time ago? Who had carefully and tenderly brought her to such a state of ecstasy that she had lost all control of her senses?

She gave an inward shudder at the mere thought of allowing *this* cold and cruelly taunting man such liberties with her. 'I assure you I thought no such thing.'

'No?'

'No!' Whatever kindness Arabella might have allotted to Darius earlier, in his concern for the inn-keeper, was completely erased by his reminder of how easily she had succumbed to his kisses and caresses.

'Have you been thinking that perhaps *I* am responsible for starting this fire?' he asked roughly.

'I will not even deign to answer such nonsense!' Once again the idea was a ridiculous one; Darius could as easily have perished in the fire as anyone else. Including Arabella. Her chin rose proudly. 'I am ready to leave whenever you are.'

His mouth thinned. 'That would be now.'

'Very well.' Arabella gave a haughty inclination of her head before turning on slippered feet and walking in the direction of the stables situated at the back of the inn.

Darius didn't move for several seconds, but instead stared grimly up at the fire as it continued to rage unchecked.

He realised he'd been overly harsh with Arabella just now, but after this second near miss in as many days Darius had been in no mood to coax and cajole her into continuing with their journey to Winton Hall tonight. They had to leave. They had to reach the relative safety of Winton Hall, where Darius would hopefully be able to put more stringent security in place.

As added security he also intended sending one of the grooms back to London with news of this second accident. Better by far that Bancroft was alerted now to the continuing danger rather than informed later of Darius's and Arabella's demise.

For as surely as Darius knew this inn would be completely razed to the ground by morning, he had no doubt that it had been intended that he and Arabella should burn along with it.

'I shall be busy about estate business for the rest of the day,' Darius informed Arabella as he prepared to take his leave after personally escorting her to the bedchamber at Winton Hall that adjoined his own. 'I suggest you use the time to rest and recover after your ordeal.'

To Arabella's relief there had been few witnesses to the arrival of the dishevelled Duke and Duchess of Carlyne when they'd reached their home some five hours later; most of the household servants had been still abed, and the few maids who were already up and about had been too busy cleaning and lighting the fires in preparation for the arrival of their master and mistress to be aware that Arabella and Darius had already arrived and gone straight upstairs to their bedchambers on the third floor of the house.

It had been an ignominious arrival to say the least. In all her imaginings of this day Arabella had envisaged herself and Darius arriving with all due ceremony and the servants lined up outside the house so that they might wait in turn to be introduced to their new mistress.

Instead of which the carriage had barely come to a halt and the door been opened before Darius had alighted onto the gravel driveway, leaving one of the grooms to help Arabella down. He had marched up the steps at the front of the red-stone mansion and thrown open the huge front door before striding into the marbled hallway. Somehow managing to display the same arrogance as if he were dressed in elegant finery instead of clothed only in his brocade nightrobe!

Having suffered through a wakeful journey, with the silence between herself and Darius of an awkward rather than a restful kind, Arabella had felt chilled both inside and out. She had pulled her cloak more firmly about her and chosen to follow her husband at a more leisurely pace, taking the time to look at the magnificent proportions of what was to be her new home.

The main house of red stone stood four storeys high, with wings of similar proportions curving the driveway on either side, and so giving the appearance of welcoming elegance.

There was no evidence of that same welcome on the present Duke of Carlyne's handsome face now, though, as he looked down his arrogant nose at his wife!

Nor did Arabella know to which ordeal Darius referred. That of having their earlier lovemaking interrupted so decisively? Or that of the fire itself, including his later questioning as to whether she had believed him responsible for it? Or perhaps he meant the cold and awkward carriage ride that had followed?

Whichever it was, Arabella was not disposed at that moment to spend any more time in her husband's company, and her eyes snapped angrily as she glared at him. 'If you will observe, Darius, you will note that your own appearance is no less…disreputable than my own.'

Darius was well aware of Arabella's displeasure with him—both with his behaviour earlier before they'd left the inn and with his preoccupation during the long and tedious hours of the carriage ride that had completed their journey to Winton Hall.

He wished it could be different. Wished that he might confide in Arabella about his own worries concerning both the carriage accident two days ago and the fire the previous night. But the oath he had made eight years ago dictated that he could not do so, which left him to continue his immediate enquiries without alerting Arabella to what he was doing.

Darius's first task of the morning, once he had bathed and dressed, would be to question all the servants who had accompanied them yesterday. From the grooms to Arabella's maid and his own valet. The thought that one of the servants he trusted, or possibly Arabella's own maid, might have been indiscreet, whether accidentally or on purpose, was highly distasteful to Darius. But the possibility had to be followed up before it could be discarded as an option.

'Perhaps so, Arabella,' he allowed. 'But I am no doubt more accustomed than you are to a night in which I have had little or no sleep.'

Colour blazed in Arabella's cheeks and her hands tightened into fists at her sides. 'You would *boast* to me of such things?'

Darius raised an eyebrow at the conclusion she'd jumped to, and couldn't help but tease her for thinking that he was mocking her by referring to his stamina as a lover! 'I wonder, can it be called boasting when one is only stating the truth?'

Arabella was so tired, so disheartened by the way things now stood between them, that she feared at any moment she might burst into loud and humiliating tears. 'I think it best if you leave me now, Darius,' she said fiercely. 'Before one or both of us says something we might later regret.'

He sighed heavily. 'I assure you, Arabella, I rarely have reason to feel regret for anything I do or say.'

Unlike Arabella, who now deeply regretted the way she had responded to Darius's kisses and caresses the night before! He was a self-confessed rake. A womaniser. A man who cared for no one and had no desire that anyone should care for him.

A fact that Arabella would do well to remember…

The worst thing she could possibly do was to fall in love with her own husband!

'Then you should consider yourself fortunate amongst men, Darius.' Her tone was sweetly insincere.

'Oh, I do, Arabella,' he drawled. 'I most certainly do!'

Arabella did not at all care for the speculative gleam she could see in those sky-blue eyes. 'I will wish you good day.' She placed a hand delicately against her lips as she gave a deliberate and dismissive yawn.

'Not so hasty, my dear Arabella.'

Instead of leaving, as she had hoped, Darius took a step towards her. Making her completely aware of the fact that they were both still wearing their nightrobes.

Arabella had already discarded her cloak on entering the magnificently furnished green and cream bedchamber reserved for the Duchess of Carlyne. A mistake, Arabella now realized, as she glanced down at herself and saw that the white nightgown and robe did very little to cover the curves of her body. The opposite, in fact, as the sheer material draped revealingly over the full curve of her breasts and clearly outlined the pouting thrust of their rosy tips!

Arabella felt her cheeks burn as she looked up and saw that Darius's gaze had followed her own. Her body was betraying her awareness of his hungry gaze in a way she had no control over, and she felt the pouting tips of her breasts harden to the fullness of ripe berries that begged to be eaten.

She drew in a sharp breath even as she wrapped her arms protectively about herself. 'I really would like to rest now, Darius.'

Seconds slipped slowly by as he minutely regarded her flustered and overheated face. 'Your body says otherwise, my dear,' he finally said.

Her eyes flashed darkly. 'My body responds to *my* commands, not the other way around!'

'Really?' Darius murmured, even as he took another step closer to her. A move that caused those betraying breasts to pucker in ever-increasing expectation. 'I believe you will find, my dear Arabella, that it is *I* who now has command over your body and not you.'

Her chin rose proudly even as she met his gaze unflinchingly. 'If you believe that then you are a fool,

Darius,' she bit out contemptuously. 'Or perhaps just overly conceited.'

Despite the fire the night before—the sooty black streaks still upon Arabella's cheeks were a clear reminder of that event, if Darius should need one—and the long and uncomfortable hours of the night they had spent riding in the carriage, Arabella still managed to look every inch the proud and haughty duchess she now was.

So much so that Darius did not have the heart to taunt her any longer. 'Perhaps,' he allowed curtly, and he stepped away from her to stride over to the door. 'As I said, I will be busy for the rest of the day. No doubt we will meet again at dinner.'

'No doubt.' Arabella nodded abruptly, determined to hold on to her tears long enough for Darius to open the door and leave her bedchamber.

He paused in the open doorway. 'You will inform either myself or one of the servants of your movements if you should decide to go outside to explore when you awaken from your nap.'

She frowned. 'I am to inform one of the servants if I wish to go outside?'

'Or myself.'

'I will do no such thing!'

'Oh, I think that you will.' The steely threat beneath the softness of his tone was unmistakable.

Arabella held on to her temper with effort. 'I have been surrounded by arrogant men all my life, but neither my father or Hawk ever felt the need to tell me what

I should and should not do. As such, I am accustomed to come and go as I please in my own home!'

Darius's mouth tightened. 'Then you will have to become unaccustomed, will you not? I am your husband, Arabella, not one of your over-indulgent older brothers,' he said harshly as she would have voiced a second protest. 'You gave me every right to tell you what to do two days ago, when you vowed before God to obey me!'

'Not when it is your intention to make me a prisoner in my own home!' She met his gaze defiantly.

'Obedience is obedience,' Darius snapped, but his expression softened slightly as he suddenly saw the pallor of her cheeks. He said more gently, 'Arabella, I am doing this for your own good—'

'Is that not the claim of all tyrants and despots?'

His mouth tightened at the accusation. 'You do not know the area, Arabella, and have no idea of the pitfalls or—or dangers of the surrounding countryside. And until you do—'

'Considering that Mulberry Hall, my brother's home, is only in the county adjoining this one—'

'You will not argue with me any further on this subject, Arabella!' A nerve pulsed rapidly in Darius's tightly clenched jaw.

She swallowed hard. 'So I am to be subject to your whim as to whether or not I may so much as walk outside in the grounds?'

It was far from an ideal situation, Darius knew. So far removed from what he had hoped for his marriage to Arabella…

But the carriage accident, and the fire last night, along with William Bancroft's warnings the night of their wedding, had ensured that Darius's suspicions were well and truly roused. And until he apprehended the person responsible some of Arabella's personal freedoms must necessarily be curtailed. Much as she might dislike Darius for enforcing such rules on her.

He nodded. 'That is exactly what I am saying.'

Her eyes glittered deeply gold in her anger. 'I believe you will find that I am your wife, Darius, and not a dog upon your hearth or a horse in your stables! As such—'

'As such you will do precisely what you are told!' Darius cut in forcefully, determined not to be thwarted in this. He dared not. Not when it had been made obvious to him that her own life was in as much danger as his own. 'Do not force me into locking you in your room in order to ensure your obedience, Arabella,' he warned darkly.

Those glittering golden eyes widened in alarm. 'You would really do that?' she gasped.

'If you insist on defying me, then, yes, you will leave me with no choice but to lock you in your bedchamber!'

Arabella stared at him incredulously and she realised by the rigidity of Darius's expression that he meant what he said.

Had she known anything at *all* before today of the man to whom she was now married? Arabella wondered dazedly. Or had she merely allowed herself to be dazzled by his golden good-looks? Challenged by his arrogant disregard for the women of the ton, who had thrown themselves at him before his brief first marriage and afterwards? Could it be that Arabella had behaved totally recklessly in her determination to ignore all the gossip that had circulated amongst the ton concerning Darius this past year, which should have warned her away from him?

What if that gossip were all true, after all?

As Arabella looked at the cold and remorselessly unbending man who had just threatened to lock her in her bedchamber if she did not obey him, she could well believe that it might be…

Chapter Nine

'Am I going to be subjected to this sulky silence all evening, Arabella, or do you think that at some stage you might indulge me by engaging in a little polite conversation?' Darius eyed his wife down the length of the highly polished table in the candlelit dining-room, with a warm fire crackling in its hearth.

They had eaten their soup, followed by the fish course, and were now enjoying perfectly cooked roast beef—all without Arabella doing any more than answering yes or no to Darius's attempts at conversation.

'I never sulk, Darius.' Brown eyes glittered as Arabella stared back at him.

Darius raised sceptical brows. 'No?'

Arabella took a sip of her wine before answering him. 'From what I have observed one has to feel strongly about something in order to sulk over it.'

'Ah. I see.' Darius sat back to rest his elbows on the arms of his chair to look at her above steepled fingers. 'In that case I am gratified to hear you do not feel strongly enough about anything I have said or done today to feel the necessity for such an emotion.'

'You are welcome.' She bestowed on him a sweetly insincere smile.

What a little liar she was, Darius mused ruefully. If there had been a knife handy earlier today, when he had instructed Arabella that she was to stay within the confines of the house unless she informed a servant, then Darius had no doubt he would have found it buried up to the hilt between his shoulderblades as soon as he had dared turn his back on her!

His bride looked absolutely enchanting this evening, in a long-sleeved gown of golden-brown silk which was an exact match with her eyes as they changed colour with her mood, with a ribbon of the same colour threaded through her honey-gold curls. Her throat was bare, as were her earlobes. Arabella's only jewellery was the plain gold wedding ring Darius had placed upon her finger but two days ago.

Deliberately so? Probably, Darius acknowledged ruefully, even as he determined to pierce the frosty politeness with which his wife had been treating him all evening. 'Then you acknowledge I had a perfect right to confine you to your bedchamber earlier today?'

A nerve pulsed in the tightness of her suddenly clenched jaw. 'As I recall, you confined me to the *house*, not my bedchamber.'

Darius would have much preferred to confine

Arabella to her bedchamber for the day, and to have joined her there so that they might continue their love-making of last night.

Instead of which he had spent an unsatisfactory day questioning his grooms, Arabella's maid and his own valet, in an effort to see if any of them had any information concerning the carriage accident or the fire. As was to be expected, all had denied knowing anything.

Darius could only hope that his time had not been completely wasted, and that whoever was responsible would at least now be alerted to the fact that his suspicions were aroused concerning both incidents.

His mouth tightened. 'I trust you are well rested now?'

Arabella looked down the table at Darius from beneath lowered lashes and searched his face as to any hidden meaning to his question—for instance, if she were 'well rested' enough not to be in any immediate need of further sleep!

Arabella had been far too angry to sleep after Darius had left her bedchamber this morning. Instead she had paced the room restlessly for some time as she plotted and planned suitable retribution for his high-handedness. It had been several hours later before she'd come to the conclusion that most if not all of those plans were impossible.

Boiling him in oil was not practical. Throwing all his clothes in the bathtub would no doubt only result in his choosing to walk about naked. As for causing him physical damage… Darius was obviously so much stronger than she that that idea was rendered as impractical as boiling him in oil.

Another plan had occurred to Arabella as her maid had helped her to dress in preparation for joining Darius downstairs for dinner. That of leaving Winton Hall altogether by commandeering one of Darius's own carriages and travelling to her family's home in neighbouring Gloucestershire. Once there, she could claim sanctuary with Hawk and his wife.

Of course it would cause the most terrible scandal if Arabella were to leave Darius so soon after their wedding, and she knew that Hawk would try to talk her out of it once he learnt of the circumstances under which Arabella had left Winton Hall. What had Darius done, after all, but suggest Arabella stay in her bedchamber and rest following the burning down of the inn in which they had been staying the night before?

Hawk would have behaved in exactly the same autocratic manner, and he would not see that Darius had bullied or intimidated her. But Arabella understood it only too well. And she would not stand for it. She would not stand for it at all!

The decision made, Arabella knew she must somehow try to avoid her husband's lovemaking for one more night at least; she wasn't sure she would be able to leave Darius at all once he had fully made love to her…

She placed her knife and fork carefully down upon the virtually untouched food on her plate and now avoided meeting Darius's piercing gaze. 'My nerves are still rather—unsettled by the upset of the last few days.'

'Really?'

Arabella looked up sharply as she heard the sarcasm in Darius's tone. 'Yes, really,' she echoed firmly.

'Perhaps a soothing bath before bedtime?'

'Perhaps.' She nodded coolly. 'Although I believe a night of undisturbed sleep would be more beneficial.'

'You do?' Darius drawled, not fooled for a moment by the demureness of his wife's demeanour.

Arabella was the least demure woman Darius had ever met in his life!

Rather, she was stubborn. Headstrong. Far too outspoken for a man's comfort. Arabella was all of those things and more. But demure? No, he did not think so!

Which meant there had to be a reason for her appearing to be so now. 'I believe we might try the bath first,' he suggested. 'Perhaps followed by massaging a little perfumed oil into—'

'Darius!' Arabella gasped, her creamy cheeks blushing hotly.

'Into your temples,' he completed wickedly. 'My late stepmother certainly believed in its restorative powers whenever she had the megrims. Which was often.' Darius's top lip curled back with distaste at the memory of Clara Wynter, his father's third wife, as she languished upon her bed or a chaise in a pose of deep suffering. Usually as accompaniment to something Darius had supposedly said or done!

Arabella's eyes flashed darkly. 'I do not have the

megrims! I am merely fatigued— You have a step-mother?' She frowned down the table at him, suddenly diverted by what he had said.

'No longer, thank God.' he replied.

'She died?' Arabella pressed softly.

'Oh, yes,' Darius murmured without regret. Why should he feel regret at the death of a woman who had made his life hell from the age of five until he was ten? 'My father married three times in his lifetime,' he expanded, as Arabella continued to look at him enquiringly. 'He adored his first wife, my brother George's mother, and was happily married to her for almost twenty years, until her death. I have no idea how he felt about my own mother as she died only hours after giving birth to me. After which I was raised by a series of wet-nurses and nursemaids. George was more than twenty years older than I, already away from home when I was born, and I rarely saw my father for the first four years of my life. So perhaps it is safe to assume that he adored his second wife too, and as such blamed me for killing her.'

Arabella frowned. 'Babies do not kill. God decides these things.'

'Or conversely the Devil.'

Arabella felt a stab of guilt as she recalled it was not so long ago she had thought Darius was the Devil disguised as an angel! 'And did your father adore his third wife too?' she prompted huskily.

'She was certainly beautiful enough,' Darius replied harshly. 'I was five years old the first time I saw her. I thought she was an angel come to earth.' His face hardened into sharp, forbidding angles. 'I was wrong!'

Arabella drew in a sharp breath. This was the most that Darius had ever talked to her about his early life, his childhood, and the picture he painted was not a pleasant one. In comparison with her own indulged childhood it sounded very unpleasant indeed.

Perhaps it explained some of Darius's excesses in his adult life—that devil-may-care attitude that had labelled him both a rake and a wastrel…?

No! Arabella must keep firmly in mind that Darius had treated her most shabbily earlier today, and not allow her softer emotions to be touched by the things he had just told her.

As such, she repressed the impulse she had to rise and go down to the end of the table where he sat. To put her arms about him. To assure him that he would never be alone again.

An impulse totally at odds with Arabella's decision to leave Winton Hall—and Darius—in the morning!

'Your stepmother ignored you, too?' she said instead.

Darius's eyes glittered deeply blue. 'It would have been far better for me if she had,' he ground out. 'But, no, my dear stepmama enjoyed nothing more than comparing her six-year-old stepson unfavourably with the son she produced within a year of her marriage to my father.' His mouth twisted distastefully. 'I was sly. Deceitful. Utterly wild. Not at all a good example for her own darling Francis to emulate.'

'I had totally forgotten that you have a younger brother!' Arabella exclaimed.

'Most people do—to his extreme annoyance,' Darius commented.

Arabella vaguely remembered Francis Wynter as being a pale, nondescript version of Darius himself. 'But he was not present at our wedding, was he?'

A nerve pulsed in Darius's tightly clenched jaw. 'Francis is currently travelling on the Continent. For his health,' he bit out.

Arabella eyed him knowingly. 'Is that not what a man usually does in order to avoid a scandal of some kind?'

'Is it?' Darius's expression was grim as he lifted his glass and took a sip of the red wine.

'You know that it is.' She smiled reprovingly. 'What did Francis do? Run up gambling debts he could not pay? Engage in a scandalous affair with a married lady? Or perhaps he killed a man in a duel?'

'Nothing so honourable!' The harsh denial was spoken before Darius could stop himself, and it visibly startled Arabella. To the extent that Darius knew he had said too much. Far too much, taking into consideration Arabella's sharp intelligence.

Although her innocence concerning Francis's movements had at least served to confirm Lucian's claim that he had not discussed the events of the previous April with any of his family—least of all his young sister…

Darius forced himself to relax and smile pleasantly. 'There is reputed to be a black sheep in every family, Arabella. Or perhaps you had assumed that to be me in the Wynter family?' He raised mocking brows, knowing by the becoming flush that appeared in her cheeks that that was exactly what she *had* thought!

Arabella was totally unnerved by the guilty flush that darkened her cheeks. She wondered what misdeed Lord Francis Wynter could possibly have committed that was worse than his older brother's notorious and well-noted exploits in gambling clubs and ladies' bedchambers…

She raised her chin challengingly. 'You must admit it is a reputation you have long nurtured.'

'Must I?'

Arabella scowled at his obvious amusement. 'It is not something of which you should be in the least proud!'

Darius laughed softly. 'My dear Arabella, you look so very beautiful when you are indignant.'

'Do not attempt to cajole and flatter me, Darius,' she scorned. 'After your behaviour earlier today, I assure you I am beyond being charmed by you.'

'I thought we had agreed that you did not feel strongly enough about my behaviour earlier to be in the least concerned by it?' he teased.

'I am *not* concerned by it!' Arabella snapped frustratedly. 'But neither do I intend to forget it.' The softening she had felt towards Darius a few short minutes ago had completely disappeared.

'What—never?'

'No!'

'I cannot…*persuade* you into thinking more kindly towards me?' he asked.

Arabella eyed Darius uncertainly, not in the least reassured by the way his gaze had darkened and warmed to the colour of cobalt as he looked at her so intently. Or the way those chiselled lips had softened so sensually. Nor by the languid ease of his muscled shoulders and chest beneath his black superfine and white linen. No, Arabella was not reassured at all!

She became even less so as Darius rose slowly to his booted feet to walk slowly, confidently, down the length of the table until he reached her side. 'Perhaps it is time you retired to bed, after all,' he murmured throatily, as one of his hands moved up to curve warmly against the smoothness of her cheek.

It was all she could do to stop herself from melting against that caressing hand. From purring like a kitten at the touch of his fingers against her skin and moaning softly at the shaft of pleasure that coursed through her traitorous body.

She was still so angry with Darius for his high-handed treatment of her earlier today, and had every intention of leaving Winton Hall—and Darius—come the morning.

Yet her body now responded to his lightest touch. Her breasts swelled, and she felt a fierce rush of heat between her thighs that made her shift uncomfortably against the brocade cushion of the dining chair.

She moistened dry lips, and in doing so felt how their swollen sensitivity betrayed her arousal. 'I believe I am old enough to decide for myself when I wish to go to bed, Darius.' Her voice was sharp with self-disgust.

How could she possibly allow herself to be physically

aroused by a man who made her as angry as Darius did most of the time?

Darius didn't answer her immediately. Instead he moved both his hands so that they rested on the arms of Arabella's chair and turned that chair towards him and brought his face down to within inches of her own. 'I was suggesting that we *both* go to bed, Arabella,' he whispered, his wine-scented breath warm against her cheek. 'But I will be just as comfortable making love to you here, if you that is what you wish.'

She blinked nervously. 'The footman will be returning at any moment to remove the dishes…'

Darius smiled. 'I have instructed the footman—in fact, all of the servants, inside the house and out of it—not to interrupt us until they are called for whenever the two of us are alone together.'

Having spent the day in her bedchamber, attended only by her own maid, Arabella had not had the chance to meet any of the other servants at Winton Hall. An oversight Darius had corrected when Arabella had joined him downstairs before dinner. All of the servants, from the cook to the butler, had been lined up in the hallway to be introduced to his duchess.

To say that Arabella had been surprised at the appearance of some of those servants would be an understatement!

All the cooks Arabella had known at the St Claire residences, both from childhood and now, were jolly and plump—usually from tasting too many of their own creations. The cook at Winton Hall was a thin and wiry woman, with a pinched face dominated by a sharply enquiring gaze that seemed to see altogether too much as she stared boldly back at the new Duchess of Carlyne.

The maids were all much older than Arabella would have expected too, and the footmen had the rough and ready appearance of labourers rather than refined household servants.

Even so, the butler, Westlake, had to be the most surprising of all. A tall and burly man, his muscled torso and arms straining the seams of his tailored frock coat, his face pocked and scarred, and his nose looking as if it might have been broken on more than one occasion, he gave every appearance of being a prize fighter rather than the butler of a duke!

Arabella knew that Hawk, as the aristocratic Duke of Stourbridge, would not have countenanced allowing *any* of Darius's servants to step foot inside a single ducal household—let alone be employed in one!

'After all, this *is* our honeymoon, Arabella,' Darius added at her frowning silence.

Arabella's bosom visibly swelled as she drew in an indignant breath. 'How *could* you have done such a thing, Darius?' Her cheeks were red. 'Whatever will the servants think of us? Of me?'

'They will think that your husband finds you so desirable that he cannot keep his hands from you,' Darius assured her huskily.

Arabella shot him a confused glance. 'But that is not true!'

Darius had been amused by Arabella's obvious bewilderment earlier, when he had introduced her to the household staff. She had smiled graciously to each in turn, her smile becoming even more fixed when he at last presented Westlake to her. The man looked exactly what he was: an ex-pugilist—a fact that any of her brothers would no doubt have been able to tell her if they had been present. Big Tom Westlake had been a champion fighter of some repute until his retirement from the ring two years ago.

To Arabella's credit she had not shown by word or deed that she found any of his household staff out of the ordinary. So much so that Darius had found his admiration for her increasing considerably. And his desire to make love to her even more so!

'I assure you it is true, Arabella,' he murmured as he easily held her gaze captive. 'We have already been married for two days and two nights, and I have yet to make love to my wife.' A fact that Darius was all too aware of.

'Yes. But—'

'Which is something I now intend to rectify,' he continued.

Every shred of anger left Arabella, every trace of even a thought of repulsing her husband's advances deserting her as Darius's lips caressed the side of her throat. Arabella gave a low moan of surrender as she felt the hot sweep of Darius's tongue against the lobe of her ear.

Everything else ceased to matter when Arabella felt the nip of teeth against that lobe, and pleasure grew and spread throughout all of her body.

Darius drew back slightly as Arabella whimpered

slightly. 'Come with me?' He straightened to hold his hand out to her invitingly.

'Where are we going?' Even as she hesitated Arabella placed her hand in his much larger one.

'Nowhere outside of this room, I assure you.' Darius grimaced as he pulled Arabella effortlessly to her feet so that she now stood in front of him. 'I have no intention of allowing anything to interrupt us this time, Arabella.' His hands moved up to cradle either side of her flushed and beautiful face. 'Not even if the house should burn down around our ears.'

The fact that the latter was more than a possibility at the moment—despite the protection of men like Big Tom Westlake—only made Darius all the more determined in his intentions. He had wanted to possess this woman for far longer than he cared to admit. Least of all to Arabella herself. Darius intended allowing nothing, and no one, to stop him from finally making her his own.

'There is no need to be apprehensive.' He reached up to gently smooth the frown from between her expressive eyes. 'You liked what we did together last night, did you not?'

Arabella's cheeks burned as she remembered how the previous night Darius had touched and kissed the most private parts of her body. 'I— Yes, I liked it. It is only—'

'Would you like me to kiss you in that way again?' Darius prompted intensely.

Arabella felt almost faint as she recalled the touch of Darius's mouth and tongue against that sensitive part of her body. 'Are such things completely natural? Do all married couples engage in such—such intimacies together?' Her curiosity was such that for the moment she did not care that the question betrayed her own lack of experience.

Darius gazed down at her indulgently. 'Are you asking me if your brothers and their wives enjoy those same pleasures together?'

Was she? Did Arabella really want to know of the intimacies between her brothers and their wives? No, of course she did not! She'd had Darius's first marriage more in mind when she'd asked that particular question…

'No,' she answered firmly. 'I merely wondered as to the—the propriety—'

'My darling Arabella.' Darius's interruption was indulgent. 'Any degree of intimacy, as long as it is by mutual consent, is permissible between married couples. Or not,' he added more seriously.

'What do you mean?'

Darius shrugged. 'Many married couples, whilst tolerating each other's company socially, do not enjoy each other in the bedchamber. That is not going to be the case between the two of us, I hope?'

Arabella knew that she should stop Darius's lovemaking now. That not doing so would make her leaving Darius tomorrow so much harder to do.

It was only that she was still so curious, and she ached to know what came next when a man and woman made love together. And if she did go ahead with her plan to leave Darius tomorrow, bringing an end to their marriage, then tonight might be her only chance of ever finding out…

Darius's face darkened as he misread her hesitation for reluctance. 'Be assured, Arabella, that I will never force you into suffering intimacies which you find abhorrent.'

Arabella didn't even want to know what those intimacies could possibly be, let alone experience them! 'I did not for one moment suppose that you would,' she came back tartly. 'Nor would I let you!'

This was more like the Arabella that Darius admired and desired. Most especially desired…

He chuckled softly. 'Allow me to aid you in taking down your hair and removing your gown.' He suited his words to his actions, his gaze holding hers as he removed the pins from her hair before unthreading the ribbon from her curls and fastening it loosely about her throat.

Before this night was over Darius intended for that ribbon to be the only thing that Arabella wore!

Chapter Ten

Arabella stood perfectly still, barely breathing, as Darius moved behind her to push her silky hair forward over one shoulder before deftly unfastening the tiny buttons down the back of her gown.

His fingers felt warm through the thin material of her silk shift, his lips cool as he tasted the heated flesh he had bared, his tongue a fiery rasp against her spine, sending quivers of pleasure down its length to blossom and spread between her thighs.

Arabella's breath ceased altogether as Darius's lips moved back up to her nape before he folded the two sides of her gown apart and allowed the garment to fall down to her ankles. His hands encircled her waist before moving upwards over her ribcage and cupping beneath the fullness of her breasts.

'Look, Arabella,' he encouraged throatily. 'Watch as I touch you.'

She breathed softly as she lowered her gaze obediently to where she could clearly see his hands as they cupped her breasts through her shift. His skin was so much darker than the creamy whiteness of those twin orbs, their nipples deeply red and pouting, straining longingly against the sheer material that covered them.

Even as her gaze focused on those disembodied hands the thumbs shifted, caressing those sensitive and swollen tips, and once again sending rivulets of pleasure down to blaze into a burning need between her thighs. 'Darius…'

'Watch, Arabella,' he instructed again.

She couldn't have looked away from those caressing hands now if her very life had depended upon it. Instead she could only gaze as her swollen nipples were captured between thumb and finger, Darius exerting just enough pressure to increase her pleasure, causing Arabella's back to arch and her head to drop back against Darius's shoulder.

'Watch!'

Her breathing was ragged as she straightened to obey, her eyes widening as one of her breasts continued to be caressed and squeezed and his other hand slowly slid down over her ribcage to pull her shift up to her waist, baring her thighs and the silken golden curls nestled there.

She gasped as his long tapered fingers parted those silken curls to reveal a swollen pink nub Arabella had not even realised was there until Darius had touched her yesterday. Why would she? A lady was not encouraged to explore her own body.

'Touch yourself there, Arabella,' Darius urged.

Almost as if he had read her thoughts! As if Darius had known of her curiosity about these secret and so far unexplored parts of her body! 'I cannot.' She moved her head from side to side in protest.

'Do it for me.'

'You said you would not make me do anything that I did not like!'

'I promise you will like this, Arabella,' Darius murmured indulgently. 'Try it and see.' He kept his fingers against those parted curls as his other hand moved to take one of hers and guide it down to that exposed flesh. 'There.' He placed her finger against the swollen nubbin and moved it gently over it.

Arabella gasped as she felt the same pleasure in her own touch as she had in Darius's.

'It is possible to pleasure oneself,' Darius revealed gruffly as he continued to hold her hand in place.

'I— But— How…?'

'Exactly as you are now doing. Touch, Arabella,' he encouraged. 'Caress. Learn for yourself what gives you pleasure.'

'But you—'

'For the moment I take my pleasure in watching *you*,' he told her.

Arabella's cheeks burned and she glanced quickly over her shoulder at him, assured that Darius spoke the truth as she saw that his face was flushed and his eyes dark and feverish with desire.

'Any intimacy is possible between us so long as we both consent to it,' he reminded her huskily. 'At this moment it is my dearest wish to watch you pleasure yourself.'

Arabella had never dreamed—never imagined… 'I cannot!' She snatched her hand away. 'It is too much!' She buried her overheated face in her hands.

Too much, too soon, Darius realised. A pity—he would have so enjoyed sitting in a chair and watching as Arabella touched and caressed herself. Another time, perhaps. Once she was more familiar with intimacy. More intimately familiar with *him*!

Even as Darius took Arabella gently in his arms he wondered if she knew how completely she had given away her lack of all physical experience. Even self-exploration—something that most young men knew about long before they had a physical encounter with a woman.

It had been almost fifteen years since Darius had first made love to an actual woman. A rather beautiful lady of the demi-monde, and considerably experienced, who had seen it as her duty to tutor him well—both in his own pleasures and that of his bed partner. It was experience that Darius had since brought to all of his physical alliances.

Here and now, with his young and inexperienced wife, was not the occasion upon which to indulge in that experience. At least only in so far as to make this as pleasurable an initiation for her as was possible. Darius had no doubt that making love to Arabella tonight was going to stretch his self-control to its very limits!

'Will you help me out of some of these clothes, love?' he encouraged gently as he began to shrug out of his jacket. 'It seems a little unfair that you are almost unclothed whilst I am still fully dressed.'

Arabella was only too glad to move behind him and help slide the tight jacket down his arms, her cheeks still burning with embarrassment at her own lack of adventure. Darius must think her a complete novice when it came to lovemaking. Which she was, of course. But it was nonetheless humiliating to keep proving it to him time and time again!

He somehow appeared bigger once free of the tailored black evening jacket—his shoulders wider, his back more muscled against his shirt and the restraint of his silver brocade waistcoat.

Arabella made no effort to hide her interest as Darius quickly despatched that waistcoat, before removing his cravat and unbuttoning the three buttons on his shirt. The open neck of that shirt revealed a covering of darker blond hair on his chest.

Her eyes darkened avidly as Darius pulled that shirt over his head, tousling his hair, the muscles moving silkily beneath the hardness of his chest.

He was perfectly formed: wide shoulders, defined chest, flat stomach, tapered waist, his thighs and legs clearly long and muscled in the close-fitting breeches.

Darius was well aware of the fact that he was twelve years Arabella's senior, and he felt glad now that he had kept himself fit all these years, with regular exercise using his sword, and also in the ring—sometimes here with Big Tom. Arabella's eyes showed her admiration for his muscled form as her gaze moved over him unashamedly.

'Like what you see, little puss?'

She looked up at him quizzically. 'Why do you call me that?'

Darius's grin was feral. 'Probably because before the night is out I intend to make you purr like a contented kitten!'

'I—could we blow out the candles, do you think?' she asked shyly, averting her gaze as Darius's fingers moved to the fastening of his breeches.

'By all means.' Darius left his breeches on as he blew out the offending candles and left the room bathed only in firelight.

A delicate light that shone on the gold of Arabella's hair and through the thin material of her shift as she stood before that fire. Clearly outlining her slender curves—full breasts, narrow waist, the gentle curve of her bottom—and her legs long and slender through the knee-length shift.

'You are so very beautiful, Arabella,' Darius murmured softly as he moved to stand only inches away from her.

'So are you,' she returned huskily, knowing herself to be completely mesmerised by his unmistakable male beauty.

'Men are not beautiful,' he chided teasingly as his head lowered and his mouth captured hers.

But Darius *was* beautiful. As beautiful as that fallen

angel Arabella had once likened him to. As beautiful as—

She could no longer form a coherent thought as Darius deepened his kiss. As lips, tongue and teeth laid siege to her own and he swept her firmly into his arms, moulding the softer contours of her body against his much harder one, making her fully aware of the long length of his arousal as it pressed against her.

Leaving her in no doubt as to what Darius wanted.

He wanted her.

Arabella St Cl—no, Arabella *Wynter.* His wife.

As she surely wanted him. Darius Wynter. Her husband.

Her arms moved up and her hands became entangled in the thick golden hair at Darius's nape as she returned the intensity of his kiss. Following his lead, she nibbled upon the fullness of his lower lip before sliding her tongue into the welcoming heat of his mouth, her tongue duelling briefly with his before Darius drew it deeper inside. Arabella felt hot, so tinglingly, sensitively hot. Each sweep of Darius's hands, as they moved restlessly across her body, ignited tiny licking flames of awareness from her breast to her thigh, and then back again. Cupping beneath her breasts, thumbs caressing her hardened nipples time and time again, until she pressed against him, silently pleading for more.

Darius broke the kiss to slip the strap of her shift down her arm so that he could move to the gentle slope of her breast with his mouth. Tasting, caressing, until he reached her nipple and could take its bared fullness inside his mouth. His teeth and tongue became a dual sensual attack that caused Arabella to moan longingly even as she cupped the back of his head and held him to her.

She wanted more. Wanted— Oh, God, she wanted—

'Help me off with the rest of my clothes, love.'

Arabella stared up at Darius dazedly for several long seconds, until his meaning became clear and she looked down to where his arousal strained so obviously against the material of his breeches. Her fingers were clumsy, trembling as they moved to unfasten the buttons, her breath catching in her throat as the last button came undone and she stared down at that hot and heavy fullness as it leapt free to rest against the palm of her hand.

His arousal was so thick and so long that Arabella doubted she would be able to span the width of it with her hand. She ran her fingers experimentally along its length.

Arabella had never imagined that this part of a man's body would look as it did. So beautiful she wanted to touch it. So silky she wanted to caress it. So responsive to her touch that she longed to kiss and caress it with her lips and tongue in the same intimate manner Darius had kissed her the previous night.

'Yes, I *will* feel that same pleasure in being touched and kissed,' Darius encouraged as Arabella looked up at him questioningly once he had completely removed his breeches.

Although he was far from sure of the wisdom of encouraging that intimacy when Arabella moved down onto her knees in front of him. Darius closed his eyes, his jaw clenching as he fought to maintain control as Arabella began to move her hand, testing, experimenting, as she learnt which caresses gave him the most pleasure.

Everything about having Arabella make love to him in this way gave Darius pleasure. Everything!

Touch. Sight. Smell.

The hand about him felt like velvet. The intense expression on her beautiful face as she watched his response to her caressing hand was like an aphrodisiac to his own roused senses.

He— Dear God…!

Darius's knees almost buckled beneath him as he felt her flicking the moist end of her tongue along the very tip of him. A hot, wet stroke that caused Darius to gasp and clench his fists in an attempt to find some self-control.

He managed to withstand that caress for only a few seconds longer. 'I think not!' he managed to rasp as he bent down to place his hands gently on Arabella's arms and pull her to her feet.

She gazed up at him almost shyly. 'You did not like it?'

'I liked it almost too much,' he admitted gruffly as his hand curved gently about her flushed cheek. 'Another time, love,' he promised as Arabella frowned her disappointment. 'I have waited too long to make love with you to be able to withstand that particular intimacy any more tonight.'

Arabella looked up at him searchingly. Darius had

waited too long to make love with her? Did he mean these past ten days? Or longer than that?

She had no chance to ask him those probing questions as he slipped the second strap of her shift down her arm and allowed the silky gown to fall to her feet, resulting in Arabella standing naked before him.

Any awkwardness she might have felt at her complete nakedness was forgotten as she saw the heated admiration in Darius's gaze. He made no effort to hide it from her. Even if he had, the response of his naked body would have given him away as he seemed to grow even larger the more he continued to look at her!

'You are as perfect as a statue of Aphrodite I once gazed upon in Greece,' he murmured throatily.

Her eyes widened. 'You have been to Greece?'

He chuckled huskily. 'I have been to many places. And someday I will enjoy telling you about all of them. Just not now, Arabella.' He ran a finger lightly across her swollen lips as he teased her. 'The only thing I want to do now is kneel down at your feet and worship you.'

'I do not want you to worship me, Darius.' Arabella shook her head, emboldened by his obvious admiration of her nakedness. 'I want—I want you inside me.' Her cheeks burned at the admission. 'I need to know how it feels to have this…' her hand caressed along the length of his arousal '…inside me.'

Darius's breath caught in his throat. He had known many women intimately, but none so honest, so open in her needs, as Arabella. 'And so you shall, love,' he promised softly, and he took her hand and moved the two of them to lie down upon the rug in front of the fire.

Darius leant on his elbow to look down at his wife. Her curls were even more golden in the firelight, her body bathed in that same soft glow. 'You are beautiful, Arabella,' he said gruffly. 'So very, very beautiful.'

Her hands moved up the nakedness of his chest, her fingers becoming entangled in the hair at his nape as she gently pulled him down to her. 'Kiss me, Darius. Make love to me,' she pressed shakily.

He kissed her long and deeply at the same time as his hands caressed her, readying her, making sure that she was prepared to receive him before he moved to lie between her parted thighs. 'I do not want to hurt you, Arabella,' he muttered as he paused and rested his forehead against hers.

Arabella had questioned her sisters-in-law enough to know that Darius could not help but hurt her a little this first time as he breached the barrier of her virginity. It was a pain Arabella welcomed if it meant she truly became one with him. If he felt unable—or unwilling—to take that final step because he did not want to hurt her, then Arabella would have to do it herself…

She allowed her hands to move caressingly down the muscled column of Darius's back before spreading her fingers over his buttocks, able to feel the way he tensed at her touch. Her fingers tightened about him at the same time as she arched her hips in a thrust that brought Darius fully inside her.

He lifted his head to frown. 'What are you doing?'

'I want this, Darius,' Arabella told him determinedly.

'I want all of you!' She thrust again, at once feeling the barrier of her innocence tear beneath that invasion.

The pain was sharp and brief. The length of a sharply indrawn breath and passing just as quickly. To be replaced by the wonder of knowing that Darius was finally inside her.

'Easy, love.' He soothed Arabella into stillness as she arched again in her need to take all of him inside her. 'I want us both to savour this moment.'

He slowly kissed the tips of her breasts, licking the tightness of her puckered nipples, then gently biting. His hand moved between them to touch that swollen nubbin nestled amongst her curls, fingers lightly caressing as he increased Arabella's pleasure.

She gasped, her eyes widening as that pulsing pleasure centred hotly between her thighs. She clung to his shoulders as she moved instinctively to meet the thrust of Darius's thighs.

'Yes, love. *Yes*!' he urged through gritted teeth as he began to move his hips, pulling back slightly before surging inside her, again and again until he was so deep it felt as if he touched the very centre of her, sending Arabella into a vortex of unimagined pleasure.

Darius tried to hold back, fighting to control his own release, wanting this never to end. But as she convulsed around him Darius knew it was a battle he was destined to lose, and he rushed towards his own climax before he collapsed weakly onto her breasts, breathing heavily, both their bodies hot and slick from the exertion.

* * *

Arabella smiled in dreamy satisfaction as she ran tender fingers through Darius's hair, loving its silky feel as he lay with his head upon her breasts.

She was no longer a virgin!

She was now officially a woman. Darius Wynter's woman.

It was glorious. Wonderful. Unimaginably delightful.

No wonder her brothers and their wives so often walked about with silly smiles upon their faces if *this* was what they shared in their marriage beds. And Arabella was convinced that they did.

It was like being a part of some exclusive club, its members privy to a secret too special, too excruciatingly wonderful, to be shared by any but themselves.

'Your Grace?' A knock sounded on the dining room door in accompaniment to the urgent demand.

Arabella's movements stilled as she recognised the burly butler's rough tones as he spoke on the other side of the closed dining-room door.

'What the hell?' Darius was scowling darkly as he raised his head to look across at that closed door.

'I am sorry to—to disturb you, Your Grace.' The unlikely-looking butler sounded more than a little anxious.

'He's going to be more than sorry when I have done telling him what I think of him,' Darius muttered beneath his breath. 'Give me a minute, man,' he called out.

'I am sure Westlake would not have disturbed us if

he did not have an important reason for doing so.' In truth, Arabella was having difficulty holding back the bubble of laughter inside her that was threatening to break loose.

She and Darius had been married three days. Three days of constant interruptions, for one reason or another, to every attempt at intimacy between them. And now, when they had at last managed to find some privacy for their lovemaking, the butler at Winton Hall had interrupted them yet again. Even after Darius had assured Arabella that he had instructed the servants to do otherwise!

Darius's scowl deepened. 'Did you hear a shot being fired? Or perhaps a herd of wild elephants, loose and threatening to trample down the house with all of us inside it?'

Arabella giggled at the unlikelihood of either of those things ever happening here in the safety of the Worcestershire countryside. 'You know I did not.'

'Well, I assure you, Arabella, they are the only two reasons I gave Westlake for interrupting us this evening,' he grumbled.

Her giggle developed into a fully fledged chuckle at his disgruntled expression. 'Admit it, Darius, it *is* very funny,' she encouraged, as her husband continued to look distinctly unamused.

'You would not have thought so if the interruption had occurred five minutes earlier,' he retorted.

'No,' Arabella acknowledged, with remembered frustration at the previous interruptions to their lovemaking. Even more so now that she was fully aware of what she had been missing all this time!

Darius gave an impatient shake of his head and gently disengaged himself before standing up. 'I am beginning to think someone is deliberately trying to sabotage even the consummation of our marriage,' he growled as he reached for his breeches.

Arabella made no effort to disguise her curiosity concerning Darius's nakedness.

Her fingers ached to touch him again. To caress and handle him until he was once again hard and throbbing with the need to be inside her. Perhaps this time to be allowed to use her lips and tongue to taste and arouse him.

Darius groaned as he obviously saw the intent in her expression. 'Do not look at me like that when there is no chance I am going to be able to make love to you again—in the next few minutes, at least.' He settled his breeches on his hips before fastening them.

Arabella stretched languidly, feeling and no doubt looking much like the satisfied kitten Darius had earlier promised to make of her. 'I am sure, no matter what the problem, that it will not keep you from our bed all night.'

Darius pulled his shirt on over his head before looking down at Arabella once more, relishing the fact that she obviously did not feel the need to cover herself, but instead seemed completely comfortable being naked in front of him.

'Perhaps you should dress too, love?' he suggested gently, reluctantly.

Damn it, if Westlake had not interrupted them Darius knew he would even now be enjoying making love to his wife for a second time.

Unfortunately, given his specific instructions to the butler earlier this evening, Darius was nowhere near as sure as Arabella that the reason for this most recent interruption would be dealt with as quickly as he hoped it would…

Chapter Eleven

Despite the unimagined pleasure of their lovemaking the previous evening, Arabella was not feeling in the least kindly disposed towards her husband as she swept down the wide staircase of Winton Hall at nine o'clock the following morning. On the contrary, she felt there was every reason for the frown upon her creamy brow as she crossed the large hallway on her way to the breakfast room.

Leaving Darius to converse quietly with Westlake the previous evening, Arabella had retired to her bedchamber to bathe and dress in one of her prettiest nightgowns. She had then lain awake in her bed, waiting for Darius to join her, sure that he would do so at any moment, as eager for their lovemaking to continue as she was.

Their marriage had got off to a somewhat shaky start, but Arabella had begun to believe that now they were truly one the tension would start to ease between them. She'd certainly had reason to rethink her decision to leave Darius come the next morning!

But as the minutes and then hours had passed, without any sign of Darius joining her in her bedchamber, Arabella's eagerness had turned to uncertainty. Perhaps he had not found their lovemaking as satisfactory as she had? Or had he been shocked by her obvious enthusiasm? Although she somehow did not think it was the latter; Darius had encouraged—no, positively *demanded*!—that loss of control.

That uncertainty allayed, Arabella's anger had returned with a vengeance. So much so that it had been the early hours of the morning before she'd managed to fall asleep, only to awaken an hour ago to find the bed beside her still empty. A glance into the adjoining bedchamber had revealed that Darius had not been to bed at all the previous night—in her bedchamber or his own.

Arabella most definitely required an explanation from him this morning—for the way he had abandoned her so completely the night before. And, if she were not to renew her decision to leave him, it had best be a good one!

Prepared for a verbal exchange with him, Arabella felt her ire only increase when she found the breakfast room empty except for the footman waiting to serve her. 'Has His Grace already breakfasted this morning, Holmes?' she enquired lightly, as the footman served the cup of tea she had requested.

The middle-aged man maintained a stony expression. 'I don't fink—er—I don't believe so. Er...Your Grace.'

Arabella's frown deepened. 'Has my husband been seen at *all* this morning?'

'Not that I know of, Your Grace.'

Arabella's irritation deepened at the man's unhelpful replies. 'In that case, send Westlake to me immediately.'

The footman paused in replacing the teapot upon its stand. 'You wants to see Mr Westlake, Your Grace?'

'Immediately,' she snapped. 'Is there a problem?'

She arched enquiring brows as the man hesitated. She really could not imagine where Darius had found the strange collection of people waiting upon them at Winton Hall. From Holmes's accent and the awkwardness of his demeanour, the footman gave every impression of originating from the backstreets of London!

'Er—I...I believe Mr Westlake is busy this morning, Your Grace,' the man said awkwardly.

Arabella's brows rose even higher. 'Too busy to make himself available to his employer?'

'Oh, no, ma'am,' the man assured her happily. 'Mr Westlake is always ready and willing to 'elp the Duke whenever the need arises.'

Arabella deliberately took a sip of her tea before replying, in an effort to allay the footman's suspicions concerning her increasing interest in this conversation. 'And does the need arise very often?'

'Not as often as it used to do,' Holmes confided with obvious disappointment. 'But often enough, I suppose.'

Arabella's interest was well and truly roused now. 'So, Mr Westlake is too busy to talk to me, and you have no idea where my husband is?'

'Now, I didn't say that, Your Grace,' he protested, his Cockney accent deepening in his agitation.

Arabella held on to her temper with effort. 'So which statement was incorrect? Westlake is not busy? Or you *have* seen my husband this morning?'

'Well…the second one, I s'pose. I 'asn't *seen* the Duke, you understand,' he defended as Arabella's frown returned. 'But I do know as where 'e is.'

'And where would that be?'

''e's in the Blue Salon wiv 'is guest.'

Guest…?

What guest?

The betrothal and wedding of Lady Arabella St Claire and Darius Wynter, Duke of Carlyne, might have taken place with more haste than was usual, but surely it was known here in Worcestershire, as much as in London, that the Duke and Duchess of Carlyne were only recently married and as such not yet receiving visitors?

Could the arrival of this guest be the reason Westlake had felt compelled to knock on the dining-room door, disturbing them yesterday evening? Possibly the same reason Darius had not joined her in her bedchamber the night before…?

From the way the footman was now squirming uncomfortably at the realisation he might have said too much, Arabella felt sure she would receive no further helpful information from him. 'That will be all, thank you, Holmes.' She gave the man her most gracious smile along with the dismissal; all those years as Hawk's sister certainly stood her in good stead for her role as Darius's duchess!

So a guest had arrived yesterday evening? Arabella mused once left alone. Someone important enough for Westlake to dare to disturb his employer, despite Darius's instructions for him not to do so unless it was a dire emergency.

Who could that visitor be?

And what was so urgent about their visit that Darius was still privately ensconced with them hours after their arrival?

'You have received no further word as to his whereabouts?' Darius's expression was grimly determined as he attempted to thrust his sword under the other man's guarded pose.

'We only know he left the house in Paris some days ago.' His opponent parried the thrust to make a lunge himself. A parry that Darius easily sidestepped. 'A coincidence, certainly. But his disappearance does not preclude him being the one responsible for the things that have happened these past few days, either.'

The two men had stripped down to their shirts, pantaloons and boots an hour ago in order to practise their swordplay, and Darius could now feel the material of his shirt clinging damply to his back from the exertion. 'Surely the loose wheel on my own carriage three days ago is too reminiscent of similar tampering with another carriage seven months ago for the two to be unrelated?'

'What of the fire at the coaching inn?'

'Perhaps a new innovation on his part?'

'I believe you once claimed that he did not have an original thought in his head?' the other man drawled dryly. 'Besides, Helena Jourdan is far more likely to be the one who wishes to do you harm,' the other man insisted as Darius would have argued the point.

Darius scowled. 'I should have wrung the woman's neck when I had the chance!'

'That would certainly have been one way of resolving a—a delicate situation,' the younger man acknowledged ruefully.

'Instead of which I now possibly have a vengeful woman attempting to harm not only myself but also my wife,' Darius frowned his displeasure.

'Talking of your wife…'

'Which we were not,' Darius bit out warningly, temporarily losing his concentration as he allowed his mind to wander to thoughts of his young wife, and the memory of how beautiful she had looked naked in the firelight the previous evening. That lapse was enough to allow the other man to lunge and press the tip of his sword directly over Darius's heart. 'Oh, to hell with this!' He threw his sword disgustedly onto the chaise and began restlessly pacing the room. 'How can I concentrate on swordplay when I have some madman—?'

'Or woman.'

Darius paused long enough in his pacing to shoot the

other man an impatient glare. 'Or woman,' he allowed irritably, 'attempting to do away with me the moment I step outside the damned house!'

'You are recently married, Darius, and as such have every reason *not* to step outside the house.' The younger man gave him a mocking glance as he threw himself into one of the armchairs.

Arabella had left the breakfast room a few minutes ago to walk outside onto the terrace with the intention of circling the house and joining her husband and his guest in the Blue Salon. Instead, shivering with the cold, she had come to an abrupt halt as she realised the two men were talking loudly enough for her to be able to hear their discussion. And what a discussion!

Firstly the coach accident three days ago had apparently not been an accident after all! And then the fire at the inn. Also no accident…?

Arabella had easily recognised Darius's visitor when she peeped in at the window. Lord Gideon Grayson. Tall, dark, and very handsome, a man Arabella knew to be a close friend and peer of her disreputable youngest brother Sebastian. He had also been one of Darius's guests at their wedding.

Although what possible business it could be of the rakish Lord Grayson if some woman were supposedly attempting to harm Darius or herself was totally beyond her.

'A vengeful woman', Darius had called her.

Possibly a discarded lover of Darius's?

It certainly sounded a possibility!

Recalling the intensity of their own lovemaking the evening before, Arabella felt herself bristle inside just at the *thought* of Darius being so recently intimately involved with another woman. A woman who obviously felt strongly enough about Darius having ended their affair to attempt to do him harm.

Dear Lord—could the 'he' Darius and Lord Grayson had earlier referred to so scathingly possibly be the woman's cuckolded and jealous husband…?

Arabella's previous anger with Darius returned in force, and she no longer hesitated outside on the terrace but instead opened one of the French doors to step decisively into the Blue Salon.

To say that the two men were surprised by her sudden entrance would be understating the matter. Darius's already grim expression became even grimmer, his eyes turning a steely blue, and in contrast, Lord Gideon Grayson's handsome face was uncomfortably flushed as he jumped awkwardly to his feet to offer an awkward bow at the same time as he attempted to refasten the buttons at the throat of his shirt.

'Good morning, gentlemen.' Arabella gave them a sweetly insincere smile. 'I trust I am not interrupting anything of importance?'

Darius narrowed chilling blue eyes on his wife, not fooled for a moment by the lightness of Arabella's greeting, nor distracted by her beauty in a pale lemon gown. The challenging glint in her deep brown eyes and the flush to her cheeks were more than enough to alert him as to the true state of Arabella's emotions: she was extremely angry about something.

The fact that Darius had felt unable to share her bed the night before could be the reason for that. Conversely, if Arabella had chanced to hear any of his recent conversation with Gray then she might just have taken exception to something she had overheard…

Exactly how long had Arabella been standing outside on the terrace?

'Not at all,' he answered her smoothly, and he crossed the room to draw her to his side by placing a possessive arm about the slenderness of her waist. 'Is the November air not a little cold for you to be outside dressed only in your gown?' Darius could feel the chill of her body through the gown as he anchored her to his side.

Brown eyes gazed up at Darius in what he was sure was deceptive innocence. 'I stepped outside to take some air before breakfast and decided to come and investigate when I heard the two of you talking in here.'

He nodded abruptly. 'Lord Grayson arrived late yesterday evening.'

Arabella turned to Lord Grayson. 'You rode all the way from London in one day, My Lord?'

Grayson flushed. 'I—'

'What does it matter how and when Gray travelled here, Arabella?' Darius cut in. 'He arrived yesterday evening, and we stayed up far too late last night drinking brandy together.'

Too much information, Darius, he inwardly rebuked himself as he saw the frown darken Arabella's brow. He'd just broken one of the principal rules of being a spy: reveal only as much information as was absolutely necessary. It was not necessary that Arabella be told what he and Gray had been doing last night.

'As you can see by our current state of undress, you have caught us practising our swordsmanship in order to shake off the effects of imbibing too much of that brandy. Poor Grayson is quite mortified with embarrassment,' he added mockingly as the other man still fumbled in refastening his shirt.

'Please do not concern yourself, Lord Grayson,' Arabella assured him dryly, and she neatly extricated herself from the curve of Darius's arm to step further into the room. 'My older brothers never felt any qualms about appearing in front of me dressed only in their breeches and shirt.'

'You are too kind, Your Grace,' Grayson accepted lamely.

'Will you be joining us for breakfast, Lord Grayson, or are you in a hurry to continue your journey?' Arabella enquired.

As setdowns went, this one was quite subtle, Darius acknowledged admiringly as he gazed at his wife. Very subtle, in fact, and yet it more than made clear Arabella's displeasure at Grayson's interruption of their privacy so soon after their wedding.

'I have invited Gray to stay with us for a few days at least, Arabella,' he informed her.

She raised frosty brows. 'Indeed?'

It was all Darius could do to hold back his smile at that obvious frostiness, and poor Gray looked as if he were wishing himself a hundred miles away! 'Indeed,' he echoed mockingly.

Arabella nodded abruptly. 'It can become so incredibly tedious in the country without stimulating company to alleviate the boredom, can it not?'

If they had been alone Darius would have almost certainly given in to the temptation he'd had on several occasions in this past week to place Arabella over his knee and raise her skirts before spanking her luscious little bottom!

But then if they had been alone Darius doubted he would have had reason to feel that impulse. Arabella was obviously severely displeased at the thought of having Lord Gideon Grayson as a guest at Winton Hall for the next few days!

As one of the agents who had long worked for Darius, Gray had been the obvious choice for Bancroft to send in response to the message Darius had had his footman deliver to the Earl following the fire at the coaching inn.

Now that Gray was rested from his hell-for-leather ride to Winton Hall the previous day, the two men had to discuss the situation further before deciding upon an appropriate course of action, even whilst disagreeing as to the identity of the perpetrator of these accidents. Darius still favoured his brother Francis, whereas Gray believed it to be the traitor Helena Jourdan—the Frenchwoman having escaped from captivity on the day of Sebastian St Claire's wedding to Juliet Boyd by seducing her jailer into releasing her.

Whilst Darius sympathised with Arabella's resentment at Gray's continued presence here, he also knew that the other man would be helpful in preventing any more of those 'accidents' from proving to be fatal.

Arabella's cheeks burned with obvious temper. 'I am sure Darius will appreciate having you for company after I have gone.'

Darius became very still. 'After you have gone where?' He looked across at her with flintily narrowed eyes.

Their lovemaking the previous evening had convinced Arabella into abandoning her decision to leave Darius come the morning. But his avoidance of sharing her bed the night before, and now his desire for Lord Grayson's company rather than her own, only days after their wedding, surely meant that Darius did not feel the same way about their lovemaking as she did. Besides which, Arabella had far from forgotten the existence of that 'vengeful woman' from Darius's past…

She met Darius's flinty gaze unblinkingly. 'It seems an ideal opportunity for me to visit with my family at Mulberry Hall now that Lord Grayson has arrived to amuse you in my stead.'

'Oh, I say!' Lord Grayson protested awkwardly.

Forget temptation, Darius decided grimly. The moment they were alone he *was* going to spank Arabella's bottom until she screamed for mercy!

'Would you mind leaving us, Grayson?' His voice was dangerously soft, his gaze still fixed firmly on Arabella's angrily flushed face. 'It would seem that my wife and I have a few things of our own to discuss this morning,' he added with deceptive pleasantness.

'Of course.' Gray grimaced uncomfortably. 'I should go upstairs and bathe, anyway. Excuse me, Your Grace.' He bowed formally to Arabella and received a cool nod of dismissal for his trouble.

Darius waited only long enough for Gray to shoot him an apologetic grimace and beat a hasty retreat, before crossing the room to stand mere inches away from his wife. 'You were not very polite to our guest, love.'

Arabella's eyes flashed with golden lights as she looked up at him. 'I believe Lord Grayson is *your* guest, not mine.'

'Nevertheless…'

'Nevertheless he is *your* guest and not *mine*!' she maintained with haughty stubbornness.

Darius drew in a sharp breath. 'You will apologise to Lord Grayson when he returns downstairs.'

'I most certainly will *not*!' Arabella eyed him scornfully.

'I believe that you *will*.' Darius's tone once again possessed that deceptive softness that most of his acquaintances and all of his enemies would have warned his young and defiant wife to beware.

Unfortunately for Arabella, none of those acquaintances or enemies was now at hand to administer such a warning!

'You may believe what you choose, Darius.' Arabella gave a dismissive movement of her hand. 'Now, if you will excuse me? I need to go upstairs and pack— *What* do you think you are doing?' She gasped indignantly as Darius caught hold of her wrist with steely fingers to pull her along behind him as he strode over to the settee.

'What am I doing?' Darius mused, even as he sat down on the settee and pulled a struggling Arabella face-down across his thighs. 'You have been rude to a guest in our home, Arabella. A rudeness for which you have refused to apologise. It is now my intention to administer suitable punishment for that refusal.'

'But—Darius!' she screamed in protest as her skirts were thrown up over her back and he revealed the plump cheeks of her naked bottom. 'Darius, if you do this I will—'

'Yes?' Darius prompted, as he administered the first light slap against those shapely orbs.

'I— How *dare* you?' she squealed.

'Oh, I believe when you know me better, Arabella, you will learn that I dare any number of things. Disciplining an unruly wife being the least of them!' His expression was grimly determined as he struck another light blow.

'I swear, I will kill you if you do that again!' Arabella ground out between clenched teeth, her face fiery red as she turned to glare up at him.

'You will have to get in line, love,' Darius drawled ruefully as he administered another slap to her naked flesh, the skin now flushed almost as much as her face. 'Those were for your rudeness and your refusal to apologise to Lord Grayson. Now, explain what you mean by your claim that it is your intention to leave me this morning.'

'You have made it more than obvious that you consider our marriage to have been a mistake—'

'In what way obvious?' he demanded incredulously.

'You abandoned my bedchamber last night in preference to drinking brandy with Lord Grayson. You prefer his company this morning instead of my own. You—Oh, you *monster*!' Arabella screamed as another slap resounded upon her bottom.

'We will get at least one of your complaints settled right now, Arabella,' he declared.

'Which is?' she challenged.

'I have *no* intention—of allowing you—to leave me.' Each phrase was accompanied by another light smack to that delicious little bottom as Darius held Arabella's squirming body firmly captive with his arm across her back. 'Not today. Not the next time you take it into your beautiful head to be angry with me. Not ever. Do I make myself clear?'

Arabella continued to struggle against that grasp. 'You cannot stop me from doing exactly as I please—'

'Wrong answer,' Darius said mildly.

She glared at him. 'It is the only answer you shall receive from me. No matter how much and for how long you beat me!'

Darius caught her wrist as her hand came up to strike him. 'I do not in the least *enjoy* beating you, Arabella—'

'Liar!' she accused heatedly.

Darius's arousal testified the truth of that claim. As

did his giving in to the temptation to fondle and caress that plump and fiery-cheeked bottom. Such a warm and deliciously plump bottom. So soft and smooth and—What was this…?

A light caress between Arabella's thighs revealed that his wife of four days was as aroused as Darius himself!

Arabella could not hold back her groan of pleasure as she felt Darius's caressing fingers exploring her intimately. That groan became a husky moan as one of those fingers entered her, and another found and rubbed the swollen nubbin hidden amongst her damp curls. That moan became a strangled cry as Darius continued his assault upon her senses until she became consumed in a release so long and so achingly pleasurable that Arabella felt a rush of the tears on her cheeks that she had refused to cry when Darius spanked her bottom.

She was instantly mortified at her loss of control, and kept her eyes closed as she felt Darius lifting her up and over him, so that her nakedness now straddled his thighs. Thighs that she could feel were hard and pulsing!

Her lids opened wide in surprise. 'Darius…?'

He smiled down at her. 'I want you just as badly, love.'

Arabella stared at him, not understanding how they could have gone from anger with each other to such arousal in just a few short minutes.

'You are right to feel angry with me.' Darius groaned with self-disgust as Arabella only continued to stare at him. 'I should not have struck you. You—'

He broke off with a strangled groan as Arabella reached down between them to unfasten his breeches and release his arousal.

He was just as beautiful as Arabella remembered from yesterday evening. Hard. Pulsing. With skin like velvet as Arabella curled her fingers about him.

She watched Darius's face as she slowly began to move her hand up and down his length, noting the flush that appeared in his cheeks and the clenching of his arrogant jaw. His hair was already dishevelled from his sword practice, several tendrils clinging damply to his brow, and the hair on his chest, visible at the deep vee of his unbuttoned shirt, was also slightly damp from his earlier exertion.

'God, Arabella,' Darius groaned weakly as she smoothed her thumb across the sensitive tip of his arousal. 'Are you very sore from last night, love?'

'Not at all,' she assured him as she stroked him once more.

Darius's back and shoulders were tense. 'Then will you just take me inside you and be done with this torture?'

That groan and his words emboldened Arabella, and she realised that the control, the power of this encounter, was now hers. 'How much do you want me, Darius?'

He blinked. 'How much?'

'Mmm, how much?' Arabella slowly leant forward so that she might kiss the smooth column of his throat, and was able to feel his shudder of response as her tongue licked the saltiness she tasted on his skin.

He smiled ruefully. 'Enough to know that if you

do not soon take me I may just embarrass both myself and you.'

Arabella laughed huskily. 'How much, Darius?' she persisted, and she sat up to deliberately move forward, so that the slick nakedness of her thighs now pressed against the hard throb of his arousal.

He moistened dry lips. 'What do you want from me, Arabella? You want me to let you leave today after all? Is that it?' He shook his head. 'I cannot allow that.'

Arabella was no longer convinced that she wished to leave Darius! Yes, she had been angry with him for his desertion last night. Disappointed when she discovered he had invited Lord Grayson to stay with them. Furious with humiliation when Darius had thrown her over his knee and spanked her bottom. But then Darius had touched her, giving her the pleasure that she had been craving since the previous evening—and now he was all but begging her to give him that same pleasure in return.

Arabella realised that she secretly enjoyed their heated disagreements as much as Darius obviously did. And she especially enjoyed the result of those disagreements!

'And if I agree to stay…?' Once again Arabella moved her heat against him, eliciting another groan from him. 'You may do as you wish during the day, Darius, but I *will* have your promise that in future you will join me in my bedchamber every night—'

'*Every* night, Arabella?' he cut in, with a quirk of an eyebrow quickly followed by an indrawn breath as again Arabella deliberately and torturously rubbed herself against him.

'Every night,' she repeated firmly.

'Every night.' He nodded, his jaw clenched once more. 'I really need to be inside you now, Arabella!' His teeth were bared as he clasped her arms fiercely, and his eyes glittered with intense desire.

Arabella deliberately held that gaze as she reached between them to guide the hardness of his arousal inside her, inch by silken inch, until she was fully impaled.

Arabella stilled. 'You are now inside me, Darius.'

'Dear God…!' Fine beads of perspiration broke out upon his flushed brow as he moved restlessly beneath her.

'Is that not enough?' she teased him deliberately, determined not to forgive him too quickly for his high-handed treatment of her just now. 'Is there something else you wish from me?'

'Move, Arabella,' he breathed raggedly. 'I need you to ride me!' His hands tightened about her arms as he began to thrust urgently beneath her.

Arabella's father had placed her upon the back of a horse at the precocious age of four, and as she slowly began to ride Darius, lifting up until his hardness almost slid completely out of her, then moving down to so pleasurably fully impale herself on him again, she recognised that it was not so very different.

At least not initially. Not until she became so very distracted by the force of her own pleasure, her breathing becoming as ragged as Darius's own, her fingers digging into his shoulders as she felt the heat of her own release building for a second time.

Darius reached out desperately to pull down the front of her gown and release her breasts above its low neckline, needing to taste Arabella's swollen nipples. He laved them skilfully with his tongue and finally achieved his own incredible release—only to learn she had far from finished with him!

Arabella took complete advantage of the fact that Darius remained hard inside her, riding him fiercely, wildly, until he reached a second, aching climax at the same moment as she—a release more excruciating and pleasurably powerful than Darius had ever known before.

'Dear God…' Darius rested his forehead damply against Arabella's as she collapsed forward weakly. 'If we make love like this every night, love, then I shall be dead within the week!'

Even with the most accomplished of courtesans Darius had never before reached a second shuddering climax so quickly after the first. The fact that his wife was so inexperienced, her lovemaking completely instinctive and so incredibly erotic, only made Darius's complete lack of control all the more incredible.

Arabella's senses returned slowly, and along with them came a feeling of embarrassment at her brazenness just now. Had she *really* just taunted and physically tormented Darius until he agreed to her terms? Demanding that he share her bed every night? Make love to her every night?

'Oh, dear.' She sighed shakily as she buried her face against his shoulder.

'Oh, dear, indeed.' Darius chest rumbled beneath her cheek. 'I fear I am completely unmanned, Arabella. In fact, I am not sure that a certain part of my body is still my own!'

Arabella raised her head to look at him, reassured a little by the teasing she could see in his expression. 'Was I too rough with you?'

'You can ask that after I beat you?' He gently rearranged her gown.

'You did not beat me.' She eyed him knowingly. 'You used just enough force to arouse me rather than hurt me, did you not?'

Darius gave a rueful grimace at her perception. 'Yes.'

She frowned. 'You intended making love to me all the time?'

'Not all the time, no,' he drawled lazily. 'But I admit the idea did occur to me after you had dismissed Gray with such haughty disdain,' he revealed. Instantly realising his mistake as Arabella's eyes narrowed and her mouth compressed determinedly. 'Arabella—'

'Tell me, Darius,' Arabella bit out, 'who is Helena Jourdan?'

Darius drew in a sharp, hissing breath as she so challengingly revealed that she *had* overheard far too much of his conversation with Gray than was safe. For himself. And for her….

Chapter Twelve

Darius's movements were precise and restrained as he carefully disengaged himself from Arabella before lifting her to the floor, so that she might stand up to rearrange her petticoats and gown while he saw to the fastening of his breeches.

All the time he was wondering how much—or how little—he must reveal to Arabella to stop her from probing further into the subject of Helena Jourdan.

As Gray had pointed out to him earlier, the subject of that woman was an extremely delicate one. In fact, it would have been so much better for all of them if Arabella had not so much as heard mention of the other woman's name.

His eyes narrowed. 'Have you been spying on me, Arabella?' That would surely be an irony: the spymaster being spied upon by his own wife!

Several of Arabella's curls, so neatly arranged by her

maid only an hour or so ago, had fallen down about her shoulders in the heat of their lovemaking. But Arabella ceased trying to tidy them as she heard the disapproval in Darius's tone.

Her chin rose defensively. 'Despite your denials to the contrary, the woman was your lover until a few days ago, was she not?'

Darius became very still. 'My *lover*?'

'Mistress. Courtesan. Whatever term you wish to apply to the most recent woman to have shared your bed!' Arabella's top lip curled in disgust.

Darius arched mocking brows. 'I believe *you* have that privilege!'

'So far we have not shared a bed,' she pointed out sharply.

He inclined his head in acknowledgement. 'Indeed—only a rug in front of the fire and a chaise.'

Arabella's cheeks burned as Darius's dishevelled appearance reminded her all too forcibly of the wild abandon of their most recent coupling. 'Exactly.'

'Something I intend to rectify at the earliest opportunity, I assure you.'

She frowned. 'I think not.'

'No?'

'I see no privilege attached to sharing the bed of a man such as *you*!' Arabella snapped.

Darius stilled. 'A man such as me?' he echoed dangerously.

Arabella's cheeks became flushed as once again she heard the steel beneath the softness of Darius's tone. The restrained stillness of his body was a warning that she had overstepped the line with that last insulting remark of hers.

'You have not answered my original question,' she said.

'Neither will I,' Darius retorted. 'We were married four days ago, Arabella. I see no reason to account to you for any of my actions before that time.'

'You see no reason…?' she repeated incredulously, her eyes having become a glittering angry gold. 'One of your ex-mistresses is still pursuing you, has apparently several times intended to do us both harm. but you see *no reason* to explain yourself to me?'

A nerve pulsed in Darius's clenched jaw. 'None.'

'You are an unmitigated rake, sir!'

Darius gave a humourless grin as he made a mocking bow. 'At last we are agreed on something.'

Arabella's breasts quickly rose and fell as she breathed deeply in her agitation, and her hands were curled into fists at her sides. 'I believe I might actually *hate* you, Darius!'

Something else they were in agreement on, then—because Darius hated himself at that moment.

Eight years ago, when Darius had first begun to tread this delicate path of spy for the crown, his life had been completely his own, and as such he had accepted that any repercussions and dangers his precarious career incurred would also be his own. It had never been his intention to place Arabella in that same danger.

In fact, since Hawk St Claire had refused his offer for her more than a year ago, Darius had gone out of his way to avoid showing any preference for

Arabella's company. What had occurred between them at Sebastian's wedding had been completely unplanned on Darius's part—a temptation he had no longer been able to resist when the lady herself had so obviously been more than willing.

If they had not been found together in that compromising position in Hawk St Claire's study, by none other than the morally upstanding Lord Redwood, then Darius would have simply walked away after the encounter. With regret, certainly, but nonetheless he would have walked away.

Faced with the choice of exposing Arabella to scandal once their alliance had become public knowledge—which without a doubt it would have done—or marriage, Darius had decided to marry her and be damned.

He should have recognised sooner that his actions were not protecting Arabella but placing her in the same danger as Darius was himself.

No, he *had* realised it, damn it! Had known and married her anyway.

His reasons for doing so were completely selfish, and certainly not something that the currently infuriated Arabella would be willing to hear….

Nor were they something that Darius intended even attempting to share with her until his enemy had been apprehended.

He eyed her mockingly. 'That should add a little spice to our lovemaking.'

The heat of her glare was enough to burn him where

he stood. 'You are arrogant, Darius, to believe there will be *any* further lovemaking between us after this!'

'I trust you are not once again entertaining the idea of leaving me, Arabella?' Darius jeered. 'Or perhaps you merely wish me to think that you might in order to…provoke me again?'

Arabella was sure that she had never been this angry in her life before. And since becoming betrothed to Darius Wynter there had certainly been plenty of opportunity for her to be so.

He was so arrogant. So mocking. So superior in every way. So—so wickedly handsome that just looking at him made her knees go weak!

How could she still find Darius so attractive when he made no attempt to deny what he was, or deny that the mistress he had denied having had been so upset at the ending of their affair and his marriage to Arabella that she was trying to do them both harm?

Was it really possible to love someone so much that losing them made you want to destroy the object of that love rather than allow anyone else to have them?

Arabella certainly felt violent enough towards Darius at this moment. She could quite cheerfully have hit him over the head with something painfully heavy!

But she was merely fascinated by Darius and not in love with him. Wasn't she…?

No! She would not even *entertain* the idea that she might be in love with her husband. She would not!

'I repeat my earlier statement, Darius—if you attempt to beat me again I will surely kill you.' Her gaze raked over him scathingly.

He quirked a brow at her. 'I take it you meant your comment earlier concerning lovemaking too?'

'I always mean what I say, Darius.'

'I remind you that so too do I,' he bit out brusquely.

'Meaning?'

'Meaning that if you so much as attempt to leave Winton Hall then I will come after you and bring you back.' His mouth thinned. 'I guarantee you would not enjoy the punishment that would surely follow.'

'Do not attempt to threaten me, Darius—'

'It is a promise, Arabella, not a threat,' he warned softly.

She gave him one last scornful glance before turning on her heel to stride from the room, her shoulders stiff and her back ramrod-straight.

Darius made no move to follow her, knowing there would be little point in his doing so. He could not confide the truth to Arabella—his role as spymaster prevented him from doing that—and as such had no way as yet of explaining his own actions, or Grayson's reason for being here, to his wife.

The sooner Darius established whether it was Helena Jourdan arranging these 'accidents', as Gray seemed to think it was, or—as Darius himself was more inclined to believe—his own exiled brother Francis, the sooner he would be able to attempt to heal the rift that now existed between himself and Arabella.

Attempt to—because Darius was not at all sure he would be successful….

* * *

'I had not realised that you and my husband were such…close acquaintances, Lord Grayson.' Arabella arched questioning brows at her guest as she presided over the teapot later that afternoon.

Teatime was a social nicety that only the two of them had bothered to attend, the footman having informed Arabella that the Duke was about the estate somewhere. No doubt with Westlake, as the butler was once again absent from his duties.

'No. Well…' Gideon Grayson looked decidedly uncomfortable at finding himself alone with his hostess in this way. 'We have visited the gambling clubs together a time or two, I dare say.'

Arabella's mouth was tight as she handed him his tea. 'With Sebastian, perhaps?'

His gaze avoided meeting hers. 'I'm not really sure…'

'No? But I had the impression when we were all at Lady Humbers's ball earlier this year that you and Sebastian were good friends.' Arabella eyed the young Lord over the rim of her teacup.

'We are. At least…we were.'

'Were?'

He gave a pained frown as he glanced awkwardly about the drawing room. 'The weather is tolerable for this time of year, do you not think?'

What Arabella thought was that the rakishly handsome Lord Gideon Grayson was avoiding the subject! 'Tolerable.' She nodded coolly. 'Can it be that you and my youngest brother have suffered a disagreement?'

'Not at all,' Lord Grayson denied sharply. 'I—Look, I apologise if my being here is inconvenient.' His expression was anxious as he sat forward in his chair. 'Normally I would not have dreamt of intruding upon a newly married couple in this way. It was only—I felt—'

'Yes?' Arabella prompted.

'Stop browbeating the poor man, Arabella,' Darius drawled as he strolled lazily into the drawing room, his appearance impeccable in a dark green jacket worn over a muted gold brocade waistcoat and snowy white linen, his legs long and muscled in thigh-hugging buff-coloured pantaloons above black brown-topped Hessians. 'No doubt Sebastian and Gray have fallen out over a woman, and now Gray is too embarrassed to admit to it. It is what we rakes do, you know.' He eyed her sharply and paused beside the tea trolley to pour himself a cup of tea as she made no effort to do so.

It was the first time that Arabella had set eyes on her husband since their disagreement this morning. Disagreement? It could be regarded as much more than a disagreement. The two of them had ended by clearly laying down their rules as regarded the continuation of their marriage!

Even now Arabella could not believe how heatedly they had made love this morning before just as heatedly arguing. Heated on her part, at least; Darius had remained coolly distant throughout. Arabella might feel more inclined to forgive him if he had not…

'Lord Grayson and I were merely engaging in social chitchat,' she dismissed evenly.

'Really?' Darius raised disbelieving brows. 'It sounded distinctly like the Spanish Inquisition to me.'

'You are being ridiculous.' Arabella shot him a venomous glare.

Darius settled himself comfortably in one of the armchairs before stretching his long legs out in front of him to be crossed at his booted ankles. 'A fault of all newly married men, no doubt. Perhaps the reason you have continued to avoid the unenviable state, Gray?' He took a sip of his tea.

Grayson looked more uncomfortable than ever as he obviously sensed the increased tension in the room following Darius's entrance. 'I— Er…'

Darius gave a hard laugh. 'My dear chap, I advise you not to even attempt an answer; whatever you say is guaranteed to offend either my wife or myself.'

Gray frowned. 'Perhaps in the circumstances it might be better if I were to take my leave of you after all, as soon as we have finished tea.'

'You see what you have done, Arabella?' Darius chided. 'You have made our guest feel unwelcome.'

'*I* have?' She eyed him incredulously.

'There, there, Arabella.' That blue gaze openly jeered at her. 'I am sure Gray perfectly understands that you are not as—as composed as you could be.' He gave the other man a bored glance as he confided, 'Arabella's nerves are understandably still a little jittery from all the preparations and excitement of the wedding.'

In contrast, Darius's own nerves were perfectly calm. With the cold inflexibility of steel, in fact. He and Westlake had just discovered that there had been an uninvited guest in the stables some time during the night. Several of the saddles had been tampered with. Including Grayson's. A fact that seemed to imply the other man's assessment of the situation might after all be the correct one; it had been the two of them who had been responsible for questioning Helena Jourdan following her arrest in the summer, and for ordering the death of her French soldier lover.

The sarcastic pleasantness of Darius's present mood served to hide the fierce anger he was feeling inside. A cold, remorseless anger that promised severe retribution for someone.

'I assure you my nerves are not in the least jittery, Darius.' Arabella answered his previous taunt with sweet insincerity. 'On the contrary, as I mentioned earlier today, I find Lord Grayson's presence a welcome diversion from the tedium of country life.'

'There now, Gray.' Darius's eyes glittered as he looked across the room at the younger man. 'I do not see how you can even *think* of depriving my beautiful wife of your company after she has so eloquently expressed a partiality for it.'

Grayson eyed him warily. 'I am sure Her Grace was only being polite.'

Darius looked across at Arabella between narrowed lids. 'Were you?'

Arabella shifted uncomfortably under that coldly direct gaze, not fooled for a moment by the mildness of Darius's tone; beneath that calm exterior he was obviously furiously angry. With her, no doubt. 'I hope that

I am always polite, Darius,' she replied noncommittally.

He gave a hard and humourless laugh. 'Oh, I believe all of the St Claire family can lay claim to being *that*, Arabella—even when they are stabbing you in the back!'

Arabella's eyes widened at the slight. 'You dare to accuse any of my family of such a cowardly act?'

'Nothing so obvious, I assure you, Arabella,' he drawled dismissively.

She bristled with indignation. 'Then what *did* you mean?'

He shrugged. 'Nothing of import.'

'I do not care for your tone, Darius.'

'No?'

'No!'

He gave an uninterested shrug. 'And perhaps I do not care to have you state your preference for another man's company in my own home.'

Arabella stood up abruptly. 'It is *our* home!'

Darius looked up at her coldly. 'As you assured me this morning, only for as long as it suits you.'

Arabella's hand itched to slap the arrogant mockery from his handsome face. 'I have reconsidered, Darius,' she snapped, 'and I have decided that I no longer intend giving you the satisfaction of leaving you.'

'I am glad to hear it.' He took another sip of his cooling tea.

She eyed him sharply; he did not *sound* pleased! 'Are you?'

'Of course.' He sounded bored by the subject. 'Now,

perhaps you might benefit from resting in your room before dinner?'

'I am not in the least tired.' Arabella stared down at him in frustration. The only reason she did not give in to the inclination she felt—to knock the cup of tea from Darius's long, elegant hand—was that they had surely already provided enough of a show of marital disharmony in front of Lord Grayson for one day.

'You will have to forgive us, Gray.' Darius turned to the younger man. 'My wife and I have not yet worked out the finer nuances of marriage.' He looked at Arabella. 'My dear, my suggestion that you retire to your bedchamber was my way of stating that I wish for you to leave us now, so that Grayson and I might talk in private.'

Arabella gasped. The insult she had felt at Darius's disparaging remarks concerning her family was now overtaken by how hurt she felt at the coldness of Darius's tone; he could not have stated any more plainly his desire to be rid of her company!

Her cheeks flushed with the humiliation she felt at his dismissal. 'No doubt so that you might reminisce over old times and old mistresses!'

'Or current ones,' Darius pointed out wickedly.

Arabella felt that heated colour leave her cheeks as rapidly as it had entered them. 'How *dare* you?'

'As I recall, Arabella, *you* were the one to introduce the subject,' he pointed out.

Only so that Darius might deny the accusation! She had not expected him to react like that!

'If you will excuse me, Lord Grayson?' Her manner

was stilted as she gave him a stiff bow. 'I believe I might go to my room and rest before dinner after all.' She had to escape from this room. Before Darius's attitude forced her to do something they would no doubt both regret.

Although Darius did not look in the least as if he regretted treating her so cruelly in front of a guest. On the contrary, he seemed to emit an icy satisfaction at the thought of her going. Leaving Arabella with no choice but to depart.

'I will see you both at dinner this evening.'

'No doubt,' her husband said as he helped himself to a dainty from the tea tray.

'I shall look forward to it.' Lord Grayson, at least, remembered his manners enough to stand up.

Arabella gave Darius a pointed stare, and received only a challenging one in return as he made no effort to emulate the other man's politeness but instead bit into his chosen creamy confection with obvious enjoyment. Inflicting yet another insult upon Arabella before she turned and left the room with an indignant rustle of her skirts.

How she hated him!

Loathed him!

Detested him!

Desired him still…

Arabella's legs almost failed her as she climbed the wide staircase to her room, necessitating in her having to grasp the dark mahogany banister in order to stop herself from sinking down weakly onto one of the stairs. She breathed deeply in an effort to calm her rapidly beating heart and the trembling of her body.

What sort of man was Darius, that he could make love so heatedly to her earlier this morning and then treat her and her family with such disdain just now?

And what sort of woman was Arabella, that she could still want Darius to make love to her like that again?

Chapter Thirteen

'Were you not…a little hard on her?' Lord Gideon Grayson looked reproving.

'I advise you not to attempt to tell me how to treat my own wife, Gray.' Darius put down the creamy dainty that threatened to choke him if he should attempt to eat another bite. In fact, the single bite he had taken, in an effort to convince Arabella of his uninterest in her or anything she did, was already making him feel ill.

'But—'

'It is for the best, Gray.' Darius stood up restlessly, his expression grim. 'Evidence leads me to believe that someone in my own household is hand-in-glove with the saboteur.' How it galled him to admit it, but he could think of no other explanation for how the stables had been broken into during the night.

The servants at Winton Hall had all been hand-picked by Darius months ago. Their obvious lack of manners showed he had not chosen them for their skills as household servants, but as men and women capable of fighting and thieving. Damn it, even the cook was Westlake's sister, and had once been taken into custody under suspicion of picking people's pockets!

'One of your own servants?' Gray frowned his uncertainty at the claim.

Darius nodded, before going on to explain the break-in of the stables during the night. 'If I am right about it being one of my own servants, then it would be as well that all of them believe I have little interest in my wife.' A nerve pulsed in his tightly clenched jaw at the lie; if Darius became any *more* interested in Arabella then he would have no choice but to take her to bed for a week. Longer! 'The charade I am playing might perhaps succeed in safeguarding her more than I have so far managed to do.' His expression was bleak.

'I can see how you might think that…' Gray still looked troubled. 'But is such a course wise? Are you not seriously in danger of alienating your wife to the point of no return? Your remark about her brothers, for instance, was so far from the truth as to be laughable. Hawk St Claire is a duke and a member of the House, a man much respected and admired. Lucian St Claire is revered as a war hero, and Sebastian proved this summer that he is a man loyal to king and country.'

'I am well aware of all the admirable traits shown by my brothers-in-law!'

Darius was also aware of the risk he was taking with Arabella's affections. If his young wife had ever felt *any* affection for him, that was. Which Darius seriously doubted. Responding to his lovemaking merely showed Arabella's curiosity on the subject, not a personal preference for Darius himself….

'What else do you suggest, Gray?' he demanded as he paced the room impatiently. 'When my promise eight years ago to king and country, as you put it,' he bit out scathingly, 'precludes my revealing the truth to Arabella?'

'Perhaps *I* might have a word with her?'

'You are bound by the same promise,' Darius reminded him harshly. 'We all are, damn it. No.' He ran an agitated hand through his hair. 'For the moment my wife will simply have to go on believing me to be the worst kind of insensitive blackguard.'

Darius would just have to hope and pray that when this mess was finally over it would not be too late to try and salvage something of his marriage….

'Yes?' Arabella did not turn from finishing tidying her appearance in the mirror on her dressing table, but instead glanced at her husband's reflection in that mirror as he leant against the open doorway that connected their two bedchambers.

Far from having forgiven Darius for his rudeness to her earlier, Arabella willed herself not to be affected by how handsome he looked in the candle-light in his dark evening clothes and snowy white linen, with his hair shining a deep gold and his eyes appearing the clear deep blue of a summer's sky.

He straightened, the expression in those deep blue eyes guarded. 'I have brought you a gift.'

Arabella stilled as she frowned her uncertainty. 'Something for me…?'

'A wedding gift.' Darius nodded as he stepped fully into her bedchamber to cross the room in strides as graceful and silent as a cat.

Arabella swallowed hard as he came to stand behind her, overwhelmingly aware of his hard and muscled body. She moistened lips that had become suddenly dry. 'Is it not a little late for that?'

'I sincerely hope not.'

Arabella raised blond brows. 'Why would you want to give me a wedding gift when you never cease reminding me that this marriage was forced upon you by circumstances?'

Darius drew his breath in sharply at the challenge, knowing how well he deserved Arabella's ridicule—and wishing that he did not. Knowing how much he wished things could be different between them. He had hoped that in the privacy of their bedchamber at least, well away from curiously interested eyes, perhaps they could be…

He shook his head at his own maudlin thoughts. 'When you know me better, Arabella, you will know that I never allow myself to be forced into doing anything I do not wish to do.'

'Really?' she said dismissively as she stood up to turn and face him, her expression aloof as she looked down her pert little nose at him. She was wearing a blue high-waisted gown this evening, her breasts full and creamy above the low neckline. She possessed a long and slender neck that, Darius noted with satisfaction, was bare of jewellery.

He reached into his jacket pocket to pull out the huge diamond pendant that hung upon a simple gold chain. 'It is my wish that you wear this tonight.'

Arabella looked down at the heart-shaped diamond pendant where it lay across Darius's callused palm, furious with herself as she felt a sting of tears in her eyes at its simplistic beauty. It was exactly what she would have chosen for herself.

And it was surely what a man would choose to give to the woman he loved…

Except Darius did not love her. He had shown by his treatment of her earlier today during afternoon tea that he never would love her.

'It is my intention to wear my mother's sapphires and diamonds this evening.' She moved deliberately to open her jewel box and take out the diamond-and-sapphire necklace her father had given to her mother—most assuredly with love!—on their tenth wedding anniversary.

She only realised once she held up the jewels in the candle-light how much the sapphires reminded her of the colour of Darius's eyes when he was aroused. And that her new gown was of that same intense colour…

Was Darius aware of it also? The expression she could see in those eyes as he gazed down at her seemed to imply that he was.

Arabella's mouth firmed. 'Perhaps you might give the pendant to Helena Jourdan instead? As an apology for your marriage to me? I am sure that any woman might be persuaded into forgiving you anything when presented with such an expensive bauble.'

Darius's gaze was flinty, his jaw set inflexibly as he laid the diamond pendant down upon her dressing table. 'Just not you?'

'I am not any woman, Darius.' Arabella eyed him scornfully before turning away to view her reflection in the mirror as she raised her arms to fasten the clasp of the glittering sapphire-and-diamond necklace about her throat, all the time aware of a similar glitter in Darius's narrowed blue eyes as he stood behind her.

'No, you most assuredly are *not* just any woman,' he acknowledged harshly. 'What would you say if I were to tell you that Helena Jourdan was not, is not, and will never be my mistress?'

Arabella raised her eyes to meet his reflected gaze. 'I would say you are a liar. Let me go, Darius!' She gasped as his hands came down heavily on her bare shoulders, squirming as his fingers held her in place. She glared furiously at him in the mirror as her efforts to free herself came to nought.

Darius had never regretted more than at that moment the promises he had made eight years ago, and the profligate and rakish reputation he had so deliberately nurtured since.

Until his betrothal to Arabella Darius had had no problem with people believing the gossip whispered about him amongst the ton. He knew that he was considered a rake and a gambler. A man who had been married to an heiress for only one month before she was thrown from her horse and died, leaving Darius in possession of her fortune. The man who had inherited the title of Duke following his nephew's death two years ago at Waterloo and his eldest brother's premature and unexpected death seven months ago. Indeed, Darius had no doubt that it was that very reputation that had caused Hawk St Claire to turn down his offer for Arabella last year!

Darius had been furious at the time, but in view of the fate of the woman whom he *had* married Darius had decided Hawk's refusal had been for the best. He doubted that he could have borne it if it had been Arabella thrown from her horse to her death.

As he could not bear her obvious scorn now… 'Whether you believe me or not, Arabella, Helena Jourdan has *never* been my mistress,' he said evenly.

Her gaze was uncertain as it met his in the mirror. 'Then what is she to you?'

His mouth thinned. 'Nothing.'

'If your conversation with Lord Grayson is to be believed, then the woman has tried to kill you—both of us—on several occasions!'

Darius drew in a sharp breath. 'It is suspected that she might have done so, yes.' He nodded tersely. 'But we have no tangible evidence that she is the one responsible.'

Arabella's eyes widened. 'You mean, there is *more* than one person who wishes you dead?'

He quirked a quizzical brow at her. 'Now that we have added you to that list, you mean?'

Arabella recoiled at the suggestion she had ever wished Darius's death. To have him horse-whipped by one of her brothers, perhaps. Rendered helpless at her feet as he claimed undying love for her. But dead? No, even now, when Arabella felt so hurt and confused by him, she did not wish her husband any real physical harm.

Because she was, after all, in love with him?

It had been a question that had plagued Arabella all day as she paced restlessly in her bedchamber.

Most of the time she was so angry with Darius, for one reason or another, that she could cheerfully strike his arrogantly handsome face. At other times she was so physically aroused by him that she could neither think nor be aware of anything else.

Was that love?

Once again Arabella shied away from giving herself an answer to that question. If she never admitted to having feelings for Darius—even to herself—then perhaps they would not exist!

She shook her head. 'It is surely your own fault if Helena Jourdan's husband also wishes to kill you.'

Darius gave her a considering look. 'Is that the best reason you could come up with for someone wishing to kill me?'

Arabella felt stung by his derision. 'It is one of the reasons, yes.'

'Except that Helena Jourdan is not married.'

Arabella frowned her frustration. 'Then perhaps it is her father, or a brother, or another lover who defends her honour?'

'No father. No brother. No lover, either.' Not any more, Darius inwardly grimaced. Helena Jourdan's

French soldier lover had been apprehended and quietly killed two weeks ago, whilst Helena herself was being held in London and questioned by Darius and Gray. It was a death that Darius did not doubt she held him responsible for…

'But earlier I am sure I overheard you and Lord Grayson mention that a man may be involved. Darius!' She gasped as his fingers involuntarily tightened around her shoulders.

'I apologise.' Darius removed his hands altogether to turn away, his expression grim; it seemed Arabella had overheard far too much of his earlier conversation with Gray than was good for her. Neither did their love-making after Gray had left them seem to have lessened her memory of that conversation… 'It is time we went down to dinner,' he said curtly. 'Gray will be wondering what has become of us both.'

Arabella's brow darkened with irritation. 'It is totally unacceptable that he should be here at all!'

'I thought you found your sojourn in the country tedious and boring and that his presence relieved that?'

She shot him a reproving glance. 'You know that I only said those things because you annoyed me.'

Darius looked at her. 'So am I to take it that you do *not* find my company tedious and boring, after all?'

'Not all the time, no.' Brown eyes glittered with repressed emotion. 'You can be…amusing when it suits you to be.'

Darius laughed huskily. 'As can you.'

'You—' Arabella drew in a calming breath. 'I wish you would send Lord Grayson away, Darius.'

He sighed. 'I could not be so rude, love.'

'Oh, yes, you could,' she disputed knowingly. 'If it suited you to do so.'

Darius shrugged broad shoulders. 'Then obviously it does not suit me.'

Arabella eyed him frustratedly. 'Perhaps we should make this into a Winton Hall house party? We could invite Hawk and Jane and baby Alexander over from Mulberry Hall. Lucian and Grace from Hampshire? Sebastian and Juliet from Berkshire. The Dowager Duchess from the Dower House. Perhaps your younger brother might even return from the Continent—'

'That is enough, Arabella!' Darius cut in harshly, his eyes glittering in warning. 'Your brothers are once again busy about their own lives,' he said, 'and my sister-in-law Margaret has not yet returned from London. It occurred to me to send her an invitation to join us for dinner this evening,' he added dryly, 'until I remembered that Margaret had said she would stay in town after the wedding, to visit George's lawyer and do a little shopping for Christmas. I thought that you might appreciate some female company to help alleviate the tedium of dining alone with two men whose company you find so boring.'

Arabella did not find Darius's company in the least boring or tedious. The opposite, in fact. As had been her hope when she'd decided to accept Darius's offer, he was far too mercurial in his moods for her ever to be bored in his company. Under other circumstances, she would not find Lord Grayson's company tedious, either. She knew from meeting him in the past that he was an amusing, as well as an entertaining companion with whom to pass the time. Just not days after her wedding to Darius, when she wished to be otherwise occupied…

'In that case perhaps we could invite your brother Francis to come and stay? Having missed the wedding itself, perhaps he would appreciate an invitation to stay at Winton Hall?' She looked a query at him.

Darius looked down his long, arrogant nose at her. 'My brother Francis is not welcome at Winton Hall. Or indeed at any of the Wynter family residences.' His mouth had hardened into a grim line.

Her eyes widened. 'Why not?'

'It is a private family matter, and as such does not concern you.'

Her cheeks flushed with temper. 'I am now part of this family!'

'That does not entitle you to know every family scandal.'

'Why bother to keep that particular one a secret when your own indiscretions are such public knowledge?'

Darious drew in a deep and controlling breath, knowing he had gone as far with this present conversation as he was prepared to go. Further than he had meant to, in fact.

Arabella showed her intelligence in every conversation the two of them had together, and intuition on more than one occasion. If she should once get it into her head to solve the puzzle of Francis's banishment to the Continent almost seven months ago he would be undone… To continue their present conversation would surely only pique that interest even further.

'I could always ask my sister-in-law Grace about him, I suppose.' Once again Arabella displayed her intelligence. 'After all, he is also related to her by marriage, is he not? As are you…'

Darius had momentarily overlooked the fact that the niece of his sister-in-law Margaret had married Arabella's brother Lucian some months ago.

His eyes shot sparks at his recalcitrant wife. 'You will refrain from discussing all private family matters outside of this house!'

'Which means I should invite Lucian and Grace to visit us here sooner rather than later.'

His mouth tightened grimly at Arabella's continued stubbornness. 'Will you just leave the subject be, Arabella?'

'And if I do not?'

Darius drew in a harsh breath. 'I will not allow your interference in matters that do not concern you.'

Discerning the cold determination in Darius's expression, Arabella could not doubt the serious intent of his warning. Even so… 'I do not recall asking your permission,' she pressed.

A nerve pulsed in his tightly clenched jaw. 'Someone should have taken you in hand long ago and put an end to your rebellious ways.'

Arabella gave a humourless smile. 'Perhaps someone did—and failed utterly.'

'*I* would not fail!'

Arabella inwardly quivered at the determination in Darius's expression. A trembling she had no intention of allowing him to see. 'You are right, Darius. It really is time we went downstairs and joined our guest for dinner.'

Darius could hardly conceal his frustration as he glared at her. 'Arabella, why will you not accept that you are meddling in things best left alone?'

'How can I know that when you refuse to discuss them with me?' Her eyes were innocently wide.

An innocence that did not fool Darius for one second as he narrowed his own glacial blue gaze on her. 'Do not attempt to defy me on this matter, Arabella.'

'Oh, I never *attempt* to defy, Darius,' she assured him dryly. 'On the contrary, I have always found it is best to just do it rather than waste precious time arguing about it.'

Given the circumstances, it was not surprising that dinner was a tense and awkward affair, with Westlake stumbling about serving the food with his usual ineptitude—Arabella really would have to talk to Darius at the first opportunity concerning the lack of ability for given tasks in all the servants he employed—and poor Gideon Grayson left to supply the lion's share of the conversation as his host and hostess glowered at each other from either end of the table.

Not that Arabella did not enjoy herself. There was a feeling of intense satisfaction to be found in being able to shake Darius's usual air of mocking amusement at those about him.

An intense and delicious satisfaction that made Arabella slightly regretful when it came time for her to excuse herself from the dinner table so that the two men might enjoy their brandy and cigars.

'As there seems little point in retiring to the drawing room alone to drink my tea, I believe I might go straight upstairs,' she announced as Westlake, belatedly remembering his manners, hurried forward to pull back the chair so that she might rise. 'I will wish you a goodnight, gentlemen.' Arabella deliberately made no attempt to look at her coldly glowering husband and instead bestowed a graciously warm smile on the now standing Gideon Grayson.

Darius rose more slowly to his feet. 'I will join you very shortly.'

'Really?' Her brows arched coolly, despite the underlying threat she heard in Darius's tone. 'I had assumed that you and Lord Grayson would once again discuss…private matters once I had left the room.'

'Let's not embarrass our guest by arguing in front of him for a second time in one day,' Darius drawled dryly, not fooled for a moment by Arabella's supposedly pleasant demeanour, having been left in no doubt throughout dinner that his young wife was still spoiling for a fight.

He should not have reacted so strongly earlier, Darius now realised, and he would not have done so if Arabella had not touched a little too closely to the truth for comfort when she had threatened to invite Grace and Lucian here, in order to quiz them further concerning the matter of Francis's banishment.

Very few people knew the truth behind Francis's abrupt dismissal from England this past summer. Unfortunately, Lucian was one of them. And possibly his wife too, now. Lucian had assured Darius only days ago as to his silence on the true events behind Francis's banishment earlier this year, but even so it could have been a promise the other man did not feel extended as far as his wife.

Darius had come to the same conclusion concerning his own wife during the excruciatingly long dinner that had just passed. He had all but decided that perhaps he owed it to Arabella to share Francis's behaviour with her, at least. After all, what Francis had done had nothing to do with the life Darius had necessarily led these past eight years. He would be breaking no confidences by sharing it with Arabella.

It might also serve to divert her from pursuing the dangerous subject of Helena Jourdan any further…

'I will join you upstairs shortly,' he repeated mildly.

Arabella eyed him frowningly. 'I assure you that I perfectly understand if you would prefer to do as you did last night and stay downstairs and talk to Lord Grayson.'

'Ah, what it is to have an understanding wife,' Darius drawled. 'Be sure to ascertain that it is a quality your own wife possesses, Gray, when and if you should decide to marry!'

'What a flatterer you are, Darius,' his wife came back sharply.

'I only state the truth, Arabella.' His gaze easily

met the challenge he could see in the dark glitter of her eyes. 'A patient and understanding wife is surely to be valued above—'

'Diamonds?' Arabella put in tauntingly.

Darius's mouth tightened as he recalled the way in which Arabella had refused his gift earlier this evening. Forced to sit through this long and boring dinner, Darius had amused himself by imagining Arabella wearing *only* that diamond necklace later tonight when he made love to her…

'Most assuredly.' He gave her a mocking bow.

Arabella's mouth thinned. 'I have always preferred emeralds to diamonds.'

Darius raised one arrogant brow. 'And yet this evening you chose to wear sapphires…'

She shot him an irritated glare. 'I have no idea why.''

'Perhaps they reminded you of my eyes…?'

Her scathing snort was less than elegant. 'I fail to see the connection.'

'Little liar!'

Arabella glanced pointedly in Gideon Grayson's direction. 'We are once again embarrassing our guest, Darius.'

Darius gave an unconcerned shrug. 'Leave a candle alight for me, love.'

Her chin rose. 'I believe I am still so tired from our travels that I may fall straight to sleep as soon as my head touches the pillow!'

Darius gave a soft laugh. 'In that case I shall very much enjoy waking you up again.'

Arabella could find no suitable reply to this comment, instead addressing Westlake as he hurriedly crossed the room with a candle to light her way. 'Please inform Mary that I will not be needing her this evening,' she instructed the butler, and he held the door open for her to leave; if she had to turn Darius away from her bedchamber then Arabella certainly did not need her maid as witness to it!

How dared Darius call her 'love' in that casual way? As an announcement that it was his intention to make love to her, it was far from subtle.

Perhaps if she really *were* Darius's love she would not mind the endearment so much?

No, she would not mind at all. In fact, she might like it more than she ought! But, as that was never likely to happen, it simply irritated her to hear Darius address her with such insincere familiarity.

Her husband was an unrepentant rake who steadfastly refused to explain another woman's role in his life, and if he thought for one moment that it was Arabella's intention to go up the stairs and meekly await him to join her in her bedchamber, then he was going to be disappointed.

Arabella held the lighted candle aloft as she entered her bedchamber, turning to close the door behind her before she felt a silencing hand placed across her mouth at the same time as an arm curved in restraint about her throat…

Chapter Fourteen

'Arabella?'

Darius was not the least surprised to enter his wife's bedchamber some twenty minutes later to find that she had not left the requested candle alight for him. But the moonlight shone so brightly through the window, the curtains having not been drawn, that it was possible for him to see that the bed was empty and the bedclothes unruffled—evidence that she did not await him there, either.

'Let us not be childish about this, Arabella.' Darius gave a weary sigh as he moved to open the door into her dressing room; it had been a long and tiring day, and the last thing he wanted was yet another fight with his wife.

Where was the peace and ease one was supposed to find in marriage, he wondered ruefully? The calm? The wifely concern? The warmth and affection?

If Darius had truly required those things from his wife then he should not have married a woman as fiery and rebellious as Arabella St Claire!

Darius came to a halt as he entered the dressing room and found that also empty of her presence. Had he so infuriated her earlier that she had decided to leave him after all? Despite his warnings that he would come after her? Or possibly *because* of his warnings that he would come after her?

He moved back wearily into the bedchamber to sit down upon the bedside. Where would she have gone? How would she have left? The answer to those two questions was all too obvious; Mulberry Hall, Hawk's home, was but a short horse-ride into the neighbouring county of Gloucestershire.

Damn it!

Darius's hands clenched into fists at his sides. He was going to throttle Arabella—strangle her with his own bare hands when he caught up with her! How dared she just take off into the night in this way, leaving no word as to her destination?

Arabella would dare do anything she chose!

The question was, did Darius follow her tonight or should he wait until morning? His instinct was to go after her now—and when he caught up with her he would do much worse than throw her across his knee and paddle her backside! That was his initial instinct. Inner caution advised against it. Warned against the wisdom of following her until his own temper had cooled. If it ever did!

Darius dropped back onto the pillows to stare up at

the pale canopy above the bed, groaning as he realised that her leaving him was all his own fault. If he had but explained Francis's banishment to her, given her at least some of his confidence, then she might not have felt compelled to take the drastic action of leaving him only days after their wedding.

He stilled as he smelt her perfume on the pillow beneath him, turning his cheek to breathe it in; erotic femininity overlaid by a light floral scent. Darius knew he would always and for ever associate it with Arabella.

His anger returned with a vengeance and he sat up abruptly, his expression grim as he looked about the empty bedchamber. Damn it, how *dared* she do this to him?

Then Darius frowned darkly as his gaze was caught by the moonlight reflecting off something that glittered and sparkled near the leg of the dressing table. What was that?

He stood up to cross the bedchamber on soft and silent booted feet before bending to pick up the object, recognising it instantly as the sparkling sapphire-and-diamond necklace that Arabella had worn earlier instead of the one he had given her. A necklace that Arabella had informed him had belonged to her mother....

Even with only the moonlight to see by Darius could tell that the clasp of the necklace had been broken rather than carefully, lovingly unfastened.

Darius accepted that Arabella had been angry enough to have accidentally broken the fastening of the necklace as she removed it, but to leave it discarded upon the floor was surely not something she would ever have done to a piece of jewellery she valued so affectionately.

Darius's fingers tightened about the necklace and he looked up sharply, his narrowed gaze grimly searching the shadows of the bedchamber. All was tidy—not a comb or a glove out of place…

Not so. There was something else on the floor, near the door. Something Darius had missed stumbling over when he entered the bedchamber because it had been pushed aside by the opening of the door.

Darius placed the necklace down distractedly on the dressing table and then quickly lit the candles in the candelabra on the bedside table, his frown darkening thunderously as he crossed the room and saw that the object on the floor was the single candle Arabella had carried upstairs earlier, in order to light her way.

Another quick glance about the room showed that the gown Arabella had worn this evening was not in evidence, either. Which it surely would have been if she had prepared for bed without the help of her maid. Darius seriously doubted that the blue silk evening gown was what she would have chosen to wear on a cold midnight ride on horseback.

Darius picked up the glowing candelabra to carry it through to the adjoining dressing room, flinging open the doors to the wardrobe to hold the candle aloft as he searched quickly through the many gowns hanging there for the blue one that Arabella had been wearing this evening. Searching a second time, just to make sure.

It was not there!

Darius stepped back abruptly, his hands shaking slightly as he accepted the possibility—the absolute horror—that Arabella had not departed Winton Hall voluntarily!

Arabella's initial fear at having something dark thrown over her head so that she was unable to see, before being dragged from her bedchamber along the hallway to what she believed was the servants' stairs at the back of the house, and then outside into the icy cold wind—all totally against her will as she repeatedly tried to kick her assailant—had turned to indignant disbelief in the last hour or so.

Once outside, Arabella had been tied up and thrown down into what she was sure was the straw of an empty stall in the stables. Several of the horses who shared her captivity had given her enquiringly friendly snorts as they sensed her presence.

She was trussed up like a chicken ready for roasting, with her hands tied behind her back and her ankles bound together, and the cowl had been raised slightly and a piece of rag tied tightly about her mouth before she was once again plunged into darkness. Arabella had been left to lie on the mound of what she could only hope was *clean* straw. Several pieces of it stuck into her uncomfortably in various places through the thin silk of her gown.

Why she should have been dragged from her bedchamber and then abandoned here in the stables was totally beyond her comprehension. But the why was not really important at the moment; it was when Darius would decide to come looking for her that concerned her the most!

Surely he must have gone to her bedchamber by now and realised that she was not there? Unless, of course, Darius had taken her at her word after all and decided to let her sleep undisturbed tonight? It would be just her luck if he should choose tonight of all nights to show her some husbandly consideration!

Arabella stilled, her thoughts frozen, as she heard the sound of voices outside the stables. Was it her abductor and a cohort returning? Or could it be that Darius had come looking for her at last? Until she had confirmation one way or the other Arabella had no intention of drawing attention to herself.

'I tell you, Gray, we have searched the house from top to bottom and back again, which means Jourdan has to have taken Arabella away somewhere!' Darius rasped harshly as moved across the cobbled yard towards the stables with the younger man trailing behind him.

'We do not know that for certain,'

'I am well aware of that!' Darius turned on the other man fiercely, his eyes glittering dangerously in the moonlight. 'I warn you, if she has harmed one hair on Arabella's head—'

'There is no way Helena Jourdan could have kidnapped Arabella on her own,' Gray reasoned, for what had to be the dozenth time in the past hour. 'Your wife is young and healthy.' He grimaced awkwardly at the unflattering description. 'She is also not a woman to be taken against her will without protest.'

Darius smiled grimly at how true a statement was that. That smile faded as he recalled the broken necklace and dropped candle in Arabella's bedchamber. As he thought of the last frantic hour of searching the house for her. Unsuccessfully.

'I have already told you that someone in the house has to be helping Jourdan.' He glowered at the thought of any of the people he had hired to protect them actually being involved in such treachery. Cut-throats and thieves they might be, but after employing them for many months Darius had believed them to be loyal cut-throats and thieves.

'Riding off into the night without any idea of your destination has to be the height of folly.' Gray followed him into the stables. 'Much better to wait until morning and see if we cannot find a trail to follow. You—'

'Quiet, Gray!' Darius ordered as he stilled, listening intently. 'Did you hear that?'

'Hear what? I—' Gray broke off again as there came the sound of a second muted thud. 'I heard it that time.' He nodded. 'One of the horses moving, perhaps?'

'Perhaps. Perhaps not!' Darius bit out as another, louder thud was heard.

'Careful, Darius,' Gray warned softly, and he raised the pistol he carried.

Darius's expression was watchful as he raised a similar pistol. One he had carried about the house with him for the last hour as he searched from attic to cellar in case Arabella was being held prisoner somewhere. All to no avail. The house was empty of all sign of her. Only the broken necklace Darius had placed in the pocket of his waistcoat confirmed his belief that she could not have left Winton Hall willingly.

'It came from over there.' He pointed the pistol in the direction of the furthest stall. 'Light one of the lamps and bring it with you,' Darius instructed the other man tersely, waiting until Gray had done so before moving silently down the length of the stables.

The lit candle inside the lamp wavered behind Darius in the darkness, sending eerie shadows down the stables and onto the back wall, giving him the appearance of a monster ten feet tall.

His movements were soft and stealthy, his heart pounding loudly in his chest, and he raised his pistol in readiness as he rounded the end stall—and saw the tiny figure in a blue silk dress lying in the straw, hands and feet tied, face covered by a dark sack.

'Arabella!' Darius hurried forward to pull the sack from Arabella's head—only to find himself the focus of a pair of angry brown eyes that glared up at him indignantly from beneath the untidy tumble of her golden curls.

Darius ignored that glare as he threw his pistol down in the straw before pulling his wife up into his arms. 'My God, Arabella!' He crushed her thankfully against his chest.

Arabella allowed herself to fall into that comforting embrace for several seconds, so relieved to see Darius again that she happily ignored the discomfort of her tied hands and feet and the horrible gag across her mouth.

Except Darius continued to hold her in his crushing embrace long after she had ceased her trembling. 'Mmumph!' she finally muttered frowningly against the suffocating material of his jacket. 'Mariush, unnie ne!'

'What, love?' He moved back slightly to look at her.

'Unnie ne!' she repeated around the confining gag.

Darius frowned darkly. 'I'm sorry, love, I cannot under—'

'I believe your wife wishes for you to untie her, Darius,' another voice suggested dryly.

Arabella looked up to see Lord Gideon Grayson leaning against the wall of the stall. 'Neth!' she encouraged impatiently before turning back to her husband. 'Unnie ne, Mariush!'

'Oh, God…' Darius groaned as he realised what an idiot he was being; of *course* she wished to be untied. He had been so relieved to find her, apparently unharmed, that he simply hadn't given a thought to untying her. He hurried to do so now, removing the gag from about her mouth first.

'Well, at least *one* of you has some intelligence!' Arabella rebuked the instant her mouth was free. 'Honestly, Darius.' She gave a disgusted shake of her head as she glared up at him. 'How could you not have realised that I needed to be untied?'

Her curls were in complete disarray, there was a smudge of dirt on one of her cheeks, her lips were slightly swollen and red from the piece of material tied about her mouth, and there were pieces of straw struck to her gown. To Darius, however, she had never looked more beautiful.

Although her ordeal did not seem to have affected the sharpness of her tongue!

Darius gripped her shoulders. 'What happened, Arabella? How did you get out here? Did you see who did this to you?'

'Could you finish untying me so that we might go back into the house before I answer any of your questions, Darius?' She looked up at him imploringly. 'I have been out here for some time dressed only in my gown, and I am so very cold.' As if to prove her statement she began to shake uncontrollably.

As reaction to her ordeal began to set in, Arabella was not sure whether that trembling was from the cold or the relief of being rescued at last. The latter, she thought.

She was barely aware of Darius untying her hands and feet before he rose to lift her up into his arms. 'I am perfectly capable of walking,' she protested awkwardly.

'I am fully aware of all you are capable of doing,' he replied, his eyes glittering silver in the lamplight. 'For once in your life will you just be silent and allow someone else to take care of you?'

Arabella was instantly cowed by the obvious fierceness of his anger; Darius looked perfectly capable of wringing someone's neck at this moment—and for once it did not appear to be her own!

'I suggest you stay here and check out the rest of the stables, Gray,' Darius instructed the younger man, before turning to stride down the stables with Arabella held securely in his arms.

She was glad of those arms about her as Darius stepped outside into the cold and windy night. She had overheard one of the servants predicting this morning that there would be snow before the night was out, and from the icy chill in the air she could well believe it.

She closed her eyes and snuggled deeper into his embrace as the warmth emanating from his body began to melt some of the chill that seemed to go right through to her bones. She had absolutely no idea who had abducted her. Or why. She was just pleased to be safe once again. So much so that she could feel the prick of hot tears behind her closed eyelids.

She must not cry. It would be most unbecoming of a duchess to show such weakness. For Arabella St Claire—no, *Wynter*!—to show such weakness.

Even so, to her mortification, Arabella felt the hot burn of tears as they began to cascade unchecked down her cheeks.

Darius's arms tightened about her as he entered the house and saw the wet tracks of tears falling down the pallor of her cheeks. 'Bring some brandy into the Blue Salon, man,' he told the hovering Westlake before taking Arabella into the room where they had made love only that morning.

The heated fierceness of their lovemaking seemed so long ago now, and Darius's emotions were not in the least carnal as he laid her gently down upon the chaise before sitting down beside her to take both her cold little hands into his own and trying to instil some warmth into their chill. And all the time the tears continued to trail down through the dirty smudges upon Arabella's cheeks, as evidence of the fright she had so recently suffered.

Darius's mouth thinned grimly as he thought of the things he would like to do to the person who had taken her. 'Did you see who did this to you?' he asked again.

'No.' She released one of her hands, attempting to wipe the tears from her cheeks but only succeeding in smearing those dirty smudges further. 'He attacked me from behind. Put a hand over my mouth and an arm about my throat.' She shuddered delicately. 'I was so frightened, Darius,' she admitted shakily as she looked up at him with huge brown, tear-wet eyes. 'So very, very frightened!' She sat up to throw herself against his chest, fingers clinging tightly to his waistcoat as the tears fell in earnest.

Darius's thoughts were murderous as he held her tightly in his arms and rested his cheek against the softness of her hair. Arabella always gave the impression of independence. Of being able to take care of herself and needing nothing and no one. Most especially not a man to take care of her. The fact that she sobbed so brokenly against his chest now told him just how very frightened she must have been earlier tonight. How frightened she still was.

He glanced up as Westlake quietly entered the salon with a tray containing the decanter of brandy and two glasses. His expression was telling as he gave the other man a fierce glance.

Westlake's face was just as grimly drawn as he glanced down at the sobbing Arabella in Darius's arms before giving a firm nod. Telling Darius that, although she had only been at Winton Hall a matter of days, she had nonetheless managed to creep into the affections of the hardened pugilist. Reassuring Darius that Westlake, like himself, would leave no stone unturned in his search for her abductor.

Darius reached down to put Arabella away from him before he stood up to pour brandy into the two glasses, allowing Arabella to take a reviving sip from her own glass before questioning her again. 'You must have seen something, Arabella.' He frowned. 'Could you tell if it was a man or a woman who—?'

'It was a man, of course.' She looked up at him indignantly over the rim of her glass. 'I would not have been taken at all if it had been a woman.' Her free hand clenched into a fist at her side.

Darius did not doubt her ability to defend herself for a moment. Unfortunately, the fact that she believed her abductor to be a man did not help in the least in identifying him. It could have been Francis, of course. But, as Darius had told Gray earlier, it could just as easily have been a man working for Helena Jourdan. Someone in his own household, who could easily get in and out without suspicion…

Darius's mouth tightened. 'Do you remember anything about this man? Was he tall or short? Fat or thin? Did he have a distinctive smell of some kind?' It was a sad fact of life that servants did not wash as often as they ought.

Arabella took another sip of the warming brandy before closing her eyes as she tried to recall in detail those few moments in her bedroom when she had had that hand placed over her mouth and the arm about her throat. 'He was tall, I think. As he stood behind me his arms came up easily over my shoulders to hold me so that I could neither move nor shout for help. Neither fat nor thin, I would say, but muscled—like you,' she continued. 'As to smell? I *do* recall something… Something slightly floral, I think. Which is no help at all.' She gave a disgusted shake of her head as she opened her eyes again. 'That could be either a man or a woman.'

'Not quite, love,' Darius drawled. 'Did the muscled chest have any breasts upon it?'

Colour warmed her cheeks as she answered. 'No.'

'A man, then.' Darius nodded his satisfaction. 'The jacket of the arms that came about your shoulders—was it made of a soft and expensive material, or something rough, like a labourer or servant might wear?'

'It was…soft.' Arabella nodded eagerly as she recalled the fabric. 'Like a velvet or fine wool.'

'Good.' Darius praised her with a small smile. 'Did he speak at all? Even once?'

'I am afraid not.' Arabella sighed her disappointment before taking another distracted sip of the reviving brandy. 'There is one thing that puzzles me, though…'

'Yes?'

'Why do you suppose that someone went to all the trouble of abducting me from my bedchamber only to leave me trussed up like a chicken in the stables?'

Once again Arabella showed the intelligence that Darius both applauded and feared. He could not have borne to be married to a stupid woman, but her obvious intelligence was making it very hard for him to continue hiding the truth from her.

Recalling his earlier decision to tell Arabella about his brother Francis, Darius knew that, with her abduction tonight, the time had come to confide *that* truth to her, at least….

Chapter Fifteen

Arabella held out her glass for Darius to refill it with brandy even as she stared up at him in disbelief for the things he had just related to her. 'You are saying that Francis was responsible for the death of both your first wife *and* your brother George?' she repeated breathlessly.

Her husband looked severe. 'That he caused Sophie to fall from her horse to her death and George to have a fatal seizure of the heart? Yes, that is exactly what I am saying, Arabella.'

She stared up at him wide-eyed. 'I— But— You—'

'I am well aware that most of Society believes *me*—to be guilty of killing my wife—as Francis intended that they should—and a few even whisper that I had a hand in causing George's death too,' Darius said simply. 'They are wrong.' His arrogantly handsome face hardened noticeably as he looked down at her in challenge.

Arabella took another hasty sip of brandy, wondering if it could be the alcohol, along with her earlier ordeal, that was causing her to have hallucinations. Darius could not *really* have just informed her that his own brother had maliciously killed two people and deliberately implicated Darius as being responsible for those deaths.

People—*gentlemen*—did not just go around randomly killing other people....

But of course they did! For years gentlemen of the ton had been known to 'go abroad for their health' after they had committed some crime or other punishable by law. Had not Arabella herself made some such teasing remark to Darius when she'd learnt of Francis Wynter's banishment to the Continent?

'*You* were wrong, Arabella,' Darius added softly.

Arabella looked at him from beneath lowered lashes, feeling guilty as she recalled that in a fit of temper she had more than once accused Darius of being involved in the death of his wife.

Yet since coming to know Darius better—since becoming his wife, since making love with him—Arabella had known there had to be some other explanation for those rumours. She could no longer believe Darius guilty of killing anyone, but she had not dreamt the true explanation would somehow involve Darius's younger brother!

She moistened dry lips. 'It has been some time now

since I believed you capable of doing anything like that.'

'Oh?'

'Yes.' Arabella was not in the least daunted by the disbelief she could read in Darius's expression. 'Since our marriage I have come to realise that you are every bit as arrogant as my own brothers, and that if you had truly killed someone then you would feel no qualms about admitting you had done so.'

Darius raised an eyebrow. 'Even at the risk of imprisonment or worse?'

'Yes.'

'I am unsure as to whether that is a compliment or yet another of your insults!' Darius's mouth twisted ruefully.

'It is a simple statement of truth,' Arabella assured him briskly. 'You say it was always Francis's intention that you be thought responsible for the deaths?'

'Yes.' Darius sighed heavily. 'I realised how neatly that guilt was to be laid at my feet last summer, when it became obvious that Francis intended to kill me too and make it look as if I had taken my own life because I could no longer live with the guilt of what I had done.'

Arabella gasped. 'That is truly terrible! He is a monster, Darius! How could you have simply let him escape to the Continent? Tacitly accept the blame for the death of your wife and brother when the guilt really lay elsewhere?'

'He is my *brother*, Arabella.'

'He is a *murderer*!' she retorted hotly.

'Yes.' Darius frowned darkly.

'And now you think he is back in England and once again attempting to kill you?'

'Perhaps,' Darius allowed. 'Which is why we have to now discuss why his actions, both past and present, are of import to you.'

'To me?' Arabella echoed sharply.

'You are now my wife,' he pointed out gently.

'I fail to see what that has to do with—' She broke off, her eyes widening even as her face paled. 'You are believed guilty of those two crimes because the death of your first wife left you in possession of her fortune, and the death of your eldest brother left you as heir to a dukedom...' She spoke softly, deep in thought, for the moment ignoring the look of distaste upon Darius's arrogantly handsome face. 'When in reality the fact that your first wife was already dead when you became Duke of Carlyne—'

'*Conveniently* dead, remember?' her husband drawled dryly.

'Stop it, Darius!' Arabella gave him an irritated frown as he reminded her of her own accusation.

'I apologise.' He grimaced ruefully. 'Please proceed.'

Arabella shot him a narrow-eyed glance. 'Because you had been widowed by the time George died, you had no wife with whom you could provide a legitimate heir. And so if you were also to meet an accidental death then Francis would inherit the title...'

Darius revealed none of his admiration for his wife as he looked at her from beneath hooded lids. Which was not to say he did not admire her—very much. In only a matter of seconds, it seemed, she had managed to grasp the motivation behind Francis's causing the death of two completely innocent people. For also, possibly, being the cause of the most recent 'accidents' involving Arabella and Darius.

'Until you remarried you were not in danger,' she continued slowly. 'But now our marriage once again allows for the eventual appearance of a legitimate heir…'

'I am not sure that I altogether like your repeated references to a "legitimate" heir, Arabella,' Darius said. 'I have already assured you that to my knowledge, I have no illegitimate heirs, either!'

Once again she felt the warmth enter her cheeks. 'It was only a figure of speech, Darius.'

'One I do not care for,' he muttered.

'You are grasping at irrelevancies—'

'It is *not* irrelevant to me!'

'Very well.' Arabella gave a cool nod. 'Is the rest of my theory a factual one?'

She could see that Darius's jaw was clenched and his teeth gritted as he obviously fought back his temper. Although why he should be so annoyed by it Arabella had no idea; Darius's numerous affairs over the previous ten years had become legendary—so was it not logical to assume that there might have been one or two unwelcome consequences to those alliances?

'It is,' he said curtly.

'Why did you tell me—? Why did you deliberately

lead me to believe that you were responsible for Sophie's death?' She eyed him reprovingly.

'Because I *am* responsible,' Darius snarled. 'If I had not married Sophie then Francis would not have felt the need to be rid of her.'

'That does *not* make you responsible—'

'I disagree,' he cut in, that coldness back in his expression. 'I did not know it at the time, but I placed Sophie in danger just by marrying her.'

Arabella eyed him guardedly. 'You have already indicated to me that you were not in love with her. Why not?' She drew her breath in sharply, uncertain whether she would be able to withstand hearing that Darius *had*, in fact, been in love with his first wife after all…

'We…respected each other for the honesty of our… needs.' Darius's jaw was set tensely.

'I do not understand.'

Darius placed his clenched hands behind his back. 'It was a marriage of convenience. Sophie wished for a title, and I was obviously in need of her fortune.'

Arabella frowned.

Darius looked rueful. 'Unpleasant, is it not?'

It had not been a love-match, certainly, but many a match was made amongst the ton for far lesser reasons. Except… 'Was it for financial gain that you also offered for *me* last year?'

Darius lowered heavy lids to hide the expression in his eyes. 'I do not believe this conversation to be of any relevance to the here and now.'

'It is relevant to *me*!' Arabella insisted.

'Why is it?' Darius eyed her quizzically. 'What do

you wish me to say, Arabella? What do you wish to hear? That I offered for you prior to offering for Sophie because I had need of *your* fortune? Or that I offered for you because I have loved you, been obsessed with you, since the moment I first set eyes on you?'

Arabella felt a painful twisting in her chest. 'We both know that the latter is not true.'

'Then it must be the first, must it not?' Darius rasped harshly.

Arabella's heart felt heavy. 'You are right. This conversation is not helping our present situation.' She drew herself up proudly. 'If my abductor tonight *was* Francis, then why do you suppose he only took me from my bedchamber before leaving me tied up in the stables? Surely the death of a second wife in little over a year would have sealed your guilt in the eyes of the law, as well as the ton?'

Darius should have felt relieved at this sudden return to the events of this evening, but what he really felt was a cold and icy shiver down the length of his spine at the thought of Arabella being at Francis's questionable mercy. 'Perhaps he did it to show me that he could?'

He had thought that by banishing Francis to the Continent he had solved the dilemma of his younger brother's despicable actions. But these last few days of 'accidents', to Arabella, as well as himself, and then her senseless abduction, served to convince Darius that if Francis were the one responsible for these things then the mental sickness that so obviously held him in its grip must be worsening; his brother was becoming a danger to himself, as well as to others.

Unless, as Grayson preferred to believe, Francis was not the one to blame, but rather it was the vengeful Helena Jourdan?

Darius had to admit that the fact that Arabella had been taken from her bedchamber this evening to be left in the stables, tied up but unharmed, did not seem like something that Francis would have done. Surely once Francis had got his hands on Arabella he would have arranged for her to die whilst he had the chance?

'Perhaps he did,' Arabella agreed distractedly now. 'But just because Francis is your brother it does not seem sufficient reason to me for you to continue to allow the ton to believe that you are the one guilty of these awful deeds!' She looked up at him searchingly.

His mouth twisted ruefully. 'Believe me, Arabella, my reputation is well able to withstand the scandal.'

'But—'

'It really is better left as it is,' Darius insisted firmly.

'Better for whom, exactly?' she shot back.

'For everyone.' His expression was bleak. 'Have you forgotten the existence of my sister-in-law, Margaret?'

Ah. The Dowager Duchess of Carlyne. George's widowed wife.

Arabella's gaze sharpened. 'You prefer that she continues to believe that *you* rather than Francis may be guilty of killing her husband?'

Darius stood up impatiently. 'Margaret does not believe me responsible for killing anyone.'

'I appreciate that she has remained here at the Dower House since her husband died, but surely once she returned to town for our wedding she would have heard the gossip about you.'

'If she did then she will have dismissed it,' Darius said, his gaze glacial. 'My sister-in-law knows me, you see, Arabella. She knows unequivocally that I would never have harmed George in any way. He was my brother, Arabella.' His voice deepened emotionally. 'I have already explained that he was older than me by twenty years and more. What I did not tell you is that he and Margaret effectively became parents to Francis and myself after our father died. We grew up here with their own son, Simon, and we were all treated exactly the same by them. As such, I loved both Margaret and George. I deeply respected them, and would never, ever have wished George harm. Margaret may very well have heard the gossip whilst in town for our wedding.' His expression was grim. 'But I assure you that she will have dismissed those rumours as the mere tittle-tattle that they are.'

Arabella cheeks flushed uncomfortably as she heard the underlying accusation in Darius's tone. 'But the truth would exonerate you completely in the eyes of Society—'

'I do not give *that*—' he snapped his finger and thumb together dismissively '—for what Society thinks of me!'

'And my family? Should *they* not be told the truth?' Arabella looked up at him in frustration.

Darius looked haughty. 'Why?'

'Because—well, because—'

'Because you do not want them to think badly of your husband?' he taunted. 'Or because you no longer want them to think badly of *you* for marrying the man Society believes me to be?'

Arabella flinched. 'You are deliberately twisting my words, Darius.'

'Do you not think that Margaret has already suffered enough, with the death of her only son two and a half years ago, followed by that of her husband but seven months ago? What good would it do now to start the gossip all over again by publicly claiming my innocence of any wrongdoing? For Margaret to learn that, although George was ill, he still need not have died when he did? That but for Francis's actions she would almost certainly not be alone now and widowed?'

Once again Arabella felt the prick of tears behind her lids as she thought of all that Margaret Wynter had suffered.

Her expression softened as she looked up at her husband. 'Why do you choose to keep your kindness to your sister-in-law, your love and loyalty for your family, hidden behind a social mask of arrogance and coldness?'

'Because I *am* cold and arrogant, damn it!' Darius glared down at her fiercely. 'The fact that I choose to avoid even more of a family scandal by not revealing the truth does not make me any less the selfish man Society believes me to be.'

Arabella knew Darius was often arrogant and mocking. That he could be cold and hard, too. But he was *not* selfish. Far from it.

Once again Darius seemed to have overlooked the fact that she had three older brothers who were just as outwardly arrogant, and who could also be cold and hard. But as their sister, Arabella knew there was so much more to them than the faces they chose to show to Society.

Just as there was so much more to her husband….

Darius's determination to protect Margaret Wynter from the truth more than proved that. Making her curious as to what else he chose to keep hidden. And why…

'No,' she accepted softly. 'But your kindness as regards your sister-in-law does allow for there being another, softer side to your nature that you choose not to share with Society.'

Darius grimaced. 'Arabella, please do not attempt to bestow virtues on me where none exist.'

Was that what she was doing? Perhaps. And yet…

'As for your own family being privy to the truth,' Darius continued, 'I believe you will find that Lucian, at least, knows I am not guilty of killing anyone.'

Arabella gave him a startled glance. '*Lucian* does?'

Darius had meant only to reassure her, but as he saw the way her eyes darkened with suspicion he accepted that he would have to share *all* the events of seven months ago with her.

'Grace is Margaret's niece, and she and Lucian were here at Winton Hall in April when I confronted

Francis,' he explained. 'Lucian is sworn to secrecy over the matter, but…' He gave a rueful shrug. 'I doubt, as with most men, he has managed to keep all of the truth from his own wife.'

'Can that be the reason, do you suppose, that Lucian did not disapprove of our marriage?'

'Perhaps.'

'Only perhaps?' she teased.

Darius shrugged taut shoulders. 'Lucian and I have been acquaintances for many years. He and my nephew Simon were at school together. As such, Lucien stayed here often at Winton Hall when we were all children. We have also passed many an evening together at our clubs, or elsewhere, since we became adults,' he added dryly.

She had no wish to know the details of this 'elsewhere'—either in regard to Darius or her brother! 'In other words, even if Lucian had not been present last April when you confronted Francis, my brother knows you well enough to realise you could not have been responsible for killing either Sophie or George?'

'As I have said, Arabella, do not bestow virtues on me where none exist!' Darius insisted. 'I assure you I am more than capable of killing if I feel that any member of my family, or myself, is being threatened.'

Arabella felt a shiver down the length of her spine as she saw the icy determination in his expression. 'Perhaps we should not discuss this any further tonight?' She stood up to cross the room to his side, the slenderness of her body almost touching his much harder one. 'I need you to hold me, Darius,' she encouraged gruffly. 'To hold me close so that I know I am once again safe.'

Darius knew he was lost the moment he looked down into the depths of her warm brown eyes. Her gaze was both direct and vulnerable—a combination guaranteed to captivate. And it certainly did captivate Darius, ensnaring him into experiencing an instant aching sensuality that made even continuing to breathe difficult.

Arabella's lips were so full and pink, so soft and succulent, and the swell of her breasts moved gently above the low neckline of the blue silk gown as she breathed shallowly. Expectantly. As if waiting for, anticipating the intimacy that would surely follow.

Darius's gaze moved to the pale creaminess of her throat. Her pulse was a wild flutter just beneath the surface of her smooth and silky skin, that same pulse beating at the delicacy of her temple as his gaze moved slowly across her face. Even as he looked at Arabella her lips parted expectantly, a pouting encouragement that instantly caused his thighs to harden.

'If I were to hold you now, I cannot guarantee that is all I would do.' His voice sounded harsh in the tense and expectant silence that now surrounded them.

Her answer was to move closer still, an inviting smile curving those full and swollen lips as she did so. It was a warm and totally trusting smile that cut right to the heart of him.

'You have already been through so much tonight, Arabella, and I may not be able to be as gentle with you as you need me to be,' he warned her as his hands reached out to grasp the bare tops of her arms to hold her slightly away from him.

She had suffered a terrifying ordeal this evening, but Darius knew that he felt that fear on her behalf no less sharply. As such, his own emotions were raw and fierce, and he was not sure he would be able to control those emotions if he took her into his arms.

Once the dropped candle and broken necklace had convinced him that she had not left her bedchamber willingly, Darius knew he had behaved like a madman as he'd searched the house from top to bottom in an effort to find her. That heated anger had turned to an icy fury in his chest the moment he'd realised she was no longer in the house, but somewhere outside in the darkness, most probably the prisoner of someone who wished to do her harm. At the very least in the power of someone who thought to wound Darius by taking her from him.

To now have her back, obviously shaken but unharmed, was almost more than he could bear, and if he started making love to her he knew that he was in danger of losing all restraint. Of possibly frightening her with the depth of his need to possess her in an effort to keep her safe from further harm.

She shook her head now. Several of her silky curls had fallen loose about her shoulders during her captivity. 'It is not gentleness I require from you tonight, Darius.'

His breath caught sharply. 'Then…what?'

The boldness of her gaze met his unflinchingly. 'I wish to *feel*, Darius. To experience…everything. Every kiss and every caress.' She moved to press the softness of her body against him, her breasts a voluptuous crush against his chest. 'I want to feel all of those things and know that I am truly still alive and safe in your arms.'

A nerve pulsed in his clenched jaw. 'You may find yourself less safe with me than you would wish!'

She looked totally confident. 'I do not believe you would ever do anything that might hurt me.' She lifted one of her hands to trail her fingertips down the hard hollows of his cheek. 'Take me upstairs and make love to me, Darius. Please!'

He swallowed convulsively, knowing he was not strong enough to withstand her pleading. Yet also knowing, no matter what the cost to himself, that he would do everything in his power to show her the gentleness she needed from him.

He swung her up into his arms and carried her out into the hallway—to find Gideon Grayson standing there, talking to Westlake. Arabella's arms tightened about his neck and she buried her face against the hardness of his chest as she also saw the two men. The fierce expression on Darius's face was warning enough for neither man to attempt any further conversation with him tonight.

'What will they think of me?' Arabella groaned in embarrassment as Darius carried her effortlessly up the wide staircase.

'They will think, as I do, that you are a very brave young woman who at the very least deserves to be carried upstairs to her bedchamber,' he said indulgently.

Her arms tightened about his neck. 'Your own bedchamber, please, Darius. I cannot—I do not wish to go back into my own room tonight.'

His mouth tightened grimly as he thought once more of the fear Arabella must have suffered when last in her bedchamber. His eyes glittered fiercely as he recalled her mention of that silencing hand placed across her mouth and the restraining arm about her throat. That she was still alive and safe here in his arms was almost enough to bring Darius to his knees.

As it was, his arms tightened about her as he carried her down the hallway. His own bedchamber was bathed in a golden glow from the single candle that his valet had left burning on the bedside table. A glow that bathed Arabella in that same golden light as Darius placed her carefully on top of the bedcovers.

Her arms remained tightly locked about his neck as she pulled him down with her, his fully clothed body half lying across her own as she raised her mouth to his invitingly.

It was an invitation Darius had no will or desire to resist, and his mouth gently claimed hers, that gentleness blazing into fierce desire as her lips parted beneath his and Darius felt the soft, encouraging stroke of her tongue against his own.

Their kiss was urgent, hungry as they tasted each other. Darius's hands moved up to cup either side of her face, his body above hers pressing her down into the bed.

Arabella could feel the hard need of Darius's thighs pushing against her as he kissed her long and deeply.

Her hands tangled in the heavy thickness of his hair as she returned the heat of that kiss. There was only the heavy sound of their increasingly ragged breathing to break the silence as they began to throw off their clothes, both of them needing, aching for even closer contact.

Arabella gasped as Darius returned the heavy weight of his naked body to her own. He was burning hot. Searing. Her nipples hardened like berries against the heat of his chest. Her thighs undulated against the hard length of his arousal and her legs parted in immediate invitation.

'Yes, Darius!' she pleaded as he would have pulled back slightly. 'I need you so very badly.'

'You are not ready yet, love—' he broke off with a strangled groan as she thrust her hips upwards to take an inch or two of him inside her.

'I need you inside me now,' she moaned urgently.

Her need was enough to send their lovemaking into a wild frenzy as they kissed and touched, caressed, devoured. Arabella felt at that moment as if their hearts and minds were joined in the same way as their bodies, the pleasure rising higher and higher, and then higher still, until they reached the pinnacle together in a hot burst of blinding pleasure.

Darius blew out the candle before falling back onto his pillows with a groan. He took Arabella with him, his arm firmly about her waist as he held her tightly against his side, her head resting on his shoulder as she continued to run a lightly caressing hand across the heated dampness of his chest.

Their silence was companionable, satiated, and as Darius heard Arabella's breathing start to slow, to deepen, and felt that caressing hand become still against his chest, he knew that she was falling asleep.

Darius wondered if he would ever sleep again. If he would ever again feel able to relax his watchful vigil. His determination to keep her safe was so strong that he knew he wouldn't be able to fully rest until their enemy was caught. He could not—

'Darius?'

He glanced down in the moonlight at the pale oval of Arabella's face, surrounded by those wild golden curls. The heavy weight of her lashes against her cheeks showed him that her eyes were still closed. 'Yes, love?'

'Westlake is not really a butler, is he?' she murmured sleepily.

Darius chuckled huskily before relaxing completely against her and allowing the darkness of sleep to claim them both.

Chapter Sixteen

Arabella was pale but composed as she walked lightly down the staircase of Winton Hall the following morning. Darius had not been beside her when she woke in his bed an hour or so ago, but feeling the warmth of the sheets beside her Arabella realised he had not been gone long, that he had probably left her sleeping so that she might rest as long as possible after her ordeal the previous night. She was also aware that he would want to be up and about early this morning, wanting to see if he could learn any more of her abductor now that it was daylight.

'I trust you are feeling better this morning, Your Grace?'

Arabella turned to smile at the butler-who-she-was-sure-was-not-a-butler as he appeared in the cavernous hallway below. 'I am, thank you, Westlake.'

'His Grace told me to inform you that he will be

outside with Lord Grayson for a time.' The man's battered face was creased into kindly lines of concern as she stepped down to join him in the reception hall.

She smiled up at him warmly, more than ever convinced—even if Darius's laughter the previous night had not already confirmed her suspicion—that this man was not what he pretended to be. In fact, she now believed that he had been hired to act as an extra protection against any attacks.

The almost guilty look on Westlake's battered features as he continued to look at her told her that he was less than pleased with himself at this moment. 'Would you care to join me for a cup of tea in the breakfast room, Westlake?' she invited.

He looked stunned. 'Your Grace?'

'Please do come,' she encouraged as she tucked her hand into the crook of his arm and smiled up at him mischievously. 'I am simply longing to know what profession you enjoyed before my husband persuaded you into coming to Winton Hall!'

Darius came to a stunned halt in the doorway of the breakfast room as he beheld his young wife and his butler sitting down at the table, drinking tea together as they chatted like old acquaintances.

Having spent the last two hours unsuccessfully scouring the cobbled courtyard, the stables, and the grounds of the house for any sign as to how last night's intruder might have got inside, the last thing Darius had expected to find when he decided to join his wife for a late breakfast was Big Tom and Arabella sitting together as if they were the best of friends!

As if sensing Darius's presence, Arabella ceased talking to glance towards the door. The warmth of the smile she bestowed upon him revealed no lingering shadow of the fear and distress she had suffered during the previous night's ordeal.

'Darius!' She stood up to cross the room to his side and link her arm companionably with his. 'Do come and join us. Tom has been regaling me with wonderful tales of his experiences in the fighting ring.' Her eyes gleamed up at Darius teasingly as he glanced across the room to where Westlake had just risen uncomfortably to his feet.

'Stay where you are, man,' Darius urged as he walked further into the breakfast room.

The ex-pugilist gave a self-conscious shake of his head. 'I'd best be about my duties now that you've come back, Your Grace.' He shot Arabella an awkward grimace before beating a hasty retreat.

Darius smiled. 'Arabella?'

Her laughter deepened. 'And to think I had decided yesterday that I must needs talk to you about the unsuitability of the household staff you have employed here!'

Darius shook his head ruefully as he sat down at the breakfast table. 'I do not believe you will in any way help with the disciplining of that staff when you invite them to take tea with you.'

That laughter still gleamed in the deep brown of her

eyes as she strolled over to join him at the table. 'But Tom has led such an interesting life.'

'A life the details of which your brothers would all be deeply shocked to learn you have been made privy to,' Darius groaned.

She chuckled softly. 'Did you know that Tom won his first fight when he was only thirteen? That he—?'

'Arabella, please.' He winced. 'I assure you, as soon as this—this situation is resolved, we will see about replacing the servants now presently in our employ with others more suited to the task.'

Arabella paused in sipping her tea. 'You cannot be thinking of replacing Tom?' she protested. 'He confided in me but a few minutes ago that after years of fighting for a living he actually enjoys the work here.'

Darius did not miss the determined light in her eyes. 'But he has proved time and time again that he has no idea how to be a butler—'

'Oh, please, Darius!' She looked across at him imploringly. 'He is far too old to return to the ring, and I am sure that with a little advice and guidance from me he will soon learn all he needs to of how to be butler in a ducal household.'

Darius had absolutely no doubt that she was well up to the task. That she was capable of doing anything she set her mind to. Their present conversation was also succeeding in keeping her attention diverted from the previous night's events. He set himself to be deliberately provocative…

'And what will we do when your brothers visit—especially Hawk, as he surely will, if only to assure himself that I have not done away with his sister!—and they all recognise Tom for who and what he is?'

'What he *was*,' Arabella corrected firmly. 'I think you underestimate my family, Darius. I am sure they will all come to appreciate Tom as I do. Even if they do not, it is of little real import; we are at liberty to choose our own household staff, I trust?' She looked effortlessly proud—a true duchess.

Darius gazed at her admiringly from between narrowed lids. While she was a little pale this morning, she otherwise appeared delicately lovely in a gown of buttercup-yellow. Yet it was a delicacy that Darius knew to be totally deceptive!

'We will talk on this subject again some other time,' he said briskly. 'For the moment we must decide what to do next. I believe it best if you depart for Mulberry Hall after breakfast so that you might stay with Hawk and—'

'No.'

He quirked one arrogant brow. 'No?'

'Absolutely not.' Arabella met his narrowed gaze unwaveringly, her back and shoulders very straight. 'I will not be forced into running away, Darius. Into leaving what is now my home.' She gave a firm shake of her head, blond curls dancing at her nape and temples.

'And if I insist?'

Arabella looked at Darius speculatively, knowing by the grim set of his face—narrowed eyes, unsmiling mouth, clenched jaw—that he *was* insisting. 'Then I will have no choice but to try to persuade you otherwise.'

'Only *persuade*, Arabella?' Darius's mouth twitched. 'That does not sound at all like you!'

'Yes. Well.' Arabella's gaze dropped from that probing blue one. 'It is not always necessary for us to engage in an argument in an effort to make my own views known.'

Darius gave a disbelieving snort. 'This is the first I have heard of it.'

She frowned her irritation. 'Is it any wonder I so often feel the need to disagree with you when you are always so sure you are right?'

He chuckled softly. 'That is more like the Arabella I have come to know!'

Her cheeks flushed hotly. 'You are not taking me seriously, Darius.'

'On the contrary, Arabella, I am taking your involvement in this situation, and in what happened last night, *very* seriously.' Darius sat forward, his expression once again grim. 'Hence my suggestion that you travel to Mulberry Hall later this morning.'

'A suggestion I have already informed you I find totally unacceptable.'

Darius scowled as he saw her stubborn determination in the tilting of her little chin and the firming of her mouth. 'I am endeavouring to keep you safe, you stubborn baggage.'

'And if I prefer to remain here with you?'

'Then, as last night has already proved, you will *not* be safe.' He stood up to pace the room restlessly. 'Do not be so ridiculously mulish about this, Arabella. Once I know you are safely ensconced at Mulberry Hall I will be able to concentrate all my energies on apprehending your abductor.'

'Are you saying that I am a distraction to you?'

He shot her a knowing look. 'I am saying your presence here is a distraction.'

'Is that not the same thing?'

No, it was not, Darius acknowledged with a frown. Worrying about Arabella's safety was a total distraction for his mind. Her presence was a distraction to his body, as he found himself desiring her both day and night! 'I cannot concentrate on apprehending your abductor if I constantly have to worry that it might happen again. With less satisfactory results.'

'You mean, that if I am taken again I might be killed?'

Darius had fallen into a satiated sleep the night before, only to awaken suddenly in the darkness minutes later. His arms had tightened about Arabella and they had remained about her all night long as he had lain there awake, holding her safely against him. He'd spent the night imagining someone somehow taking her from him again. Finding her broken and lifeless body after searching for her not just for hours, but for tormented days and nights…

'It is a risk I am unwilling to take.'

'But it is not *your* risk, Darius.' Arabella spoke softly.

His hands clenched at his sides. 'Of course it is my risk! No matter what our reasons for marrying each other, you are still my responsibility. Mine to protect!'

How awful that Darius should only consider her his 'responsibility'. His 'to protect'.

Arabella was aware of exactly what he meant by 'no matter what our reasons for marrying each other'. Knew that he had to be referring to his belief that she had only married him because he was now a wealthy duke rather than a penniless lord. As for his own reasons for marrying her...

'Why did you marry me, Darius?' She looked at him searchingly.

He shot her an irritated scowl. 'This is hardly the time—'

'There may not be another time, Darius.' She shook her head sadly.

A white line of tension appeared beside his thinned lips. 'That is precisely the reason I am insisting you leave here today.'

'I have said no.'

'Arabella—'

'I will not go, Darius, so you may as well cease repeating yourself. You—'

'I am sorry to interrupt...' An uncomfortable Gideon Grayson stood hesitantly in the open doorway.

'What is it, Gray?' Darius turned to the other man with considerable thanks for interrupting his disagreement with Arabella; she would leave here later this morning if he had to tie her inside the carriage to achieve it!

Gray winced. 'A rider has just arrived with a letter. From London. He refuses to give it to anyone but you,' he added tellingly.

Darius looked concerned. 'Did he say who had sent it?'

'He refused to tell me that, either,' the other man revealed.

'Very well.' Darius nodded tersely as he walked to the door. 'Stay here and keep Arabella company, would you?'

'I am not a child who needs to be watched every minute of the day,' his wife commented dryly as she overheard his muttered comment to Gray.

Darius turned to look at her. 'Would you deny our guest the opportunity to eat breakfast?'

Her cheeks flushed at the rebuke. 'No, of course not.'

'Then I am sure Gray will be only too happy to keep you company whilst you finish eating your own meal.' The glittering intensity of his gaze challenged her to defy him again.

'I had not realised until recently, Lord Grayson, how tedious husbands can be,' Arabella remarked lightly as she resumed her seat at the breakfast table.

Darius scowled darkly as he saw that Gray was having trouble holding back a smile at his expense. 'If she tries to leave, Gray, you have my permission to tie her to the chair!'

The younger man looked scandalised. 'I could not possibly—'

'I believe my husband is playing with you, Lord Grayson,' Arabella cut in, taking pity on him. 'With us both.' She shot Darius a glare that warned of retribution for his high-handedness.

'You cannot be so sure of that…' Darius drawled mockingly, before taking his leave, leaving an awkward silence behind him.

Arabella found herself the focus of the embarrassed gaze of Gideon Grayson. 'Please do sit down, Lord Grayson.' She indicated the chair opposite her own that Big Tom had so recently vacated. 'Darius does so love to tease,' she remarked casually as she poured him a cup of tea, all the while wondering precisely why this man was still here… 'You stopped here on your way elsewhere, I believe, Lord Grayson? Will your hosts not be concerned by your delay?'

'Oh, no! Well—I—'

'You were not on your way to anywhere but Winton Hall, were you?' Arabella's shrewd gaze pinned him where he sat.

Gideon Grayson gave an uncomfortable start. 'I really cannot talk about it, Your Grace.'

'Call me Arabella,' she invited. 'And of *course* you may talk about it. I am Darius's wife now, and any business that you have with my husband you may also discuss with me.'

The young Lord looked even more ill at ease. 'I am afraid I cannot. No.'

Exactly as Arabella had expected. Just as she suspected there was much more going on in Darius's life than he had so far confided in her. 'Then perhaps you would prefer to discuss the weather, as we did yesterday?'

'I would, yes.' His Lordship looked much relieved by the suggestion.

'Did you and my husband find any evidence this morning of how the intruder could have entered the house yesterday evening?'

'But— That is hardly the weather, Your Grace!' He shifted restlessly in the chair.

Arabella gave him a sweetly saccharine smile. 'I merely asked if *you* would prefer to discuss the weather, Lord Grayson. I did not say *I* intended doing so.'

He gave a reluctant laugh. 'It is easy to see now that you are indeed Sebastian's sister!'

Arabella's smile deepened. 'You find my youngest brother as amiable as I?'

'I find he is as full of surprises,' Lord Grayson contradicted wryly. 'The most recent, of course, being his marriage to Lady Boyd.'

'No doubt you will miss Sebastian's company about Town?'

'Your brother and I have not been as…close of late as we once were.' He looked less than comfortable with the admission.

'So Darius has remarked.' Alerting Arabella to yet another mystery; her brother Sebastian was outwardly the most charming of men, and he and Gideon Grayson had been friends for years. She no longer believed Darius's hint that Sebastian and Lord Grayson had fallen out over a woman, either. As far as Arabella was aware Juliet had been the only woman in Sebastian's life for some months now. 'Perhaps you were also present at the Bancroft house party in the summer?'

Lord Grayson stiffened, his expression now wary. 'Perhaps.'

'Either you were or you were not?'

He gave a slow and reluctant inclination of his head. 'I was.'

'I see… Darius has been rather a long time, has he not?' Arabella frowned her concern as she realised it must be ten minutes or more since Darius had left them. She stood up abruptly. 'I believe I will go and see if—'

'Carlyne expressed a wish for you to remain here.' Lord Grayson also stood up.

Arabella raised haughty brows. 'I trust you are not about to attempt to physically restrain me from joining my husband, My Lord?'

'Of course I am not.' His face flushed uncomfortably. 'I just think it wiser if you remain here until Darius comes for you.'

Arabella shot him a derisive glance. 'You have known Sebastian for some years now, and during that time you must surely have come to realise that the St Claires are not always wise?'

Grayson grimaced. 'I have found that to be the case on occasion, yes.'

'You see my point, I hope?'

'Yes. But—'

'There is no *but*, Lord Grayson. I intend to go and look for my husband now. My advice to you is that you continue with your breakfast until Darius sends for you.' Arabella gave him one last challenging smile before turning on her slippered heel and leaving the room to go in search of her husband.

* * *

Darius sat behind the desk in his study, his face pale as he attempted to accept the significance of the note he had just received from William Bancroft.

'Darius…?'

The contents of Bancroft's note were so disturbing that Darius was not in the least surprised he had not heard Arabella open the study door and enter the room before quietly closing it again behind her. Nor was he surprised that she had not done as he had asked and stayed in the breakfast room with Grayson; Arabella had not obeyed any of his suggestions to date, so why should he have expected that she would obey that one?

'What is it, Darius?' She glanced at the note that lay open upon the top of his desk. 'Have you received bad news of some kind?'

His laugh was completely lacking in humour. 'Not just bad, Arabella, but earth-shattering!'

'What is it?' Arabella's concern deepened as she took note of the pallor of his face. 'Darius, what has happened?' She crossed the room to his side.

He did not answer her with words, but instead held out the note for her to take.

'Read it, Arabella!' He stood up abruptly to move away from her and stand in front of the window, his hands gripped tightly together behind his back, his expression as grim as the cold and frosty weather outside.

Arabella's hand shook as she held the note, her emotions too disturbed for her to immediately be able to focus on the words written there. She had never seen Darius like this before. So bleak. So utterly lost to all hope, it seemed.

Her heart sank as she read the note signed by Lord Bancroft. Helena Jourdan was dead. She had been drowned over a week ago, when the ship taking her back to France had floundered and sunk in a storm off the Normandy coast. The bodies of those who had died were only now being washed ashore and identified.

Darius looked so bleak, so helpless, because Helena Jourdan had died…?

Arabella crumpled the note in her hand to stare across the room at her husband. 'You cared for her after all, then.'

'Do not be ridiculous, Arabella!' Darius exclaimed as he turned impatiently back into the room, his eyes ablaze with emotion.

She shook her head. 'But you are so upset—'

'Of *course* I am upset.' Darius began to pace the small confines of the room. 'Do you not see what this means, Arabella? Can you not see that if Helena Jourdan has been dead this past week then she cannot be the one trying to harm us? It must be Francis after all.'

Now that Darius had pointed it out to her, of course Arabella did see. But it was not that realisation that made her face pale as she stumbled to the chair placed in front of the desk and sat down abruptly. No, that was for quite another reason entirely.

Even the thought of Darius being in love with another woman, of his being devastated at learning of that woman's death, had been almost enough to bring Arabella to her knees in aching anguish.

She *was* in love with Darius!

She had known herself to be fascinated by him during her first Season. Had imagined herself to be slightly infatuated with him, and been infuriated rather than saddened when he'd married Sophie Belling the previous year. But Arabella had not known, had not realised until this moment, that she had really been in love with him all along.

Even when he had felt himself forced into offering for her she had fooled herself into believing that she was only accepting him because he would make her a much more interesting husband than any of the other men she had met during her two Seasons.

How could she have been so stupid? So blind to her own feelings?

'Arabella?'

She looked up to find Darius frowning down at her, and was at once engulfed in feelings of panic. Darius could not know how she felt about him! He must never learn that she had been foolish enough to fall in love with him when he was a penniless lord, and that she was still in love with him now that he was a wealthy duke!

She drew in a deeply controlling breath. 'I realise this must be disturbing for you, Darius. But surely it is as you imagined?'

'Imagined, perhaps. But I never gave up hope it would not be the case.' He sighed heavily. 'We will, of course, both have to return to London immediately.'

Arabella blinked at the sudden change of subject. 'We will?'

Darius nodded. 'Immediately.'

'But of course I shall come to London with you if you think I can be of any help to you—'

'It is not *I* who is in need of your assistance, Arabella, but your newest sister-in-law, Juliet.'

Arabella looked bewildered. 'Juliet?'

'Of *course* Juliet,' Darius confirmed impatiently. 'Your sister-in-law will need the support of all of her family to help sustain her through this difficult time.'

'I had not realised that anyone but close family yet knew of Juliet's…condition.' Arabella was completely at a loss as to Darius's train of thought. Perhaps having confirmation of his brother's perfidy had unhinged him slightly? No, Darius was not a man to become unhinged by anything, and she had no doubt that when he finally apprehended Francis he would deal with his brother in the same calm and collected way he had dealt with him seven months ago.

Darius looked confused. 'What condition?'

'Why, she and Sebastian are expecting…' Arabella trailed off into silence. She knew by Darius's blank expression that he'd had no idea Juliet was with child. 'Darius, why exactly do you think that Juliet needs her family around her at this moment?'

Darius had been so weighed down by the evidence of Francis's guilt that he had spoken without thinking. Without practising his usual caution. Arabella, being Arabella, was now starting to draw her own conclusions from that slip. No doubt they would be the correct ones!

No matter. Darius had thought long and hard as he'd lain awake the previous night, holding her safe in his arms, and the conclusion he had come to from all that thinking was that as a married man it was now time for him to withdraw his services from the crown. He had enough to occupy him in being Arabella's husband and the Duke of Carlyne. Most especially in being husband to the wayward Arabella!

Darius had never known another woman like her. Her beauty was all too apparent. But she was also self-confident. Self-willed. So high-spirited. A young woman, in fact, who refused to be cowed or frightened by anything or anyone. Even her scare the previous night—something that would have reduced a lesser woman to tears and hysteria—had only shaken her momentarily before she returned to being her normal stubborn self. As for the way she had sat down this morning and drunk tea and gossiped with Big Tom Westlake…

No, Darius had never before known a woman quite like her…

He grimaced. 'Arabella, have you not wondered why William Bancroft should be the one to inform me of Helena Jourdan's death?'

'Well, I… That *is* rather strange,' she agreed. 'What is the Earl of Banford's connection to her?' Her gaze was suddenly sharp with suspicion.

'I will explain that in a moment.' Darius sighed.

'Arabella, Helena Jourdan was Juliet's cousin and companion.'

Arabella gasped.

Darius nodded. '*And* a French spy.'

A frown appeared on Arabella's creamy brow, and her eyes widened before just as suddenly narrowing again. Her beautiful pouting lips thinned indignantly as she glared up to at him. 'The same French spy arrested at Lord and Lady Bancroft's house party this past summer?'

Having made his decision to leave off working for the crown, Darius knew the time for prevarication as regarded his young wife was over. 'Yes.'

Arabella went from being indignant to blazingly angry in a matter of seconds, and she stood up with an impatient ruffle of her skirts. 'Why did you not tell me before? Why did you not explain?'

'I could not, love.'

'Do not "love" me, you—you—'

'Diverting as this conversation no doubt is to the two of you, I find that I am becoming rather bored by it!' a contemptuous voice suddenly interrupted.

Darius turned sharply to stare into the shadowed corner of the study behind him, his eyes widening with disbelief as he saw the man standing there, looking back at him so disdainfully.

His brother Francis!

Chapter Seventeen

Arabella turned to frown at the man who had somehow joined them in the study without either of them having been aware of it until he spoke to them. She recognised him instantly, of course: young and handsome, with golden-blond hair and pale blue eyes, Francis Wynter really was a weaker-looking version of his brother.

'How convenient that I should find the two of you alone here together,' Francis remarked mildly as he stepped out of the shadows to reveal that he held a raised pistol in each hand. 'Recognise these, Darius?'

Darius nodded tersely, a nerve pulsing in his tightly clenched jaw. 'They are our father's duelling pistols.'

'One for each of you, yes.' The younger man gave a mocking inclination of his head. 'I apologise, my dear. We have not as yet been introduced.' He turned that bold blue gaze upon Arabella. 'I am—'

'I know who *and* what you are.' Arabella looked back at him scornfully.

'Oh, dear, Darius, what *have* you been telling your young wife about me?' Francis gave his brother a taunting look.

'Darius did not need to tell me anything about you,' Arabella assured him disdainfully. 'I know from your previous actions what a monster you are, and your cowardly behaviour of last night only confirms that belief.'

'Arabella—'

'Oh, please, do let her continue, Darius.' Francis Wynter calmly interrupted Darius's words of warning. 'I am all agog to hear what the haughty Lady Arabella St Claire thinks of me.'

Arabella drew herself up to her full height. 'I am Arabella *Wynter*, Duchess of Carlyne, and as such you will address me as Your Grace!'

Those pale blue eyes narrowed with dislike. 'Not for very much longer, my dear,' he assured her evilly.

Arabella felt a shiver of apprehension run down the length of her spine. 'You, sir, are—'

'Arabella, please!' Darius stepped forward to push her behind him in an attempt to shield her with his body, all the time keeping his steely gaze fixed firmly upon his brother. 'How did you get in here, Francis?' He asked one of the questions that had been plaguing him these last few tense minutes as Arabella had kept Francis occupied in conversation and Darius's mind had raced as to how he was to reach his own loaded pistol hidden in the top drawer of his desk.

Francis gave a humourless smile. 'Because you and our cousin Simon, and frequently Lucian St Claire—' he shot Arabella another look of intense dislike '—chose to habitually exclude me from joining in your diversions outside, I was left to stay indoors and fall back on my own devices. In the process of doing so I discovered several secret passageways that had obviously been installed in the house when it was first built. In order to aid escape if the inhabitants of the house were ever attacked, one presumes. You see?'

He balanced one of the pistols so that he might reach out and touch the rose design in the centre of one of the panels on the wall, resulting in the whole panel silently opening.

'Ingenious, is it not?' He pressed the rose and closed it again before resuming his previous position, having both pistols levelled on Arabella and Darius. 'God knows what our ancestors got up to that they needed such an escape, but I have certainly found those passageways helpful for my own plans.'

It explained how Francis had managed to enter the house the previous night undetected, at least. Without, as Darius had previously suspected, the aid of one of his own servants. That was something, at least. 'What do you want here, Francis? Have your past actions not already caused enough unhappiness to our family?'

'My dear Darius, I have not even begun!' his brother said coldly as he pointed one of the pistols directly at Darius's chest. 'Now, for this to work properly, I am afraid you will have to step aside.'

Darius felt his heart turn to ice. 'What do you mean?'

Francis smiled. 'First you will shoot your wife in a fit of temper, and then you will take your own life.'

'A fit of temper?' Arabella was the one to repeat it incredulously as she stepped out from behind Darius. 'I assure you Darius is far too much in control of his emotions to resort to anything so childish as a fit of temper!' she dismissed contemptuously.

At that moment Darius wished that his wife were a little less outspoken and more in control of her *own* emotions! 'Would you please allow *me* to deal with this, Arabella?' he asked mildly.

'"This" being your disgrace of a brother, I presume?' She shot Francis another contemptuous glance.

Darius winced as he saw the murderous glint that had now entered Francis's eyes. 'Arabella—'

'No, please allow her to continue, Darius.' His brother continued to look venomously at Arabella. 'It will make it so much easier to shoot her when the time comes!'

That lump of ice in Darius's chest became even heavier. 'You will never get away with this, Francis. No one will believe that I shot my wife of but a few days before taking my own life.'

'But of course they will.' Francis gave them a confident, insane smile. 'Once the rumour is circulated that your wife and Grayson were involved before your marriage, and that she invited Grayson to be with her here as early as your honeymoon, I have no doubt that the ton will believe every word of it!'

Darius's eyes narrowed to icy chips of blue. 'Lord Grayson has a perfectly legitimate reason for being here.'

'I'm sure,' his brother drawled knowingly.

This was not going well, Darius realised frustratedly. Not that he expected Francis's story to be believed for a moment; too many people of influence knew of his true relationship with Grayson. But if he and Arabella were already dead it really was going to be of little interest to either of them what anyone believed! If Darius could only get to his own gun in the drawer of his desk. Perhaps if he could distract Francis?

'Have you been hiding in the house this whole time, Francis?' he enquired lightly, only to receive a frowning glance from his wife. He once again managed to move so that his body acted as a shield for hers.

'At the Dower House, actually.' Francis smiled. 'The few servants that Margaret retains apparently do not talk to the lower class of servants you have engaged here since becoming Duke of Carlyne, and conveniently saw no reason to enlighten anyone as to my presence there.'

His brother really was insane, Darius realised heavily. Completely. Utterly. Which was not going to make the slightest difference when Francis pulled the trigger on his pistol and killed both him and Arabella!

'Can we not sit down together and talk about this?'

'How magnanimous of you, Darius.' Francis gave him a derisive glance. 'I seem to recall that as a child you were always one for doing the right thing. I made sure my mama never believed it of you, of course,' he added. 'Young as I was, I still remember her talking of how I would make a far better duke than either George, Simon or you could ever be.'

Arabella now understood the need Darius felt for caution; his brother was obviously not in his right mind. Had not been so for some time, from the sound of it. No doubt he had been helped along in that insanity at a very young age by the ambitions of a mother who had proved herself to be vicious and unforgiving to the young and vulnerable little boy who had been her stepson.

'Margaret is expected back tomorrow.' Francis gave a contented smile. 'I have decided it will be more convenient for all if, when she arrives, she is able greet me as the new Duke of Carlyne. If you would kindly step aside so that I have a clear shot, Darius?' He made a waving motion with one of the pistols.

So that he had a clear shot at *her*, Arabella realised with horror. This man, Darius's own brother, intended to calmly and cold-bloodedly kill both of them! As he was the only one of them holding pistols, Arabella could not see how they were going to deflect him from carrying out that plan, either.

Perhaps if she were to pretend to faint? No, Arabella doubted that would ruffle the obviously deranged man in the slightest; he would probably just take advantage of her prone position and shoot her where she fell.

Francis gave an impatient sigh as Darius continued to shield Arabella with his own body. 'I really would have preferred for you to see your duchess die before your eyes,' he said in disappointment. 'But ultimately it is of little import which of you dies first.'

Once again he levelled the pistol at Darius's chest.

'No!' Arabella screamed as she saw that finger about to squeeze the trigger, moving to grab Darius's arm in order to pull herself round in front of him. She clung firmly to both his arms as her hungry gaze ate up every handsome inch of her husband's angry face, and then she heard the sound of breaking glass and the loud report of the pistol being fired…

'Arabella! Arabella, for God's sake open your eyes and speak to me!'

Her first thought was that she had failed and Francis had succeeded after all. That she and Darius were both dead. How else could he now be talking to her? Her only consolation—if it could be called such—was that she and Darius were still together.

'Arabella, I *know* you are awake because I saw your eyelids move just now. Now, open your eyes, damn it!' Strong hands clasped hold of her arms and she felt herself being shaken.

She had never given particular thought to what it would be like in the afterlife. There would be angels, of course. Celestial music, perhaps. But never in any of her imaginings on the subject had Arabella thought to hear Darius cursing at her. Or that she would still be able to feel his strong fingers around her arms…

Her lashes flickered before she opened heavy lids to gaze upwards, blinking dazedly as she found herself looking at the canopy above the bed in her bedchamber.

Was this what heaven was like? she wondered dreamily. Did the same life continue? With the same surroundings…

'Arabella, *look* at me!' The pale yet fiercely angry face of her husband moved into her line of unfocused vision as he bent over her. 'Do you hear me, Arabella?'

'I hear you, Darius,' she managed to croak out between stiff lips. 'I imagine that the whole of heaven can hear you when you are shouting so loudly.'

'*Heaven?* Damn it, you are not dead!' He scowled down at her darkly. 'Although God knows how you are not! How *dare* you place yourself in front of me in that way? How *could* you deliberately put yourself in danger?' He shook her once again, before just as suddenly pulling her up into his arms, his expression anguished. 'Oh, Arabella, I thought he had killed you! I thought you were— Oh, God…' He buried his face in her golden curls and began to shake uncontrollably.

She was *not* dead!

She could not be dead when Darius felt so solid and warm against her. When she could feel his body shaking as he held her so tightly against him.

'Darius?' Arabella reached up a hand to wonderingly touch the soft golden reality of his hair and the hardness of his jaw. 'Darius, you are not dead, either!' She buried her face against the warmth of his jacket as she clung to him.

'Neither one of us is dead, love.'

As if to prove the point Darius began to kiss her throat, her earlobes, her cheeks, her eyes, her nose, and then finally her lips. They kissed hungrily, desperately, deeply, for long, wonderful minutes.

'Why did you do that, Arabella?' Darius finally pulled back slightly to glare down at her fiercely once again. 'Why did you deliberately put yourself in the path of danger?'

His eyes were dark and pained with the memory of that few seconds in time when Arabella had moved in front of him to place herself directly where Francis had been aiming the pistol.

'You really are alive, Darius!' Arabella's eyes glowed as she looked up at him wonderingly. 'You—' She broke off as he gave a pained wince. Her fingers had tightened on his arm. 'You are hurt!' Her eyes widened in alarm as she removed her hand and saw blood darkening the material of his jacket.

'It is unimportant. A flesh wound only,' Darius dismissed. 'Arabella—'

'I wish to see this flesh wound.' Arabella pushed him gently back so that she might sit up on the side of the bed. 'Take off your jacket.'

'Arabella, you will not deflect me from my chastisement of you by attempting to change the subject,' Darius warned her harshly. 'You will explain yourself.'

'Take off your jacket immediately and let me see your arm.' She ignored his rebuke as she concentrated on trying to peel his jacket from his shoulders.

Darius's expression softened at her concern. 'It really is only a flesh wound, Arabella, and can easily be dealt with later.'

She looked up at him uncertainly. 'How is it that we are both still alive?'

He grimaced. 'Because Francis is the one who is dead.'

'How?'

'Grayson,' he told her. 'He went outside after talking with you, and as he passed the study window he saw Francis in here, pointing the duelling pistols at the two of us. He shot him at the same time as Francis pulled the trigger on his own pistol, jerking Francis's aim and so deflecting the bullet into my arm instead of your back.' Darius's face was ferocious at the memory of what had so nearly occurred.

Arabella remembered the sound of breaking glass that she had heard a mere fraction of a second before the loud report of Francis's pistol. 'Then the danger really is over?'

'Francis's death has brought that whole sorry business to an end, yes.'

'I am so sorry, Darius.'

'I am not.' His jaw was rigid with tension.

Her eyes were wide. 'But what will happen now? How will you explain Francis's death?'

Darius shook his head. 'I have not had a chance to work out the details as yet, but I think perhaps it might be arranged in a few days that my brother has met his death by contracting influenza whilst travelling abroad.'

Arabella frowned. 'Arranged how?'

'I have said I have not worked out the details as yet—I am sorry, Arabella.' He sighed as he saw how hurt she looked at the harshness of his tone. 'It is only that at this moment I am more interested in why you threw yourself in front of me in that reckless way.' Darius looked down at her searchingly.

Those few seconds, when he had held the limp Arabella in his arms, had been the worst of Darius's entire life. A moment of utter and complete despair. Before he'd felt the pain of the wound to his own arm and realised that Francis's bullet had not struck and killed her after all. Then had come the most euphoric moment of his life…

'Tell me why you did something so stupid? So unbelievable? So utterly selfless!' His eyes glowed down at her fiercely.

She swallowed hard, her gaze not quite meeting his. 'I could not stand by and let that monster kill you.'

'Why not?'

She looked up sharply. 'You would rather I *had* let him kill you?'

Darius gave a rueful smile. 'I would rather that you answered my question, Arabella.'

Tiny white teeth worried at her lower lip. 'Will you not just accept that—?'

'Arabella, it is time that you knew how much I have always loved you,' he cut in. The time for prevaricating about his feelings for the courageous young woman who was now his wife was as over as his career spying for the crown. 'I have loved you, been obsessed by you, since the moment I first set eyes upon you eighteen long months ago.' He sincerely repeated his statement of the previous evening, which he had then said mockingly in order to put her off the scent of the truth.

Her eyes widened. 'Is that true, Darius?'

'Impossible to believe, is it not?' His mouth twisted.

'I—but you married Sophie Belling!' She frowned her confusion.

'Yes,' he confirmed harshly. 'And all I have been able to selfishly think since then is that if I had married you in her stead a year ago then it would have been you that Francis killed!'

'You loved me even then?'

'Long before then.' Darius admitted stiffly.

'Then I do not understand why you married someone else.'

'Sophie was not all that she seemed. Besides...' Darius's expression became bleak. 'What did it matter whom I married once you had refused me?'

'But I did not—what do you mean, she was not all that she seemed?' Arabella looked even more confused.

Darius stood up abruptly, knowing that he had to put some distance between himself and Arabella while he told her of his years working for the crown whilst deliberately fooling the ton into believing he was nothing more than a fortune-hunter and a rake. Besides, Arabella had not yet told him that she returned any of the feelings he had just confessed for her, so perhaps she did not...

'Sophie was an agent for the crown. As am I,' he added softly. 'Our marriage was one of convenience, as I have already explained. But it was a convenience meant to confirm my own apparent desperate need for a wealthy wife, and Sophie's need for a titled husband, whilst allowing us both to continue our work for the crown without alerting the ton or anyone else as to those less public activities.'

Arabella appeared to have been rendered speechless by his revelation. Although, characteristically, she did not remain so for very long! 'Your *apparent* need for a wealthy wife?' she questioned.

Darius shrugged. 'The rumours of my bankruptcy were vastly over-exaggerated, I am afraid.'

'Deliberately so? By you?'

'Yes.' He sighed. 'I have always been in possession of rather a large fortune, love,' he assured her dryly, as still she frowned.

'I— But you— How long have you worked as an agent for the crown?'

'Eight years,' Darius told her bleakly.

'Eight years!' Arabella gasped, shaking her head in disbelief. 'And the Earl of Banford and Gideon Grayson?'

'Also agents for the crown. Obviously ones who have been allowed a more respectable reputation than I,' he added with a humourless smile.

'All this time—all these years—you have *deliberately* allowed Society to think the worst of you!'

He grimaced. 'I did not deliberately allow them to think anything; eight years ago, when I was asked to work for the crown, I was very much the rake everyone believed me to be.'

'And in the years since?'

Darius gave a rueful shrug. 'Once a rake always a rake, you know.'

Except he was not, Arabella realised. Darius was no longer a rake, or a gambler, and had never been a fortune-hunter, or responsible for the death of his wife and brother, or indeed any of the awful things that Society had believed of him for so long. Instead he was as much a hero if not more, as any of the gallant soldiers who had publicly taken up arms to fight for their king and country.

'How can you bear it, Darius?' she choked emotionally. 'How can you stand the gossip and sneering of people who should instead be thanking you for their very freedom?'

He shrugged wide shoulders. 'I have never much cared for Society's opinion of me, Arabella.'

'And my own opinion of you?' Did *that* matter to Darius?

Only minutes ago he had told her that he loved her. That he had loved her for this past year and a half! Arabella stood up slowly to cross the room so that she stood only inches away from him. From the heat of his body. From the warmth of the arms he kept firmly behind his back.

'Darius, I have loved you, been obsessed by you, since the moment I first set eyes upon you.' She met his deeply searching gaze unblinkingly as she repeated his own words back at him and allowed him to see her love shining in the depths of her eyes.

A nerve pulsed in his tightly clenched jaw. 'You refused my offer for you over a year ago.'

'No.' Arabella knew there must be absolute truth between Darius and herself now. 'I did not even know of that offer,' she explained at Darius's questioning look. 'I had no idea of it until Hawk told me of it on our wedding day.'

Those blue eyes narrowed. 'Your brother did not even *consult* with you that first time before refusing me?'

'No.'

Darius drew in a harsh breath. 'What would your answer have been if he had told you of it?'

Arabella smiled. 'I have no doubt, no matter what my feelings for you, that I would have considered long and hard before aligning myself with the disreputable Lord Darius Wynter. But ultimately…' Once again love glowed in her eyes as she gazed up at him. 'Ultimately I know I would have said yes!' She put a hand on his arm. 'I love you so very much, you see, Darius. I always have. And I always will.'

Darius closed his eyes briefly as he attempted to take in the wonder of Arabella having loved him all along. 'Do you think that perhaps we *are* both dead and gone to heaven, after all?' he murmured wonderingly as he took her into his arms to hold her tightly against him.

Arabella gave a husky laugh as she pressed into the warmth of those arms. 'If we are then I hope we will both stay here for ever!'

For ever with Arabella.

It was all that Darius had ever wanted and more.

Chapter Eighteen

Mulberry Hall Seven weeks later.

'Come along, Arabella, it is Christmas Day and all of your family will be expecting us to join them downstairs for breakfast some time before lunch!'

Arabella stretched sleepily as she lay naked in her husband's arms, realising they both must have dozed off for several minutes after having indulged in some rather wonderful lovemaking.

'I have not given you your Christmas gift yet.'

'No?' Darius grinned down at her.

'*That* was not your Christmas gift.' Arabella returned the warmth of that smile as she moved up on her elbow to look down at him. 'I thought that since you have now given up spying you might appreciate having some other diversion with which to keep busy.'

'You are not enough?' Darius teased indulgently.

'Perhaps,' Arabella allowed huskily. The past seven weeks of knowing how much they loved each other had been more wonderful than she could ever have imagined. 'But I would not wish you to become too bored at Winton Hall with just me for company.'

Darius sobered, his gaze intense as he assured her, 'You could never, ever bore me, love.'

'Does that mean you do not want your Christmas gift?' Arabella swirled the hair upon his chest with the tip of her finger, instantly reigniting Darius's desire for her.

He eyed her speculatively, noting the teasing glow in her eyes and the secretive smile that curved her kissable lips. 'What mischief have you been up to now, love?'

'Have *we* been up to,' she corrected. 'Although I am afraid I will not be able to properly place your gift into your arms for another seven and a half months…'

Darius frowned his confusion. 'I do not understand—Arabella?' His voice sharpened as she took hold of his hand and placed it against the flatness of her stomach.

Her smile was one of complete happiness as she announced. 'I am with child, Darius!'

'I— But— Are you sure?' Darius sat up abruptly to look down at her in utter disbelief.

'Jane's physician confirmed it only yesterday. Do not look so concerned.' Arabella laughed indulgently at his look of stunned disbelief. 'I believe it is a perfectly natural occurrence when couples make love as often as we have this past seven weeks!'

Those weeks had been blissfully happy ones for Arabella, as she knew herself well and truly loved by Darius. It was a love she returned just as deeply.

Darius had resigned from spying. After a suitable time Francis had reportedly become 'ill in France', and then been buried in the family crypt—a necessary fabrication for both Margaret Wynter and Society.

Arabella's family had been wonderful throughout, Hawk having had a quiet conversation with Darius some weeks ago in which it had been revealed that Hawk's new position in the government had finally allowed him access to knowledge of what Darius had really been doing this past eight years. Darius had been rendered speechless by the other man's apology for any heartache he might have caused Darius or Arabella by refusing Darius's first offer, and for his disapproval of their marriage two months ago.

Altogether, it had been as if those first few dangerous days of their marriage had never been. And now they were to have a baby. A child they had made together with the deepest of love.

'Is it not wonderful, Darius?' Arabella glowed up at him.

'*You* are the one who is wonderful, my darling Arabella,' he said huskily. 'I love you so very, very much,' he murmured gruffly, and once again he took her in his arms.

'As I love you,' she assured him fervently as she threw her arms about his neck and drew him down to her.

Breakfast, Christmas Day and her family could all wait….

* * * * *

HISTORICAL

Regency

LADY FOLBROKE'S DELICIOUS DECEPTION

by Christine Merrill

Lady Emily Longesley married the love of her life and hoped that he would learn to love her. Instead, he upped and left! Confronting her errant husband three years on, she sees that Adrian, Earl of Folbroke, has been robbed of his sight! If she plays his mistress by delicious deception, can he finally learn to love his wife?

Regency

HOW TO MARRY A RAKE

by Deb Marlowe

Heiress Mae Halford has mended her heart after her friend Stephen Manning's rejection. She's ready to find herself a husband, but the first man she bumps into at a Newmarket house party is Lord Stephen himself!

BREAKING THE GOVERNESS'S RULES

by Michelle Styles

After being dismissed from her post as governess for allowing Jonathon, Lord Chesterholm, to seduce her, Louisa Sibson has rebuilt her life. She lives by a rulebook of morals—and will not allow the devastating Jonathon to break them again!

On sale from 4th March 2011
Don't miss out!

Available at WHSmith, Tesco, ASDA, Eason and all good bookshops

www.millsandboon.co.uk